Cruel Enchantment

The Succubus smiled, her lips as red as the stain of pomegranate juice. Her huge wings, now folded, arced above her head, the black velvety flesh and spines like those of some Queen of Bats.

'Gregory,' she murmured, 'I know exactly what you want.'

'You're here to tempt my soul into damnation,' growled the young monk. 'Don't think I don't know that, demon.' She was sexuality incarnate, everything that Gregory had forsworn and denied himself. She was an ancient goddess come to earth – a goddess of night and mystery.

'I'm here to give you what you need,' she said softly, looking at his lap.

Cruel Enchantment

JANINE ASHBLESS

Black Lace novels are sexual fantasies.
In real life, make sure you practise safe sex.

First published in 2000 by
Black Lace
Thames Wharf Studios
Rainville Road, London W6 9HA

Reprinted 2000, 2001

Typeset by SetSystems Ltd, Saffron Walden, Essex
Printed and bound by Mackays of Chatham PLC

ISBN 0 352 33483 5

Contents

To Chris: This is all your fault . . .
And Phil: For making it possible.

Loud Sing Cuckoo

*I*t was unseasonably warm that week in May. Sevran was working the rows of plants behind the longhouse and had been since noon, pulling the young weeds from where they had flushed between the clumps of herbs. The heat of the sun beating into the clearing in the wood made it seem more like a summer task than a spring one.

A blackbird was singing noisily in the elderbushes at the edge of the clearing. The smell of hawthorn blossom, half honey and half rancid, thickened the air.

She worked without pausing except at the ends of the long rows, straddling the low mounds, trying not to think of the heat or her thirst. Her legs were straight and she bent forwards from the hips, arse in the air in an undignified manner, but it was easier than kneeling her way along. She had hitched her full skirts up to clear the tender leaves, tucking them at the sides into the waistband, and had discarded her tunic, leaving only her linen undershift to cover her back – that was for the sake of coolness, but the skin between her breasts was still damp where the deep neckline of her shift all but bared them to the sunlight. Her long, firm

1

legs were exposed too by the hitched skirts, almost to the thigh, but it did not matter; there was no one to see. If anyone were to pay a visit to the herbalists' house they would be out at the front, talking to old Metta. Sevran had taken advantage of this; she had enough to do without worrying about her modesty, too. Her mind was half on the weeds her brown hands were twisting from the soil, half on the earthen jug of water waiting for her at the end of the row. If the heat kept up like this, she knew she would be out again watering the garden in another day. She paused momentarily to scratch at her prickling breastbone and left a streak of dirt on the pale linen. Her full, unbound breasts brushed together as she bent over the bright new leaves of feverfew and tansy and yarrow.

Sevran reached the end of the row and straightened gratefully, arching her back. It ached, but she was young and lithe and her muscles would take more abuse than that. She seized the jug and savoured the pure, innocent pleasure of the cool water flooding her parched mouth and throat. Her hair itched with heat, too; she had bound it back behind her but most of it had escaped in thick wriggly coils that now clung to her neck; brown, it was a shade darker than her skin, with copper streaks where the sun had caught it already this year. With a sense of almost guilty enjoyment, she raised the jug over her head and let the water spill down through her hair and over her face. It trickled coolly on her breasts and darkened the linen. Sevran laughed.

A horse whickered softly.

Sevran turned with a gasp, letting the jug fall from her hands. There was a huge grey horse standing motionless at the edge of the clearing – on its back, equally motionless, a man. His hair was long and white, the colour of ashes, his skin yellow as old bone. He and Sevran stared at each other. There was no telling how long he had been there; she had not looked up as she worked. Suddenly, despite the water she had just drunk, she could not swallow, could hardly breathe. Her eyes took in the details before her – the sword sheathed across the saddle, the gaunt, ungainly look of the horse with its too-big head and hooves, the bitless bridle – but she seemed unable to think. She waited for something to happen that would free her from the awful limbo, but the man did not move; the horse did not move. Birds whistled in the wood. Eventually, for there was no other choice, her own body moved without any instruction. She began to walk back down the row towards the longhouse, never turning her face away from the stranger. As she strode forwards her hands plucked the skirt hems from her waist and let them fall to cover her legs, but it was too late for that.

As soon as she started to walk, without any discernible instruction from the rider the grey horse eased into motion too and paced alongside her down the rows. He made no attempt to overtake her and, as she was closer to the house, she reached the corner of the building first. She had to drag her gaze from the rider and turn one corner, then another, not able to run, knowing it was all but useless to retreat.

She reached the front of the house. Old Metta was sitting alone by the front door, her hands busy crumbling herbs in her lap, her face turned up towards the sun. Sevran's heart sank; she had hoped that there would be people up from the village, a pedlar, the trader from the city – anyone to make up a crowd, to bear witness, to show defiance. There had been peace between the nations for a year now, but Sevran had never expected to test it herself, and she had no trust in any warrior. She stumbled towards the old woman, but stopped part way. There was no safety in numbers here, and Metta could not run.

'Sevran?' said Metta, turning milky eyes towards her.

3

Her hands kept busy at their work, independent creatures that did not need the herbalist's last vestiges of
sight to do their tasks. Sevran opened her mouth to
speak but found no words. She felt so heavy in every
limb that she might have sunk into the hard-packed
earth.

Hoofbeats sounded and the horseman rounded the
corner behind her, unhurried, and drew to a halt.
Sevran turned to face him.

'I hear a man on horse,' called Metta. 'Have you
come for herbs?'

The man lifted one leg over the neck of the horse and
slid from the saddle. 'By your goodwill and my good
faith,' he said, 'I beg your hospitality this night.' He
shaped the words awkwardly, but they were clear
enough. Metta raised her eyebrows at the old-fashioned
formality of the greeting.

'You have my goodwill; be welcome at my hearth,'
she replied with a wry shrug. Sevran bit her lip.

'I don't recognise that accent,' Metta continued.
'Where are you from, rider?'

The man said nothing. His gaze shifted to Sevran
and she looked hurriedly away. He might have blue
eyes, and to meet those was said to be deadly misfor-
tune – though she did not doubt that her luck was to
be very bad tonight.

'Metta, he's a Northerner,' said Sevran hoarsely. She
had picked the only word she knew which was not
pejorative. Metta's hands stopped moving and she
grew very still. The man leaned against the shoulder of
his horse.

'How many of them?' said the old woman. Her face
had gone grey.

'He's alone,' said Sevran. 'At the moment.'

'Then fetch him a drink, child,' she replied, tight-
lipped. 'Be hospitable.'

Sevran walked into the house, almost blind, and

scooped a cup of goat's milk from the crock in the corner. She was halfway back before it occurred to her that she should have slipped aconite into it. Outside, no one seemed to have moved. She passed him the wooden cup. Her hands were shaking a little, but he moved awkwardly too. Sevran looked down as the milk slopped on to the earth and waited until he had finished the dregs. He handed the cup back to her.

'Thank you,' he said, in barbarous syllables but politely enough. Then he turned back to his mount and began to untie the girth.

Sevran walked over to Metta and put her hands on the other woman's shoulders. The older woman gripped her wrist fiercely and hissed, 'Run to the village, Sevran!'

'I'll not leave you alone,' said her apprentice.

'I'm an old woman,' Metta insisted. 'He won't touch me.' Then, more honestly, she added, 'If God is kind.'

'Come into the house,' said Sevran. 'There's nothing to be done.' She felt nauseous; she did not think she could run even if she had to.

'I will pray for us,' Metta said, allowing herself to be steered towards the door.

'Pray he doesn't use a knife,' said Sevran flatly. She stopped on the threshold and watched the man finish unsaddling the horse, which he did not bother to hobble or tether. She had only seen a Losfarn close up once, and that was a corpse left behind when a band had swept through the village three years before. She had been fourteen. This one, though taller than most men she knew, was shorter than she had expected; she remembered white giants and horses that struck with hooves and teeth, a confused nightmare. Much more clearly she remembered Hettel, who had been raped by one of them. When the pregnancy had become impossible to hide, the priest had cut the child out of her. Metta had packed the wound with comfrey and yarrow

5

and done her best, but of course Hettel had died anyway, days later. Sevran would have broken her new oath of apprenticeship then, if there had been anywhere else to go. Now she was blackly grateful that she was not a virgin, that she was saved that at least. Herbalists, more than halfway to being witches in the eyes of others, did not marry – but Sevran, burning and desperate, had offered her services to a pedlar who came to the house one day. The experience had been disappointing, though the man was comely and gentle enough; over far too quickly, it had left her an itch she had had to bathe for a fortnight. She had not been tempted to repeat the experiment with any of the villagers, though there were enough men who stared and smirked at her when they met, even as they made the sign against evil behind her back. That was another reason for not running from the clearing; she did not believe that throwing herself on the mercy of the village men would save her from violence. She watched the man with the white hair and felt tension freeze like a fist of ice inside her. At the same time she saw the way he moved and realised that it was weariness that had made him clumsy. He favoured his left leg, too, walking with a slight limp. When he glanced in her direction she ducked into the shadow of the doorway, into the dusty aromatic interior.

He followed her into the house and, after looking around him, dropped the folded saddle by the door. The sword he laid carefully in front of the hearth fire. Metta, seated in her chair and mumbling under her breath, twisted away as he passed by; he glanced down at her, expressionless. Sevran watched from behind the heavy oak table that they used for all their work, as he paced the central room, looking at the few furnishings, the two great pillars that held up the high peaked roof and the many sheaves of dried herbs hanging along the walls and from the rafters. His face did not betray what

6

he thought; in fact, she had not seen the slightest trace of emotion written there since he had appeared, neither ill intent nor gratitude nor interest. When he passed close to her she could smell him, mingled scents of horses and sweat and leather, and her breath caught in her throat. He walked to either end of the house and lifted the curtains that set aside their two bedchambers, looked in, and walked back to the fireside without comment. There he sat in the other chair, her own, across the fireplace from Metta and, leaning back, fixed his gaze on her.

'Make us supper, child,' Metta said uneasily into the dead silence. Sevran moved to comply, dipping water from the bucket into the iron cauldron they cooked with. She had to use both hands to move it into the fireplace, and had to kneel in front of his outstretched feet to set it on its hook and rake the embers up underneath it. The leather of his boots was decorated with copper wire, but very worn. Likewise his clothes, though of fine weave, were now scuffed and stiff with wear; once dyed expensively black, she guessed, they had faded to grey. She did not look into his face. She kneeled within arm's reach and waited inwardly for a move on her, yet it did not happen.

She returned to the table and prepared food, parsnip and barley and salt bacon – for spring was a lean season, before the harvest set – without another word being spoken. The unleashed violence in the room made the air thin and she found herself breathing quick shallow breaths. She sliced the food with the big iron knife, wielding it fast in a silent and pathetic symbol of defence. She was under no illusion about her ability to overcome any attack; he was heavier than her, stronger and crueller. He carried a sword. She felt his gaze like a spiked weight on her skin; it was unbearable to turn her back on him, worse to look up and meet his steady, undisguised regard. She wanted to find a tunic and

7

cover her bare arms and shoulders. Her skin crawled with goose-flesh. She was shamefully aware that fear and chill had hardened her nipples to visible points under the thin linen. She saw him looking and a flush warmed her skin. She was glad Metta could see nothing of this.

Eventually, when the supper was set on to cook, Sevran slipped out into the evening sun to empty the peelings on to the midden. As she passed the man's horse, it raised its head from the grass it was cropping and bared its teeth at her. To her horror, she saw that it had sharp canines like a dog's and she shied away from it. She walked around the house and found her discarded tunic in a damp shadow, then she sat next to the patch of lovage and watched the house, chewing her lower lip, until she was too afraid to stay away longer. Her heart was beating so strongly that she could feel the pulse at her throat. She thought of him watching her, unawares, in the herb-garden, looking at her legs and breasts.

The red rays of the sunset slipped in through the west-facing door with her as she returned, outlining her in copper and setting her hair ablaze with light. In the almost-darkness of the windowless longhouse, she ladled stew out for the three of them. The man said a few words she did not understand as he took the bowl, flat, harsh-sounding syllables in his own half-human language. He ate three bowlfuls of the pottage and a small loaf of black bread swiftly, with the concentration of one who has not eaten well in days. The break from his watchfulness was a relief to her, but she only picked at her food. She noticed that he had not taken a bite until Metta had started on hers.

The two women were used to sleeping and rising with the sun. Metta yawned as she put aside her bowl, then whimpered with shame.

'Go to bed,' said Sevran swiftly. She helped the old

8

woman from her chair to the curtained alcove at the northern end of the house. 'Please sleep, Metta,' she begged as she pulled the covers over the small body.

The herbalist squeezed the younger woman's hand. 'God be with you,' she whispered.

Sevran slipped back into the room with tension singing in her body. She was entirely unprepared to find him asleep, his head turned aside against the high shoulder of the chair. His breathing was deep and regular. For a moment she sagged all over. Relief was like a blush that caressed her whole body. Asleep, the man was not something she feared. She watched him as frankly as he had watched her, seeing the gentle curves his long fingers had relaxed into on his thighs. She had thought him young at first because he was beardless; now she saw the fine lines about his eyes and mouth. Although he was still alien, his hair a pale tangle about his shoulders, the menace had gone from him – or from her perception of him. She looked for a long time, motionless. She knew she could kill him now, if she were swift. Or wake him. Both images played themselves through her head; her choice. She smiled faintly to herself and slipped away to her own bed.

Normally she slept naked, but this night she could not bring herself to remove the last layer of cloth between her and the night. She slipped under the wool and sheepskin blankets and lay curled on her side with one palm pressed between her legs. She could feel her own dampness through the cloth. Fear, perhaps. A great wave of yearning and loneliness swelled within her and she longed to bring herself to a climax, but she could not believe that the man outside would not hear, would not smell, would not feel her desire; it would tear the roof down and shake the house to rubble. Aching, her head buzzing, she slipped reluctantly into sleep.

She awoke when the door slammed. She was surprised she had slept at all. She stared at the coarse weave of the cloth that shielded her sleeping space, seeing through it the dim glow of the hearth fire. It was not much later, then. The door banged again and she sat up. The breeze was knocking it back and forth; it must be off the latch. It would wake everyone. Sevran slipped out of bed, still clad only in her undershift, and cautiously peered around the curtain. The door was a few inches ajar, and both chairs were empty; the man was not in the room.

Sevran moved swiftly to the door, silent in her bare feet, but as she laid her hand upon the bar it was pushed back in her face. She retreated a few steps as the man came into the room. His shirt was loose and his trews hitched loosely over his hips, the belt unfastened.

He stopped when he saw her. Sevran took another step back and was blocked by the edge of the table, solid against her arse. Without looking behind him, the man shut the door one-handed and dropped the latch, his eyes on her face. He moved towards her carefully. Sevran rode the rising tide of her shallow breaths, her eyes huge and pleading, her lips parted. He reached out to her with one hand and touched his fingers to her throat – she jumped at his touch, then held herself still as his hand described a caress across her collarbone, the curve of her jaw, under her ear. His thumb brushed her full lips, parting them easily, pressing into the wetness of her mouth. She slid the tip of her tongue around the callused pad of the thumb.

He moved in closer, standing over her, still wordless, pale eyes burning in a face still masklike. His other hand found the back of her neck, buried itself in the thickness of her hair, knotted it, held her, pulling her inexorably back as he leaned over her. The hand at her face drew free and sought her breasts through the linen. Her nipples were so hard that the touch of his fingers was painful; Sevran gasped with shock at the pleasure that stabbed through her as his hand passed from breast to breast, fingers and palm exploring the rich curves. When he gripped her left nipple and tugged it, a hot wave of helplessness washed over her and she moaned in her throat, closing her eyes. It was as if he had drawn hooks across her soul, snaring her in a thousand pricks of agonised delight – if he had not been holding her up, she would have collapsed across the table. Her own hands, white knuckled, lost their grip on the table edge and flew up of their own volition under his shirt, finding smooth skin over hard planes of muscle.

For a moment, in their questing, they each mirrored the other, then the man abruptly pulled her upright again and released her. Sevran's eyes flew open; she feared she had done something wrong, but he simply needed both arms free to drag the shirt across his head and discard it. Sevran's impertinence was rewarded by the sight of his naked torso, strangely hairless, lean and well muscled but scarred across chest and shoulders. She touched a silver scar tentatively and felt a shiver chase across his skin; as if to punish her now he knocked her hands away, caught both her wrists and gripped them behind her back with one strong hand. He loomed over her once more. Swiftly he tugged her undershift down across her shoulders. The deep neckline caught across the swell of her breasts but he was not going to be thwarted and pulled the cloth ruthlessly over their soft resistance, snagging the erect nipples. Stripped naked, her breasts were beautiful; full and dark nippled, their generous size emphasised by the narrowness of her waist, their firm softness contrasting with her strong, work-honed shoulders and stomach.

Sevran arched herself against the hand at the small of her back as he stooped over her, his mouth suddenly against her skin. It was a demanding, hungry mouth, teeth grazing her skin, tongue and lips devouring her, twisting her nipples, tugging and sucking across her eager body. She tried not to moan too loudly, but was barely conscious of anything but the flames of sensation and desire ripping through her flesh. He bore her over so that she lay flat upon the table, her crossed hands pinned behind her by her own weight, her legs pushed apart by the edge of the wood against the back of her buttocks. His weight was pressed down on her thighs and while his mouth was busy laying claim to her breasts and stomach, his hands, both free now, pushed the skirt of her undershift up to bare her legs. Soon it was bunched about her waist only, serving to hide nothing, only to act – twisted about her wrists and hips – as a rope to tie her helplessly so that she could not block his touch.

His hands moved over her thighs, gentle once more as they explored the brown fuzz of her pubic mound, her parted labia, the moistness of the cleft between them. Suddenly he was in no hurry, savouring each inch of her flesh. He stood upright to look down upon the body that was offered to him, touching her aching nipples, her yearning lips, her panting throat, all with the certainty, the total possessiveness of one who has inherited a kingdom that needs only to be explored, not to be conquered. He dragged one hand across the taut stretch of her stomach, making her writhe as she strained to follow his touch. He parted her legs further, entered her wet and gaping sex with one finger and then another, spread them to stretch her tightness, raised one eyebrow slightly, though at what Sevran could not say: for, although she stared at him, she could no longer think of anything but the movement of his fingers inside her. With free and unhurried fingers he coaxed more moisture from her and then spread it shamelessly from clitoris to arsehole, his touch at both making her gasp and bare her teeth in frustration.

12

Sevran felt the muscles of her vagina clench about him, pulsing with their own rhythm. He was working her harder now, more than one finger – she could not tell how many – thrusting deeper, rotating, laying her open, preparing her. She ground down on his tormenting hand, her face slack with desire, his taut with concentration. The juices of her sex coated his hands now. He caressed the puckered mouth of her arse with the wetness borrowed from her other eager hole until it yielded, then with one smooth and utterly merciless movement drove his fingers into her anus. For a moment the pain that hit Sevran was blinding – then that agony exploded, inverting into a savage orgasm that tore her apart. She came, jolting and shuddering, on his hands.

For a long moment he held her like that, watching her spasm, before he slid from her and left her bereft. Sevran felt the loss and the muscles pulsing around empty space; she gasped unconsciously with disappointment. Then, without dropping his trews, the man freed his prick from the cloth and guided it to her now sopping cleft. Sevran could see nothing of this new invader from the angle at which she lay, but she felt the hard tip of his cock running up and down her oozing slit, then pushing relentlessly into her. She welcomed it, gasping to be filled again, feeling the tides surge in her once more.

But he withdrew, just as she opened for him and before penetrating her fully. He stepped back, picked her up from the table and dropped her to her knees before him. Sevran stared, at a loss, open-mouthed. She had seen an erect penis before, but not this close. It seemed huge; surging from a nest of white hair, glistening dully at the engorged tip, it smelled of her own sex and – sharply – of the man's alien maleness. It twitched in the warmth of her breath, jerking back against the

13

rigid plane of his belly. The slit at its head wept moisture.

'Your mouth,' said the man thickly, taking her head in both hands and twisting his fingers in her hair. He guided her lips down over the end of his prick and pushed into the wetness of her mouth. Sevran began to suck eagerly, hardly knowing how it must feel for him but lapping as best she could with her tongue. Her lips gripped his shaft behind the head of his cock, engulfing him in hot velvet; she heard the barely voiced gasp of his gratification. Freeing her hands from the tangle of her undershift, she sought his crotch, playing with the full pouch of his bollocks, trying to divide her attention between their incredible heavy softness and the rock-hard rigidity of his prick. His legs and arse were rigid too with strain. She traced the ripples under her tongue wonderingly, making a delicate foray into the crack at the cock-tip. The man tightened his grip. Then he began to move, thrusting the length of his shaft into her throat, forcing her head down on him. Sevran choked. She wanted to take his length, she tried to yield to him, but her throat was not used to this treatment and she gagged. He let her wrench away after a second. They were both gasping. He tipped her face up to look into it, saw the tears spilling down her cheeks and her swollen, bruised lips. Reluctantly he released her and lifted her to her feet, the undershift falling away from her as she stood.

Sevran clung to his arms, wretched with disappointment, but he did not give her time to blame herself. He pushed her back on to the table and spread her legs. He did not bother to pinion her arms, this time. He simply entered her, pushing the full length of his aching cock into her. She was tight as a closed fist but she was wet and she was hot and she wanted him. Sevran sank her fingers wildly into his pale skin, clawing at his back then buttocks as he lowered himself down on

14

her with each successive thrust. She wrapped her thighs around his and pulled him further into her with her legs. He thrust fiercely and without restraint, but she welcomed every movement of his body within her and on her, felt him battering down the walls that separated her from the light, pushing her through, smashing down barrier after barrier –

The light engulfed her. She sank her nails in, arched and screamed. His naked shoulder muffled her cries and she bit him in delirium. He spasmed above her and his climax tore a groan out of him. Then the light died into the long pulsing throb of his semen pouring into her and the wet gulping twitches of her body drinking it up.

Slowly the man lowered the full weight of his torso on to Sevran's. They were both glazed with sweat, their groins fused by hair and hot moisture. She held him as he recovered his strength, feeling the pulse in his throat beat against her cheek. Then he withdrew and turned away from her, very slowly, his lips brushing one bruised breast as they passed. He said nothing as he propped himself against the table, and he did not look at her.

Sevran stood up slowly. Her arms and legs were shaking, the muscles jumping under the skin. She felt his seed, mingled with her own wetness, begin to ooze out of her and run down one thigh. She looked at the man shamelessly. His trews still hung on his hips; out of them, still erect, his cock rose like a spear, slick with their juices. She wanted to lick it clean. The man sat with his head bowed, lank white hair falling across his face.

'Come to bed,' she said softly. The man lifted his head to look at her. She indicated the curtain of her bedchamber with one hand and held the other out to him. Rather hesitantly, as if surprised, he laid his hand in hers and their fingers snagged together. For the first time, he smiled.

The Dragon's Bride

*T*he little cart lurched over the stones of the track and Sheldi jammed her feet against the side to steady herself, her heart jumping as she looked at the cliff-edge so close to the wheels. A crow floated in the void below her, ink-dark against the greens and browns of the heath. Sheldi was self-possessed enough to find her own fear funny, in the blackest way, and she bared her teeth in a bitter grin. Her father, walking behind the cart, saw her grimace and mumbled, 'Nearly there, my petal.' Sheldi turned her head and spat at him, but her throat was too dry and she produced only the noise of her contempt.

It was not as if bracing herself would help. Her hands were tied behind her back to one of the struts on the cart-side. If the mule pulling the vehicle should lose its footing on the narrow track that wound down into the quarry – or, more likely, throw off the two men walking at its head and bolt over the edge with fear, because it was already shivering and skittering about with nervousness, its nostrils flaring at the acrid scent of the wind – then she would be dragged down with both animal and cart into the drop. She could neither fall out nor leap to safety. Not that there was any safety left for her; the retinue of royal guards would see to that. Sheldi stared into the air that gaped to the side of the small procession and wondered why she should be afraid of falling.

She did not look into the faces of the men with her, even when the group reached the flat quarry floor and halted by the stake while she was untied and lifted down. She fixed her gaze on the cliffs around them, watching the horizon for movement. She had told herself that she would not show cowardice but it was impossible not to look about for the beast, knowing that it could lurk behind any crag or crouch above them on any height. The soldiers were looking around them too, their weapons gripped tightly – as if they would be of any use – and the priests in their white robes held down their flapping head-dresses and wheeled in tight circles, waiting for the vistas of rock to metamorphose into scale and flesh. The wind here was blustery and loud, hissing through the rocks and caves with a muttering susurration that threatened to hide the approach of any flapping creature. And the place stank of burning and of the unburied remnants of the quarrymen in the blackened ruins of their huts, so that the mule rolled its eyes and jerked at the hands of the men holding its bridle. A pink froth was dripping from its working jaws. Sheldi watched a bright gob of foam fall and splatter on the rocks at its feet. She knew they would not be able to restrain the mule for much longer if they did not lead it away soon.

Hands belonging to several soldiers seized her and pushed her back against the stake, not gently. Her wrists were retied. The men worked quickly, anxious to get away from her presence, as if she were something unclean. Her father hovered, his face grey, but as soon as she located him Sheldi looked away again, tilting her head back to stare into the cloud-streaked sky. Another hand, unseen, reached from behind her to loosen the ribbons in her hair, so that the heavy honey-coloured length of it slipped free to stream around her shoulders and wrap tenderly against the rough iron of the spike at her back. There were flowers in her hair, and gold jewellery at her throat and wrists, and her tight robe was of fine green silk worked with embroidery, which clung to her frame in emphasis of her youth and her curving figure. She was dressed as a bride would be, though this was no wedding and her partner would not be a man. But it was tradition, as was the iron stake – a tradition not called upon in fifty years, and now four times in as many months.

The oldest of the priests, and the highest ranking she supposed, stepped in front of Sheldi and offered a small flask to her dry lips. 'You may drink this,' he said as the wind tugged his long beard sideways. 'It will take away the pain.'

Sheldi looked at the flask bleakly. 'No,' she decided at last. She raised her voice so that everyone could hear. 'Tell Edwin that even if he is too afraid to send his own daughter, I can still face the dragon.'

'Impudent slut!' the priest snapped. 'You may not use such words of His Majesty!'

'Oh?' said Sheldi. 'And what will you do to me?' But her voice had failed her and was shaking now. She watched the priest turn his back, then glanced over at her father to see his reaction. Above his stiff velvet collar the man's face was pink and stricken. He's embarrassed, Sheldi thought incredulously; I've let him down because I'm not behaving like a lady! The last words she had been saving for him died in her throat and she closed her eyes. The raging wound of her betrayal shrank like a doused fire; she was numb with pain.

'In the name of His Majesty, King Edwin, and of all his subjects, I acknowledge the brave sacrifice that you make for the sake of the Kingdom and the city that you love, and I offer you our thanks,' said the priest in flat tones. He raised his right hand as if to bless her, then changed his mind and waved at the guards. 'Summon the dragon,' he said.

Sheldi kept her head bowed as the bulk of the party hurried off, not heading for the road but for some sheltering outcrop where they would be out of sight. One soldier remained, waiting until they were a reasonable distance away, holding a long trumpet before him like a snake he wanted to drop. The pause seemed interminable. Sheldi raised her head to watch him, looking for some trace of sympathy in his scarred face. His eyes were brown and met her own reluctantly, only for the space of a single breath. Nothing was said. He licked his lips, raised the trumpet and blew a long aching note.

Sheldi flinched. The soldier turned and ran, his feet scattering stones. When the noise of his flight had diminished, there was no sound but the soughing of the wind and the roar of the blood in Sheldi's ears.

The dragon came over the lip of the quarry, high up, and circled four times, banking steeply, before it stooped to land. The rocks crunched and stirred under its bulk. Its shadow was vast, as dark as a storm cloud, but the huge membranous wings folded compactly as it found its footing on the stones and crouched over her, within striking distance if it should choose to stretch out its neck. Sheldi stared, could not help staring; she felt as if her heart had stopped and she had died in a rictus that froze her with eyes open. I don't believe this is happening, she thought. It's a dragon. I'm going to die now. She did not know which concept was harder for her to grasp.

The dragon arced its sinuous neck and gazed down at her, and for all the red-and-black scaled length of its form, the spines of the neck and the talons on each of its feet and the leathery, smoky stink of it, it was the eyes that seized Sheldi's attention; eyes yellow as flame with black, vertical slits for pupils, eyes that gleamed like gold in the furnace, eyes that looked down the long, ridged length of its head, not set at the side as horses' are but forward like an eagle's; predatory, fierce, intelligent eyes that made Sheldi writhe within even as she clung motionless to the stake. The dragon opened its mouth slightly to reveal rows of curved teeth – all canines, sharp as spear-points. The ember-coloured skin of its throat worked.

'Promising,' it said. Its voice was like rocks grinding together in a river; it made the ground tremble and Sheldi could feel the vibration of its rumble thrumming into her fingers and spine through the stake. 'What are you called, little thing?' the dragon continued.

Sheldi felt her knees weakening. She had to jam her back against the iron to stop herself from falling. 'Sheldi,' she forced out. It sounded like a squeak to her ears but the dragon heard.

'Sheldi,' it rasped. 'Meaning "happiness" in the Western dialect. Are you happy, little thing?'

'Not at the moment,' she croaked. She wondered crazily with part of her mind what kind of creature liked to talk with its prey, while the other half of her mind concentrated on not losing control of her bladder. Her vision skidded down the incredible muscular length of its body, trying to assimilate the dry, scaly immensity of a creature as big as a building. It was dull red in colour, fading to grimy black about the feet and tail and head, its wings and belly the colour of dried blood. Oddly, it did not occur to Sheldi to scream; perhaps because that would be too small a response to such a monstrosity.

'Then I shall cut you free,' said the dragon. 'Hold yourself still. If you try to run away, I shall eat you.' It paced forwards to fill the whole of Sheldi's vision, the whole of her senses. It was too huge to understand. The air thrummed with the sound of its breathing and the scrape of scales on rock. The ashy stench of its breath, like dead fires and oily slate intermingled, filled her protesting lungs as it lowered its head close – so close she could see into the cavernous gape of its nostrils, black and ridged and tarry, as the head swung past her, dipped and twisted behind her. She cringed away but forced herself not to struggle, then felt the rope that bound her tug cruelly, yanking her shoulders back. A small cry escaped from her – but the rope parted and her arms fell free. Sheldi fell to her hands and knees on the rough stone and bit her lip to prevent herself loosing the tears she felt start to her eyes. When she looked up the dragon had cocked its head back and was watching her. Its immobile, bony face had the permanent expression of a sardonic smile.

'Happy now, little Sheldi?' it enquired.

'Uh,' she said as she stood unsteadily, rubbing at her wrists where the severed ends of the rope still bit into her skin. 'Are you going to eat me now?' she added miserably.

'Not yet,' the dragon rumbled. 'I am taking you back to my home.' Quick as a snake striking, it lunged out with a foreclaw and snatched her into its grip; before Sheldi could shriek it bunched itself on to its haunches, threw open its wings and leaped into the sky. If Sheldi screamed she did not hear it over the battering of the wind and the whistling crack of flapping wings. She opened her eyes into the stinging wind and saw the ground falling away below her before she shut them again, tears of pain streaming down her face. Only shock and disbelief saved her from the agony of panic in that insane flight. The dragon's claw gripped her so tightly she could hardly breathe and, although it was warm, the air itself was icy and ripped at her hair. Exposed parts of her skin – her face, lower legs and one

21

arm – chilled in minutes to a grinding ache, while the sky lurched and yawed around her. She pulled her arm across her face to shield herself and wished she could faint, just so as to escape from the nightmare. The only thing she could compare it to was an old memory of childhood when she had been climbing a tree in the garden and a branch had snapped beneath her, dropping her through layers of foliage until she had caught and clung on sturdier lower limbs. There was the same sense of battering pain, of clinging to unyielding structures that might at any second give way while the world yawned beneath her, the whole trusted foundation of the earth turned into a gaping pit, and her heart trying to burst out of her throat. Time ceased while the cold ate into her limbs and the sky spun to the beat of the beast's wings. Sheldi felt herself sinking into dizziness without colour or form.

Then it stopped. The regular motion of the dragon became a confusion and a darkness, and suddenly Sheldi was sliding across a stone floor, her pinned limbs sprawling aimlessly as they found their release. When she had stopped moving she lay as still as she could, her cheek pressed against the flagstones. She could hear the dragon moving about above her, and the yammering echoes made her think that they must be in a great cave.

'Are you alive, Sheldi?' came the dragon's voice.

'Ah – yes,' she said faintly, not daring to remain silent, despite her desire to vomit. She lay awash with nausea for a long time until she decided that she was not going to be sick, probably because she had been given nothing to eat that day. She sat up and looked about her uneasily. Her whole body was shaking.

'Welcome, little Sheldi,' said the dragon. 'This is the house of Oromon.' The beast couched like a dog on the bare stone, head and foreclaws up and alert, hindquarters sprawled away, belly exposed. Its heraldic setting was revealed to be a great hall with arched pillars and narrow windows that lanced high into the roofspace, filled now with a web of leadwork but only the remnants of glass. One end wall of the room, presumably the one through which they had entered, was broken away entirely. Sheldi looked behind her and saw a vista of treetops and a winding river valley directly below; the building was perched right on the edge of a crag. The hall was bare except for a jumble of barrels in the vast fireplace and a wooden door at the far end, far too small for the dragon to squeeze through, under the splintered remains of the minstrels' gallery. Sheldi searched her reeling thoughts for recognition.

'This is the Castle of Crows,' she said slowly. She had seen it before from the woodland road below; a ruined border keep miles from the city, gutted after the rebellion of its minor lordling decades before. It was said alternatively to be inhabited by bandits or by ghosts; she guessed that now it had become the home of a new legend.

'It is a pleasant place,' said Oromon. 'Water and farmland nearby, and deer on the moors beyond. Difficult to approach except by air. Several of your villages in the area. An excellent home for one of my people. I was quite surprised to find it vacant.'

Sheldi wrapped her arms around herself and stared into its golden gaze wordlessly.

'Are you going to scream?' it enquired. 'This is the point when your kind usually fall on the floor crying, or defecate, or jump from the edge. Sometimes your females are drugged, of course, and then they don't panic until it wears off.'

Sheldi shook her head and shivered. 'I'm cold,' she said. There seemed to be no need to raise her voice to speak to the beast; it heard her whisper well enough.

'Get up and come here, then. I will warm you.'

Sheldi saw no point in disobeying. She walked over

23

shakily until she was almost within arm's length of its ribs. She could feel the warmth radiating from its skin, true enough – it was almost comforting, after the flight. She sat down on the floor, not trusting her legs. The dragon regarded her inscrutably, its head propped on its crossed forelegs.

'Have you been drugged, little Sheldi?' it asked. 'You are very calm, for a maiden.'

Sheldi allowed herself a smile. 'No,' she told it. 'But I have drunk so much fear that I can't taste it any more.' In truth, she felt light-headed, as if slightly detached from her body, which was buzzing at the extremities with renewed blood-flow. She wondered abstractly if it were true that a dragon's gaze could catch you in a glamour. Now that she was calmer she could grasp a better picture of Oromon's true size; she noted that his lower jaw was roughly as long as she was. It was not a comfortable thought.

'Are you a princess, then?' Oromon enquired. 'I have heard that it is traditional to offer princesses to my people, though I do not know if I have ever met one.'

'I'm not a princess,' she said bitterly. 'I'm standing in for one. The King's daughter was entered into the lottery with all the other noble maidens, that's true enough. But when her name was drawn this time the King appealed for someone else to take her place. And I was chosen. It's possible my father volunteered me – though I don't know that for sure. I know he didn't protest when my name was put forward. I expect he sees it as an honour for the family.'

'Ah,' the dragon hummed, making the lead in the windows quiver. 'So who are you, Sheldi?'

'I'm no one,' she said with a slow shrug. 'My father's a trader in pepper and horses from the Middle Sea. He's very rich, for a merchant – richer than most of the noble families in the city, I'd guess – but he's not old blood. That makes me good enough to be put into the draw to be eaten by a dragon, though not good enough for anyone to want me to marry their son. I go to Court a lot, waiting for some gentleman to propose, but it hasn't happened. I don't do anything else. When I was little, my father would take me on his trading journeys, but not since I reached a marriageable age.' She shrugged again and smiled acidly, before asking, 'So why do dragons only eat noble maidens, then?'

'We do not. I have eaten all kinds of your people, male and female,' Oromon corrected her.

'Did you eat the other three before me, from the city?' she asked reluctantly.

'I did. They were too squeamish and full of panic.'

'Oh.' Sheldi looked at her feet. She noticed that her fine dress was much the worse for wear; torn now and bedraggled. She assumed that the woven strings of flowers would have fallen from her hair during their flight. 'Why do people offer you their best maidens, then? It's always the traditional way, I mean – and it's what you expect. Like a bargain, almost. As soon as a dragon appears, it's out with the virgins to the stake, and you're there waiting.'

Oromon blinked a long, slow blink before asking, 'What do you know about dragons, little Sheldi?'

'Well. You fly. You breathe fire. You sleep on mounds of gold.' She looked around briefly at the bare hall. 'You get killed by heroes or Saints, sometimes. You live for hundreds of years. And you steal away and eat noble maidens.'

'We steal away females of your kind,' the dragon said musingly. A wisp of smoke spiralled up from its nostrils. 'My people live a long time, little Sheldi. I am one hundred and forty-six years old, which makes me only a young male by our standards. It will be another hundred years before I have the size and strength to go and challenge older males in the mating dances, before any female of my people will even look at my courtship. So for a hundred more years I will be alone. I will hunt, and sleep, and perhaps talk to your wizards. They seem to like that. But I will be alone. Do you see the problem? My people have traditions too. One of them is to take away a human of your kind and train her to be a concubine. A substitute for a real mate. Do you understand now?'

Sheldi, who had thought she was beyond further shock, stared blankly into the dragon's eyes before turning to look down the length of his belly. She saw no sign of a testicular pouch, but there was a bony rigid penis sheath slung from the soft skin between his hind legs. It was half the length she was. She turned back, appalled.

'Ah, no,' she said hoarsely. 'No. I mean, it's not possible. I mean – you couldn't even start . . .' A blush rose up the whole length of her body like a second skin. Oromon chuckled, the noise throbbing in her bones and adding to her confusion.

'No need to be afraid, little Sheldi; I have no intention of mounting you. Just the opposite, in fact. But you do understand why we take your kind, now. You may be small, but you have hands, and intelligence, and imagination. And you are adaptable.'

Sheldi stared him in the eye. 'Is this going to kill me?' she said, feeling the pulse knock in her throat.

'No, of course not. However, the alternative will, as you can guess. But I will look after you very well, if we are suited to one another. You can have whatever you want, from anywhere. It could be a very happy relationship.'

'I see,' she croaked.

'Good. If you see, then I assume you have made your decision.'

'Yes.' She wondered how her voice could sound so flat and calm.

'Stand up, then,' said the dragon. 'I wish you now to remove your clothes.'

26

Sheldi stood, though it was a long moment before her hands moved to the cross-lacing at the front of her bodice and began to loosen the cords. Every movement was slow, as if her hands were weighted, as if she were trying to give her mind time to catch up with what was happening. She let the stiffened bodice fall open, then slid from it and the thin undershift beneath in one drawn-out motion. The silk pooled at her feet like water. She kicked off her little slippers, then raised her head and stood up straight, feeling Oromon's gaze upon her naked flesh like a physical touch, conscious of every inch of her skin as never before in her life. Her hair, perfectly straight, fell in a heavy cascade across her shoulders and down the long line of her back to brush the curves of her buttocks. The jewellery at her throat and wrists gripped her gently. She could feel the icy floor beneath her bare feet, the radiated warmth of the dragon on her right side, the small cool breezes that played across her skin and caused her nipples to stiffen.

'Good,' said Oromon dryly. 'Tell me, are you considered attractive by the standards of your people?'

Sheldi looked down at herself, at the firm curves so generous that they were almost a joke. Noblewomen of the city aspired to be tiny and fragile with huge dark eyes. She remembered the barbed 'She has the physique of a dancing-girl, not of a lady!' hissed deliberately just within her hearing, a lifetime away. 'Actually, I'm thought to be too tall,' she said quietly to the dragon.

'Not now,' said Oromon, bringing his head in close to her, so close she could hardly avoid touching it. His hot breath whistled around her feet. Suddenly his tongue – forked like a snake's and pale blue – slid from between the mesh of his teeth and flickered up the taut line of her stomach. Sheldi gasped and put out her hand without thinking on to the scaled ridge between his nostrils. It was warm.

'What are you doing?' she whispered.

27

'Smelling you,' he replied. 'Kneel down; you will be more stable. It is necessary,' he added as she obeyed helplessly. 'My people have excellent hearing and vision, but a poor sense of smell. And the scent of your kind is not very like that of my own. But close enough. Ahh.'

His tongue brushed across her breasts, moving in and out of his mouth, tracing a path across her shivering skin from throat to belly, exploring under her arms and across her lips. Sheldi shut her eyes and submitted, yielding to the dry, delicate touch. When it slid between her parted thighs, she made no sound, though her eyes flew open. She felt the tip of the tongue questing in the moist folds of her flesh and realised with silent shock how adroit a forked tongue could be at parting and spreading that flesh.

'Open your legs,' breathed Oromon, withdrawing for a moment, and when she complied he returned to probe deeper. And she was wet, she suddenly knew: soaking wet. His tongue was drawing slick trails of moisture down from her vagina across her thighs and she could smell herself. She flushed with shame. The dragon-tongue slipped into the hot passage of her sex, flexed there and withdrew – Sheldi bit down on a tiny moan.

'Not entirely unpleasant, then,' Oromon chuckled; then, when she refused to reply, he stabbed again in a teasing caress that jerked a cry from her lips and left her shaking.

'Oh, please,' she whispered, forced to admit her pleasure as her hips, without voluntary instruction, pressed her aching mound against his reptilian flesh.

'Not yet,' he reprimanded, pulling his whole head back into the gloomy shadows of the roofspace. Sheldi knelt still, her dignity stripped from her, her mind reeling. 'Go to the fireplace,' he told her implacably. 'There is oil there; anoint yourself.'

Sheldi rose to her feet and walked unsteadily across to the hearth. She found the oil, golden and nearly odourless, in a barrel, and as the dragon watched she poured cupfuls over her breasts and down her legs, rubbing it in with her hands until she was slick and gleaming from shoulders to toes, pressing herself shamelessly between the legs as he rumbled his amusement. 'Now come to me,' he commanded at last, but she needed no telling. She burned with frustration and curiosity. She wanted to know what a dragon's pizzle looked like. Taking a cupful of the oil with her, she walked across the breadth of the hall to the red wall of Oromon's belly.

From the rigid protective sheath his erection was beginning to protrude, white as fish-skin – shockingly pallid against the dark colours of his scaled body – and glistening with its own moisture. Whether it was her scent or his anticipation, she had begun to arouse him, and this made her flush in her turn. Sheldi reached out to touch the pale flesh, feeling it smooth and slick beneath her palm. She poured some of the oil on to the tip and began to stroke it along the length, but more emerged into sight in response to her touch.

'Harder,' growled the dragon thickly. 'You must be firm.' She obeyed at once, pressing and massaging with the heels of her hands, causing him to rumble deep in his throat and twitch his barbed tail. His penis was as thick as her own thigh and not bulbed at the end like that of a man but tapering to a point, on the underside of which was a moist slit. Sheldi was awestruck. Her oiled hands described lavish caresses down span after span of its turgid length, and the erection jumped beneath her touch.

'Climb up, now,' Oromon told her. She scrambled on to the ridged sheath and wrapped her arms around the pizzle to hold on as he rolled carefully on to his back. Sheldi found herself yards above the ground, straddling the dragon's stiff prick, her knees on the hot, soft leather of his belly. The hard, slippery pole under her was as long as her own body now and pointed out like a battering ram. Sheldi had a vivid image of how bizarre it must look, this enormous spear arising from between her thighs, and the thought made her wriggle upon her perch. She pushed forwards with her hands and rubbed backwards with her groin upon the oily surface, working up a rhythm of pressure and motion. Oromon groaned and her head buzzed from the deep tones. Her own open, needy cunt was pressed against the white flesh, hopelessly unable to encompass its girth but yawning and desperate and sliding. Waves of heat passed through her belly; without warning she began to come, frigging herself on the dragon's huge prick, loving it, exultant, gasping out her release. The pizzle bucked beneath her, lifting her from her footing – she nearly lost her balance and had to lie forwards and cling to it as the shocking vibrations of her pleasure died away.

She came back to her senses lying face down, draped around the white lance that fitted tightly between her slippery breasts. She looked up the length of it towards Oromon's head, saw the glow of his golden eyes, his teeth bared in tension. No words came from him now; he was caught on the apex of anticipation, wordless and unthinking as any beast, needing her to finish it. She smiled.

Then she began to work her way up the length of that prick to the tip, using her whole oiled and sweat-slick body to rub it, wrestling, using the friction of hands and feet and breasts and thighs and groin. She clung to his member as if it were her lover, grinding and mauling. She felt muscular spasms chase through the taut surface of his belly. She reached the tip and pushed her face into the slit, delving with her tongue as she hugged and writhed. She lay on her back, the very end of the prick between her upthrust breasts, her legs crossed over and around it and squeezing, and she dug her nails into the white skin and dragged lines of exquisite pain across the surface.

And the dragon roared and arched and spent in ecstasy, his come gushing from him over Sheldi, exploding in her face like a bucket of water, drenching her hair and breasts. It was hot and very wet; Sheldi choked as it forced its way into her open throat and she swallowed great mouthfuls. It tasted of burned sugar, bitter and sweet all at the same time. When she finally opened her eyes, gasping, she saw that the liquid was perfectly clear; it lay on her flushed skin glittering like diamonds. The dead weight of the dragon's prick settled on her outstretched body, limp and throbbing with the last pulses of pleasure.

After a long, wordless pause for breath, Oromon rolled gently back on to his right flank. Sheldi, exhausted, slid down the slope of his stomach without attempting to resist the fall and he caught her above the flagstones in one foreclaw. She nestled in the warm space between limb and body, stunned by what had happened, touching the huge scales of his cradling claw wonderingly. Oromon's head swung round on its long neck so that he could look at her collapsed form. His tongue slid out to brush her nipples, tasting his own juices mingled with her scent.

'I think I must find you food, now, little Sheldi,' he purred, 'and I suppose you will need clothes. There is a well in the courtyard for when you want to wash. A lot of the castle remains intact . . . I believe there are whole rooms below which you must look into. I have seen a library. Perhaps you could fetch out the books and read to me from them later. My people are great storytellers. Or would you rather just sleep for the moment?'

But because his tongue was probing the wet, hungry folds of her cunt and teasing her clit into fiery life again, Sheldi was unable to answer.

Renaissance

The merchant frowned at the man standing in front of him and said, 'You're a doctor? You don't look like one.' He might have added, 'Where are your robes? Where is your gold-topped cane? Why are you so young?' The object of his scrutiny was dressed as plainly as a journeyman of some respectable craft-guild, and the box on the strap over his shoulder could have held anything from pens to mason's tools.

The younger man raised his hands. 'Well, physicians are not born with long grey beards,' he said with a disarming smile. 'But I am doctor, I assure you; I studied at the University of Solerno, and I came here on the word of Raoulin of Silver Street. You can send to him for my credentials, if you doubt me.'

The merchant grunted, leaving no room for uncertainty as to his confidence in the man's story: 'That old trickster – fifteen silver pennies he charged me for his treatment, and not a moment's improvement has my wife seen from it.'

'I can see you have lost faith in the medical profession,' said the young man softly. 'Permit me to restore it, I beg you; from what I hear of your good lady's symptoms, she suffers from a malady I have treated before with success.'

The merchant's eyes narrowed with suspicion. He did not doubt that the young man had treated many women to their satisfaction; a doctor that was not old and ugly must be a singular rarity, and this was a fair-featured man before him. Not what the merchant would call an impressive or memorable face, but clean-shaven with loose brown hair and intelligent eyes – a smooth, plausible fellow to whom most men would not give a second glance, and yet, the merchant suspected darkly, one who would be good enough for many weak-willed women. He frowned again. 'What, is my wife's illness now the gossip of the city?' he grumbled. 'I have consulted many physicians, and not one of them has lived up to their promises. I see no reason to let you examine my wife.'

'Then she will continue to suffer until her death,' said the man, his voice hardening somewhat. 'And you will carry the burden of a crippled marriage.'

The merchant rubbed his hands uneasily across the straining expanse of his tunic. There was a greasy patch on the rich fabric there resulting from this habit. 'Well, I will not pour silver into your pockets to hear you recommend scourging her,' he said.

'Is that what you have been advised?' the other asked with visible concern.

'I'm told she is possessed, or under some witch's curse,' the merchant said. His expression grew heavy. 'I have been told that I will have to have the devils beaten out of her. But I am too tender-hearted to bring myself to that yet. Perhaps that is why these devils plague me, because my faith is weak.'

'Please, do not resort to torture,' the doctor said. 'I am sure that I can bring about a happier cure.'

The merchant weighed his protective instincts towards his wife with the prospect of further years

33

living with her frenzies and her silences. 'You may come upstairs,' he said at last, 'though I will attend the examination.'

'Of course,' said the younger man. He hefted his box and followed the anxious husband up the stairs out of the shadowy hall and into the interior of the opulent townhouse. His eyes missed nothing: not the rich embroidery of the merchant's ample robes; not the fashionable frescos on the plaster of the large rooms he was led through; not the tasteless but expensive glassware that was on display on every shelf or chest. It was a house too big for its occupants to fill comfortably and must keep a small army of servants in employment.

The merchant led the way down a corridor and into a room that faced south across the red-tiled roofs of the city. The room was large with a very high ceiling, and the scale of the place was emphasised by the fact that every stick of furniture bar a narrow bed and a small stool had been removed. The afternoon light slanted in through the arched windows, unimpeded by shadow or barrier, and the whole space was filled with dust-motes and tiny muttering echoes. There were two occupants in the room: a middle-aged female servant who stood up respectfully from the stool when her master entered, and a smaller woman who sat upon the bed, her knees drawn up before her. This one did not so much as stir in response to the newcomers.

'This man,' said the merchant to the servant, waving one hand behind him as they approached, 'is, ah, Michel . . .'

'Dubois.'

'Michel Dubois, a physician of this city, whom I have engaged to treat Annette. Fetch him a goblet of wine, woman. Will you be needing a bowl for the examination of my wife's urine, sir physician?'

'No,' said the doctor. 'That won't be necessary.' He placed his box down carefully, his gaze all the time on

34

his patient. She was rather short and slightly built, as far as one could tell through the shapeless tunic she had been bundled into, with pale skin. Probably two decades younger than her husband, as was to be expected. Her hair was a matted tangle, dark as a blackthorn bush in winter, her long lashes and rather full lips the only generous touches in her unpainted, somewhat pinched-looking face. Her expression was blank.

The servant ducked her head and hurried off.

Annette's hapless husband folded his arms and watched as Michel leaned over his wife, took her chin in one hand and turned her face up towards his so that he could look into her eyes. Their gazes did not meet; Annette's vision was elsewhere, her dark eyes turned slackly away from the man in front of her as if he did not exist. When he released her face, she returned to her previous position. Michel took up both her hands from her lap and examined them, turning them over. Again she showed neither resistance nor response. Her husband felt a tiny twinge of something he did not consciously identify as satisfaction.

'She's not always like this, is she, though?' said Michel, sinking on to the stool so that he was face to face with her.

'No,' the merchant said. 'This will last another few days.'

'And what then?'

'For a little while she will be normal, or close to normal, like other women. I will be able to show her at balls and dinners, if I like. She will talk and dance and dress like a human being. Then in a few weeks she will change again; that is the worst of her times. She will become uncontrollable, break things, attack people. She is so filled with rage, I don't think she knows who or where she is, or that she can recognise us. That will last a week.'

'Rage and fear, followed by a slide back through acceptable behaviour into this dark fugue,' the doctor mused.

'That is right,' the merchant said. 'You have seen this before?'

'I said that downstairs,' he agreed absently, still watching the woman. 'What is her appetite like?'

'When she is like this, she does not eat at all. When she is in her frenzy, she eats like a furnace. Anything we let her get near. She killed a cat once and tore it up with her teeth,' he finished with a shudder.

'Hmm. And her carnal appetite?'

The merchant coloured. 'Well, you can see,' he stumbled. 'I can approach her now, or when she is able to talk, but later on . . . she becomes like a lamia. I fear for my life. She has drawn blood from me. I wouldn't dare go near her at the height of her frenzy.'

'Obviously,' Michel agreed. 'Tell me, how long has she been your wife?'

'Three years now. She was from a good Burgundian family.' The merchant thought of disclosing her dowry and then decided better of it.

'And has she been suffering from this malady all that time?' asked Michel.

'No – not for the first year. It came on gradually after her fourteenth birthday.'

'So, has she borne you a child yet?'

'No,' the merchant sighed. 'I am without an heir. If I were a cruel man, I could divorce her; she is as barren as the sea-sand and it seems clear at the worst times that she is possessed by a devil from Hell. The Archbishop would be sympathetic to my plea, I'm sure.'

The servant came back into the room as he spoke these words and the merchant fell silent. She presented a goblet of brilliant blue Venetian glass to the physician, who took a few sips of the white wine within and passed it back to her.

'Do these attacks coincide with the onset of her courses?' Dubois asked the husband.

He went red, and protested, 'I have no idea!'

'Well?' said Michel, turning to the servant. 'Is she bleeding now?'

The woman glanced quickly at her master. 'Yes sir,' she said.

'And is the flow heavy or light in your opinion?'

'Very light, sir,' she said. 'It always has been for her.'

Michel nodded. 'The diagnosis is clear,' he said. 'The treatment, however, may not be. Your doctors with their whips and cudgels were right about one thing; it is a malady beyond their repair.'

The husband was alarmed. 'What do you mean?'

'I mean that the disorder, though it has a physical cause, does not have a cure in our meagre store of knowledge.' He sensed the protestations rising in the merchant's throat and moved to explain. 'Imagine wrapping a cord around a man's arm tight enough to prevent the ebb and flow of the blood. What would happen if that cord were not removed?'

'The limb would blacken and die, of course. I imagine that the man himself would succumb, if the limb were not amputated.'

'Well, your wife is in a situation analogous to that one. The tides of the humours within her are blocked, so that the blood pools and grows stagnant, and the rancid fluids poison her and drive her mad. She is not possessed by any devil, for which you may be grateful. But the disorder is serious, and she will die of it if it is not cured.'

'You suggest that we bleed her? It did not cure her before, though it does keep her quieter when her frenzy comes upon her – is that all the cure you recommend?'

Michel stiffened. 'I'm not suggesting bleeding her,' he said, his calmness fading for a moment before he

37

regained his equilibrium. 'I'm saying that I do not have the remedy for your wife. Her cure is with the Church.'

'The Church? Is there nothing to do but pray?'

Michel raised a hand to forestall his client. 'Have you heard of St Veronique the Virgin? No? She is little-known, a poor rural saint that only the peasants revere. However, God has granted her through His grace the cure for this malady that your wife suffers from. It is a sure miracle; I sent several sufferers to pray at her shrine and every one of them has returned cured. That is all your wife need do; make a pilgrimage to the shrine and pray there.'

'I have never heard of this saint,' the merchant said shaking his head.

'Nevertheless, her shrine is less than a day from your own door. It is a little chapel on the estate of the Châtelaine Marguerite, niece to the Duke. She permits the passage of pilgrims across her land, though there are few of them. As I said, it is not a famous place, but it is a holy one.'

The merchant mused, 'The Châtelaine? I sold her an entire glass service, once, and two bolts of silk for a summer gown. I suppose it cannot do my Annette harm if I take her to this chapel.'

Michel shook his head. 'Listen to me. The procedure is laid down by the Church. She must go alone, unaccompanied; do you understand?'

'Alone?' he snorted. 'Don't be ridiculous!'

'I mean it, or you will get no cure. It is less than a day's walk, and she will be under the protection of the Châtelaine, as well as St Veronique herself. There is nothing to fear for her safety.'

'I don't like it,' the merchant said. 'The roads are lawless places.'

'I'm not asking you to like it,' Dubois said curtly. 'She must go alone. She must wear the white garb of a penitent and a wooden cross upon her breast, to mark

38

her for a pilgrim. Her head must be bare. Plain shoes. Nothing else; no jewellery or relics. She is to walk to the house of the Châtelaine, and there she'll be directed to the shrine. And she should start as soon as she is able, before the choleric rage rises in her. A week from now, if she is capable of the journey. She will spend three nights praying at the shrine, and then she will return. I swear, she will be cured if she asks St Veronique with a pure heart. I know no other way for her.'

There was a long pause while Annette's husband stood staring down at the physician, weighing his words. He noticed absently that the younger man had rather curious, light-hazel eyes, now that they caught the afternoon sun. He thought of future months lying in ambush before him, the long seasons waiting for Annette to choke on her own choler or drown in her own melancholy, until he might be free to find a sane and comfortable wife once again. And so, with reluctance, he finally nodded his assent. Dubois' mouth crooked in a smile.

'Do you agree, too, Annette?' he said gently, turning to the woman and addressing her directly for the first time. He took one of her pale hands between his long brown fingers and leaned forwards to look into her eyes. 'You must want to be free of this, too. Will you go to St Veronique?' And, to the considerable surprise of her husband and her maid, Annette's withdrawn gaze slowly focused on his face. Though she did not smile or change her empty expression, she nodded very slightly.

Annette stood at the side door to her house in the morning sunshine. It was still early enough for the street-sweepers to be visible clearing horse-dung and vegetable peelings from the cobbles in front of those houses that retained their services, early enough for bread-vendors, out with their baskets of loaves, and fish-sellers, still on their way from the docks to the market place. Early enough for her white penitent's gown, made from the finest wool, to feel comfortable on her. In another few hours, when the sun was up, she thought unemotionally, the sheer unbelted robe would be too hot and heavy and she would have to find shade. A pilgrimage at the height of summer was a foolish notion; had she been driven by anything other than dire necessity, her husband would never have let her go. As it was, he had kissed her farewell a few moments ago – but chastely. She had made her confession in the Church of the Blessed Virgin at dawn, by special arrangement with the priest, and it would not do to besmirch her shriven soul now.

Annette stared up the street for a few moments, gathering her thoughts and her strength for the journey ahead. The hopeless lethargy of the week past was mostly lifted now, but lingered like a veil that separated her from the bright world before her. Everything felt unreal; she knew that if she did not force herself to act then she could easily stand all day by the wooden gate, watching the city without interest or active thought. She knew her duty, but it was a deliberate effort to apply herself to the task. She wasted some minutes staring at her feet, clasped in flat shoes she had never previously worn, before pulling a deep breath and stepping on to the road.

The gate she needed lay to the north west, across the breadth of the city. The route was direct enough that she need spare it little thought. She knew the way to the market place and the Great Square beyond it; skirting the Cathedral, she would then have to climb the hill to the gate. She watched her feet move on the cobbles, and the road in front of her, not sparing a glance for the buildings she passed – fine houses, the famous Library, the Archbishop's Palace – or for the people. She attracted many curious looks but was only dimly aware of them. To those onlookers, she must have appeared the very image of penitence, but in fact she was sunk in indifference, her awareness all turned inward. She let her mind dwell on the strange feel of her new shoes, and the harsh rasp of the woollen robe against her bare skin – for she was wearing nothing beneath it – and the oddness of being outdoors with her head bare. She had not gone bareheaded in public since she was a child; no other woman in the city would be walking as she did that day, not even the prostitutes down on Grope Lane. Now that it was cleaned and combed her rich, dark hair fell upon her shoulders like a cloud of darkness. Her inner darkness was invisible to all but herself.

She reached the gate without being challenged by any but children who were not old enough to restrain their surprise at the sight of such a strange figure, though some people crossed themselves – perhaps in response to her piety, perhaps to disassociate themselves from her sins. The streets were filling up now and around the gate the crowds bottlenecked and came to a standstill. Soldiers on the gate were taxing incomers based on the goods they were carrying and the number of legs in their party; a flock of sheep blocked the way now.

Annette stopped to wait her turn. She turned her face away from the smell of the frightened sheep and wiped the dust they were kicking up from her eyes. The gateway was filled with people arguing, grumbling and trying to retain their companions. A party of masons were causing further confusion by carrying out repairs on the side of the main arch, their scaffolding wobbling under their movements. Annette watched listlessly for a while then returned to looking at the ground. There was a large wooden crucifix hung around her neck, with which she fiddled idly with one hand. The cross nestled exactly between her breasts.

A hand fell on her arm; she looked up with some surprise. A young man was touching her; thin-featured, ill-shaven, with clothes that looked fine and fashionable but which were stained and shabby. His breath smelled of wine. He had clearly seen her from one of the taverns nearby where youths such as he sat and gambled. This one looked as though he had been gaming for days. Annette stared at him blankly as he bestowed a smile upon her.

'My lady,' he began rapidly, 'I have no idea what it is that you are repenting of, but I do sincerely hope that you enjoyed it enormously at the time. And, if I might say so, any partner that you may have had in your sins was a lucky man, and if I were he I would not repent the action if the Devil himself were upon my heels. You look somewhat tired and thirsty, if I might be so bold – I hear that repentance is hard work; perhaps you would like to join myself and my companions for a refreshing drink. It isn't far – just over here – you can recommence your journey at any point.' By now he had one hand on her arm and the other around her shoulders, tugging her away from the road. Annette stared up into his bloodshot eyes and fumbled for words. She managed to whisper, 'No', but it had little effect.

'You have beautiful hair, if you'll forgive me for saying so – I thank the angels that your husband chose to spare you it. By God, I hope it was adultery, woman – you would be wasted on anything less.'

A knot had gathered in Annette's breast; a tight knot of rage. It was like a white flame lighting up the darkness inside her. She bit down on her lip, starting to tremble inwardly. She knew she was going to strike that stupid leer off his face. She was going to smash every bone in those groping hands that were round her waist now. He could see nothing of what was happening in her, could only see some confused whey-faced girl with eyes dark as bruises staring at him in confusion. The rage swelled in her like a choking wave. She was going to kill this man.

He was yanked away from her. Another man had appeared behind him; an older man dressed in scholar's robes who pulled him roughly away from Annette.

'Don't even think about touching a pilgrim, boy,' the newcomer said. He was old, his neat beard and what remained of his hair, silver, his handsome face lined, no match for a drunk young man – but his eyes were as fierce and commanding as a hawk's.

The youth gawked in surprise, put a hand to his belt for a knife or a sword that was thankfully not there and sneered, 'And who the hell are you, old man?'

'I am Bernard de Montauban, the Archbishop's personal secretary,' the other shot back, his voice not the voice of an old man at all. 'Do you want me to call in those soldiers or do you want to go back to your cups, you sot?'

The youth started, laughed, hesitated, spat on the ground and then turned his back and walked away. Annette looked wordlessly at the older man.

His eyes were grave. 'Calm down,' he said firmly. 'This is not the time to lose your temper.' So saying, he took her arm and led her towards the gate. Strangely, Annette did not find his grasp anything but reassuring. 'You're going to the shrine of St Veronique, aren't you?' Bernard said. 'Come on; I'll walk you through the gate.'

He was as good as his word, leading her past soldiers who simply saluted and pushed other people aside to make a path for them. Annette felt her head spin. The knot of anger in her throat had died away again as quickly as it had appeared, but it left her feeling twitchily awake, as if she had been kicked from a comfortable doze.

'Follow the road north,' Bernard said, pointing up the dusty track. 'Turn off when you see the Châtelaine's house.'

43

'Thank you,' Annette murmured. He smiled briefly, took up her hand and kissed the back of it formally – then turned the hand over and kissed the palm too. His lips were warm and dry. Annette felt a shiver mount her spine.

Bernard stepped back, said, 'St Veronique be with you, child,' and then disappeared back into the crowd milling under the city walls.

Annette turned slowly round, taking in the scene about her with something like interest for the first time. She had never been beyond the city walls without a chaperon, and rarely at all if it came to that. She was a merchant's wife, not of that class of people whose women went hawking and hunting for amusement. She knew the countryside only as an interim between the secure walls of different cities, a place from which produce was brought and in which payloads were lost to bandits or weather. She had never considered a journey as an active thing, an event in which she was involved. She had never considered the weather as more than an inconvenience to her person. Now she looked at the hazed summer sky in apprehension. It was going to be very hot on the road and, worse than that, there was a humid tension in the air. To the south-west, the direction of the mountains, a bank of blue thunderclouds heaved and threatened. Annette hoped it would rain – otherwise the walk would be torture.

Under the brassy morning light the land beyond the city stretched away up the broad river valley, a golden land of hay-meadows and oat fields, striped with the brighter green of the pastures near the Argens where cows grazed, and stippled by the sombre shades of the cork-oak groves. There was little cover. The great strips of the fields were not broken by shelterbelts of trees; land here near the city was too valuable. Dark fingers of cypress and poplar marked the lines of the roads; these and a pall of yellow dust. Annette took the first

44

few steps in the direction Bernard had indicated; her path lay across the breadth of the valley and into the flanking hills.

She walked for hours, discovering for herself the taste of the dust, the novel feel of strain in her calves and the rule of the highway – give way to anything larger or more numerous than yourself or be pushed aside. She talked to no one and was in turn unmolested, though that might have been due to the fortunate presence of a severe-faced nun, balanced side-saddle on a donkey, who preceded her on the road for many miles. In the worst heat of the day she paused in the shade of a lemon grove, where she begged a drink from a family also resting in the patchy shadow. A small girl shyly passed her a skin of red wine – the roughest Annette had ever tasted, but by now she was unconcerned – and then offered a broken loaf and a damp wedge of cheese along with a request for the 'fine lady' to bless them. Annette was touched by both the peasants' generosity and the child's faith, and tried to show her gratitude with gesture and prayer. She herself did not feel sanctified in any way, but was aware only of a growing wonder at the strangeness of it all and a vulnerability she had never experienced in the care of her family or husband. As she sat beneath a tree, looking away from the nearly deserted highway to the field behind the orchard where rows of workers toiled without pause at the hay-harvest, she felt the unguarded nature of her situation like an actual presence. Her hair itched with sweat but she caught herself looking behind her before scratching it, as if she were being watched by someone she did not trust.

When the shadows had lengthened a few inches, though the day felt no cooler, she roused herself from under the tree and resumed her journey. There were fewer people on the road in the afternoon. The scythes of the haymakers flashed in the distance as they worked, frantic to bring the harvest in before the weather broke. Annette put a leaf into her mouth to relieve the dryness there, but it turned to a mucilaginous wad that did nothing to ease her thirst. The wine she had drunk had made her a little dizzy. She did not really notice when the road started rising and turning back and forth, winding up a minor valley into the hills. She did not notice until she stopped to sit on the verge for a few moments that she was passing another valley, on the flank of which was perched a large fortified house. The building gleamed in the strong light, which was becoming increasingly yellow now.

Annette looked back and saw that she had passed the road that led off to the great house. She had to backtrack until she recovered her way; it would have been too difficult to cut across the valley, which was terraced and planted with rows of vines. The land here was too steep for hay-meadows and looked very dry. The minor road she now trod was, however, better-surfaced than the main highway, and Annette paused to pick off her new shoes, which were rubbing her, so that she could tread barefoot on the smooth flags.

Almost as soon as she had started down the turn-off, the yellow-green light darkened and a sudden gust of wind threw grit into her face. She felt the first raindrops strike the back of her hand as she was wiping her eyes and in moments the storm had broken over her head and the rain was pouring down. There was no shelter, not even a lone tree near the road; Annette had no choice but to put her head down and keep walking. The day turned to premature dusk around her as the clouds rolled in and the water thundered down. It got into her hair and washed out the sweat. It soaked her robe, back and front, until she was wet to the skin and shivering in the new chill. Her wish for rain had been granted with a vengeance. Thunder grunted and growled overhead like a grumbling husband. She had never felt such elemental nakedness as she did now, hunched and slipping in the rain.

But it was only a summer storm, and it passed as swiftly as it had arrived. It left the earth wet and gasping like an unsatisfied lover, and Annette soaked to the bone. She wrung out her long hair and the hem of her dress, which was sodden. The finely spun wool clung to her now like a second skin, moulded shamelessly to her thighs and breasts and the line of her back and rounded buttocks, heavy as leather. It was disgraceful. She tried to tug it back into its former shapelessness but it held tight to her neat curves, resisting all her attempts – and at least it was warm where it clung fast. Eventually she gave up and kept walking, hoping to dry the cloth with her own body heat. She was well aware of how it must look. Her slender form outlined in white left little to the imagination: her high, firm breasts moulded in wet fabric, and even the cleft between her arse-cheeks defined by the clinging, betraying material. A rosy flush of defiled modesty warmed her pale face and she kept her head up, searching the empty road ahead, not looking down in case she should be distracted by her own flaunted curves and the sight of her nipples, hardened against the cold wool, rubbing almost painfully on the wet fibres.

She reached the gate-house of the great building far too soon for her robe to right itself, though it was actually steaming gently from her warmth beneath – as was the rich land in the renewed sunshine, giving off the organic scents of leaf-mould and animal dung. The gate-house was kept by a servant, who was poking at a piece of blocked guttering with a stick when she arrived. He turned, saw her, and stared. Annette shivered under his open regard but did not blench; she felt numb now, detached from reality once more. His gaze, roving undisguised over her displayed form, could not make her feel any more strange.

'The Châtelaine Marguerite?' she whispered. 'I am on pilgrimage to the shrine of St Veronique.'

The servant, bearded and stocky, nodded without a word, hefted his codpiece in an uncouth manner and waved her in through the gate. At that moment, a plump woman emerged from the gate-house and gaped at Annette.

'A pilgrim, wife,' the gatekeeper explained swiftly, his voice hoarse.

The woman's face, which up till now had registered only shock and distaste, shut like an iron trap. 'I will take her to the Châtelaine,' she said in a low voice. 'She is in the garden. You stay here.' Her husband obviously did not dare demur; the woman started off into the grounds at a fierce pace, waving Annette to follow her. She did not look round once at their guest. She led the way through an apple orchard and behind the stables to a wall to one side of the main building – clearly taking the most private route. No one met them as they walked. Annette caught only glimpses of the fine façade of the house, built of yellow stone. The door in the wall was stained green. The servant opened it, ushered Annette through and then shut it behind her so smartly that she jumped, fearing a trap. She looked around her.

As promised, she was alone in a garden. After the bare hillsides, stitched with well-trimmed ranks of vines outside, this place seemed as lush as Eden itself. Small paths of yellow stone led here and there between beds of flowers and what she took to be herbs. There were peach trees heavy with fruit and arches laden with sprawling, golden hops, there were rosebushes – large and small – in full bloom everywhere, so that the air was filled with the velvety musky scent of them, and there were brilliant green seats of turf placed about the raised beds, so that one might sit and fill oneself with the scent of the summer. Everything was soaking wet, with raindrops shining on every leaf and the bees questing among the freshened flowers.

Annette walked slowly through the garden, not knowing which direction to take, knocking showers of wet petals from every rosebush she inadvertently brushed against. Her hem became heavy with moisture once more. Her mind grew stiller in the rich, silent, enclosed place, to the point that, when she rounded a corner and saw two people standing before her, she could not remember without a struggle what she should say. The man and the woman, who had been laughing quietly together when she appeared, turned to observe her for a moment in silence. Annette met their keen inspection with some confusion.

That the woman was no longer young was obvious from her too carefully made-up face, but she was still possessed of her underlying beauty and a pair of startling blue eyes. Her faded yellow hair was arranged in a gilded net; blonde hair was something Annette had hardly ever seen in this part of the country. She wore a green silk dress upon her tall and slender figure, the full skirts hitched up to one side on a cord so that she need not drag them in the mud of the garden, and was holding a bunch of damp lavender in her ringed hands.

The young man with her was naked to the waist and barefoot, clad only in a pair of rough work hose and leaning on a wooden spade.

Annette felt the silent weight of their scrutiny like a pressure over her heart. She dropped a curtsey and asked, 'Châtelaine Marguerite?'

'You are?' said the woman, smiling coolly.

'I am a pilgrim, my Lady,' she stumbled, 'on my way to the shrine of St Veronique. My name is Annette Mercier. I come to ask your permission to cross your land and . . .'

The Châtelaine's smile grew warm suddenly, like the

throwing open of a door in winter to reveal a firelit room. 'My dear,' she said, advancing with arms out, 'you are very welcome here. Annette, did you say? Did Michel send you? Of course!' She kissed the younger woman lightly on either cheek; her perfume was scented with roses too. 'My dear, you must have been caught in the storm – you are soaked. Come here and sit down. I shall send for dry towels at once.'

Unable to answer, Annette was led forwards into a copse of fruit bushes and up to a stone seat near a wall. The surface of this was relatively dry and she sank down gratefully. The Châtelaine regarded her seriously. 'You look very tired, my dear. You must have walked miles. Are you hungry?'

Annette nodded, feeling dizzy. The sense of unreality was very strong; she felt as if she had fallen into the hands of a fairy queen in some ballad. If she shut her eyes, she was sure, none of this would be happening.

'Stay here and rest,' the Châtelaine commanded. 'Gaspard will look after you. I will return shortly.' So saying, she disappeared through the screen of shrubs.

Annette was left alone with the young man, who strolled easily over to her side. She cast one glance at him and then looked away deliberately, her throat tightening. She had never seen any man in her life to match this one; tall and broad shouldered, every lean inch of him was defined by muscle. His hair was a glossy dark-brown mane that fell straight as water down between his shoulder-blades, and his beard – a narrow line sketched along the angle of his chin – was as black as his brows. She sat still in her clinging wet robe and tried to ignore the smile she had glimpsed on his lips. As a married woman, she could not in modesty begin a conversation with a strange man. She fixed her gaze on a rose near her elbow. It was nearly unfurled, the white petals flushed with pink still curled over its secret heart. Raindrops bedecked its silky petals.

Annette looked away again quickly, caught Gaspard's movement and was tricked into looking at him. He had wandered round so that he was facing her directly, was exploring the wet folds of her dress openly with his gaze. When he saw her looking, his smile broadened; he had arrogant, dark eyes, the kind that it was extraordinarily difficult to look away from.

The Châtelaine must have to keep this one on a tight rein, Annette thought distractedly, but she blushed anyway.

'You're hungry?' he asked. She could not help but nod. He turned away unhurriedly to one of the bushes and began to pick the berries. He took his time, his smooth, muscular back with its sweep of hair almost challenging her not to watch him. She lost the challenge easily. She could feel her heart beating slow and hard.

He returned with a handful of red berries and squatted nonchalantly before her. Annette sat with her back straight as a rod, pinioned by his gaze. She felt as though she were melting into her seat. He held out the berries over her lap, that mocking smile in his eyes and, when she did not move, picked one out and put it between his own lips. Annette watched helplessly as his fleshy, sensuous mouth closed upon it. He raised his eyebrows. She opened her mouth to say, 'No', but she hesitated a fraction too long, and he took another berry and smoothly pushed it between her lips. His fingertips grazed her softly.

She did not recognise the fruit. It burst on her tongue, sweet and tart at the same time, and she swallowed it. It was very good. She shivered, her nipples tightening. She wanted more, but pride made her reach for the next herself, not waiting for him. Amusement danced in Gaspard's eyes. He took her outstretched hand in his own, raised it to his lips and kissed her palm. Annette gasped as the tip of his tongue slid out to caress the

51

heart line, raking across it as if it were some other, more tender flesh . . .

There was the sound of footsteps beyond the bushes. Gaspard released her hand, dropped the remaining fruit into her lap and stood, unhurried. Annette lost his face, watched his dark nipples and his firm abdomen as they rose up in front of her instead. He lingered, making it clear that he did not fear his Lady's return. The thick outline of his virile member was quite clear against his left thigh, through the rough cloth of his hose. He took three slow paces back, and Annette had to snatch her attention from him to the face of the woman behind him.

'Here we are,' said the Châtelaine Marguerite, glancing with amusement at her two companions. 'My dear Annette, has Gaspard been teasing you? You have gone quite pink.' She tutted gently and put down a broad basket at Annette's feet. 'I have here a little food for your journey. Gaspard, go about your work. I will dry our pilgrim's hair; we do not want her catching her death, this night.'

Gaspard executed a short bow, the cruel smile never leaving his lips, before striding off. Annette's head was spinning. She bowed her head in confusion, only dimly aware of the Châtelaine taking a white cloth from the basket and walking around behind her seat.

'Now,' said Marguerite softly, wrapping the cloth around Annette's tangle of damp hair and beginning to squeeze and tousle it gently; 'you have only a little way to go my dear, to reach the chapel. There is a gate at the far end of this garden; you take the path beyond it up the small valley as far as you can go, and there is the chapel of our St Veronique. Perhaps three miles, I think. You will be there before nightfall.' Her soothing voice and the firm, caressing motion of her hands were sending waves of pleasure through Annette, who closed her eyes and dared almost to relax a little. 'I have brought you a cloak, because it gets cool on the hillsides, even on summer nights,' the murmuring voice continued, as the hands stroked the hair back from Annette's forehead and throat, tickling a little. 'There is a good stream by the shrine, and I will see that food is sent up to you. It is my duty to look after pilgrims, after all.'

The Châtelaine was now patting dry Annette's throat and the nape of her neck, describing gentle curves under her chin with the soft cloth and her cool fingers. Annette gave a tiny, high moan through closed lips – the sensation was pleasant but it frightened her; it was too good, too stimulating. A frisson of longing tightened in her flesh, causing her to jerk gently on the damp seat. The Châtelaine's hands were under the wet drawstring edge of her dress now, tracing her collarbones. Annette's eyes flew open.

The Châtelaine tugged the cord at Annette's throat, and pulled the gathered neck of the dress open. With gentle, soothing movements she reached down to touch the deep valley between Annette's high, rounded breasts and expertly stroke their sensitive inner walls. The skin tightened across the young woman's nipples and those questing fingers followed across her lightning-shot skin to the points of her breasts, the foci of tormenting pleasure and needful pains. Annette gave a helpless gasp low in her throat, trying to stifle the noise. The Châtelaine pressed up against her from behind, her own breasts cradling Annette's head for a heartbeat, then pulled away so that she could lean forwards and brush the damp dress from either shoulder, down to her elbows, baring Annette to the waist.

Annette froze, every muscle in her body tensing up. That movement brought home to her the fact that the dampness between her thighs was not all from the cloth, that there was a hot aching hunger in her. But she did not move, not when her breasts were cupped by the Châtelaine and gently hefted, not even when her two rigid nipples were taken between cold bejewelled fingers and used to lift the whole weight of each rounded orb, sending knife-slashes of ecstasy through her body. This was unreal, unbelievable – even her certainty that Gaspard was only just out of sight behind a screen of leaves, watching his Lady play with her naked flesh, was not enough to penetrate the fortress of her helplessness. Her body did not belong to her. And so the Châtelaine could do as she liked, but Annette could not respond.

Marguerite gave a sigh that was almost a growl. 'You are truly beautiful, my dear,' she said, pinching the tender pink buds of Annette's nipples into delirious frustration. 'I am so glad you have come here to us.' Then – reluctantly, it seemed – she released her prisoner and drew up the fallen garment of her modesty.

Annette stood up, her face white with two hectic points of colour in her cheeks, and turned to the Châtelaine, who drew herself upright, a hungry smile in her eyes the only sign of her misdoings. 'You must be on your way,' she commanded the merchant's wife. Annette could not meet her blue eyes, but crossed her hands over her forsaken breasts in a confusion of longing and disappointment and shame. The discarded berries had left little pink stains on her robe as they had tumbled from her lap, a rosy Pleiades centred over her pubic mound.

'You must take these,' the Châtelaine warned, picking up the basket and proffering it to her. Annette accepted it numbly and left the garden by the way she was directed.

'The blessed Saint guide you, my dear,' were the Châtelaine's last words to her.

* * *

54

Annette awoke on the cold stone floor of the shrine, stiff from the chill that had soaked into her bones. She rolled over and sat up as soon as she realised that her sleep was truly lost to her. Morning sunshine filtered into the chapel through a single tiny window. The doorless entrance, which faced south down the path from the Châtelaine's house, was filled with pale light. Annette wrapped the cream-coloured cloak tighter around herself and tried to remember her arrival, with only partial success; details were fuzzy with fatigue. Her legs ached all the way from blistered feet to knotted thighs. She had walked from the Châtelaine's garden up a steep little valley, past the grounds and the fields and up into the uncultivated hillside beyond, finding and then following a stream, while her clothes had dried in the last of the afternoon sun. Evening had come quickly to the valley; the rocky walls cut out the light early. She had eaten most of the food in the parcel she had been given on her way, feeling faint with hunger as she took the first bite; a cheese tart, a cold baked fish, a small loaf of fine white bread. Some of the bread was still left on the flagstones beside her, hard as wood now, along with a leather flask that had contained good red wine. Annette murkily remembered finding the chapel with its two candles glowing on the altar, stumbling through a prayer to St Veronique and then simply curling up on the floor to sleep the sleep of the exhausted. She felt ashamed now, as well as cold; she should have stayed up to pray through the night.

The shrine was almost completely bare, now that she could see it properly – little more than a stone room built between rocks and water. There were no seats or furnishings, nothing but a stone altar upon which stood a wooden cross and the stubs of two thick candles, their tiny flames wavering in deep pools of wax. The front of the altar was carved and painted with the design of a young woman holding out a cross, as if to ward off a man on horseback. An animal of some kind – it looked like a dog or wolf – was depicted crouching at the woman's feet. On the east wall of the building, small wooden pegs had been driven into the mortar between many of the stones, and from these hung an assortment of crucifixes on chains or thongs. Most were plain wooden crosses like Annette's own.

She got to her feet and went outside to relieve herself. The valley, it transpired, unlike the arid surrounding hills, was crammed with vegetation, mostly stunted trees and sprawling, thorny bushes, all jostling around the banks of the stream. The water here was clear and deep enough even to bathe in but, to Annette's fingers, felt bitterly cold. Annette wandered along the bank uphill for a little way. By the time she returned to the chapel, she was at least warmer.

There was someone in the shrine before her, standing at the altar. Annette's heart jumped, but calmed again when the stranger turned round and revealed herself to be a young woman who grinned warmly at the sight of her.

'A new pilgrim!' she exclaimed without the slightest surprise. 'Please excuse me, lady, I am replacing the candles. Don't let me interrupt your prayers.' She was young and very dark, with masses of curling black hair that was barely contained by a tattered scarf. Her clothing was rough, simple and, like the headcloth, not quite adequate to the task of concealing what lay beneath. She had warm, wicked eyes and, if possible, an even wickeder smile.

'Is this your job?' Annette asked, looking at her bare brown feet. It was not what she had expected the sacristan to look like.

'Oh yes, lady,' said the peasant girl, wrapping up the two quenched stumps of the old candles in a cloth. 'Father Emil cannot get to the shrine every day because of his duties, so he has set me to sweep the floor and make sure the candles stay lit here. I'll tell him that there is a pilgrim present; he'll be sure to pay you a visit.'

'That's good,' said Annette weakly. She found the dark girl almost alarming; the combination of firm, curvaceous body, robust confidence and conspiratorial smiles from that generous mouth was overtly sexual, which shocked Annette in the context of this holy place. Not so much that she wanted the girl to depart, however. 'What is your name?' she asked.

'Claudette,' the other replied with a suppressed giggle. She seemed full of delight at her lot on this summer day. 'I work for the Châtelaine. I was told to bring you this food as well.' She picked up a parcel from the floor and brought it over to unwrap it in front of Annette. 'See: cheese, wine, olives and bread and a little pot of honey. Oh, she must like you; she is very careful with her honey.' This was the occasion for another giggle, and when Annette visibly blushed, she went off into a low peal of laughter which drew a smile out of Annette too.

'There you are,' Claudette finished, dropping the package into Annette's hands. 'I'll bring more tomorrow morning.'

'Have you eaten yet?' Annette asked.

'Only a drink of milk,' Claudette admitted.

'Eat with me, then,' the pale woman invited.

They could not indulge in anything so mundane inside the chapel, so they went outside and sat together on a warm rock to share the food. Claudette stretched out her bare feet to the sun and smiled contentedly at the world.

'You don't have much of an appetite,' she observed.

'No,' Annette said softly, nibbling on a piece of salty cheese, 'not today. I am supposed to be denying myself, for the Saint to listen to my prayers.' She in fact preferred to watch Claudette eat, scooping honey out of the earthenware pot and smearing it on rough pieces of bread – such as she could get there and not drip on her breast or drizzle up her bare forearm instead – before licking her fingers clean. The glistening honey was the same dusky golden-brown as Claudette's skin, Annette noted with pleasure.

'I don't see that your hunger will sharpen Veronique's ears,' Claudette said impiously, and rolled over on to her stomach. Her skirt bunched up, baring her hard calves. She is doing this deliberately, Annette thought; what is happening here?

'What are you praying for, then, lady?' Claudette enquired teasingly.

'I'm ill,' Annette said with caution. 'I'm praying for healing.'

Claudette bit her lip, her eyes huge with secrets. 'Oh, I'm sure you'll find it,' she said. 'St Veronique is very kind.'

Annette gave a token smile, wondering meantime if the Châtelaine Marguerite's aristocratic hands had ever cupped those large brown breasts. She did not doubt that Gaspard had hauled her into the hayloft and parted those rounded thighs many times. How could he resist? She looked away down the valley, her mental picture of Gaspard rooting blindly up Claudette's wanton passage kindling a warmth in her that her husband had never evoked in three years. Her voice sounded strange to her as she asked, 'What does the picture on the altar mean?'

'Hmm? That is the saint herself,' Claudette said, rolling a black olive over her lower lip and biting it neatly. 'Have you not heard the legend? When she fled from the wicked lord who wanted to ravish her, the wolves of the hills came to her assistance and fed her.'

'No, I hadn't heard that.'

'So you don't know about the Miracle of the Wolves?' asked Claudette, her eyes glinting. 'No? Sometimes all the wolves come down off the hills and into the chapel to pray to St Veronique. Nobody knows when they will choose to come. It might be tonight. It might be when you are here.'

Annette stared at her, then at the chapel. There was no door to the doorway. 'You're fooling with me!' she said quickly.

Claudette pursed her lips wickedly. 'Are you afraid of the wolves, pilgrim?' she asked, then burst into a throaty chuckle. 'Don't worry, lady – if they come, they won't hurt you. They're good Christian beasts, come to pray for their souls. They wouldn't eat a pilgrim: not a pure, pious lady like yourself.' She wriggled with delight at the thought, and Annette shook her head in disbelief.

'If I were you,' Claudette confided, getting up to her knees and leaning towards Annette so that her breath was warm on her cheek, 'I would not worry about anything while I was in the chapel, so long as I knew my heart was pure.' As she finished these words she stretched forwards just enough to allow her red lips to brush Annette's left cheek, and then silently drew those lips in a feathery stroke over to her earlobe, which she took gently between her teeth.

Annette held very still. Claudette withdrew, smiling still, then rose gracefully to her feet, turned and tripped off down the path. The last glimpse of her as she disappeared was of her mane of hair flopping on her shoulders.

It was difficult to leave the sunny rock and return to the cramped gloom of the shrine. Annette shivered as she entered, but she went to the altar, folded her cloak as a cushion for her knees, and bent her will to prayer. She stayed on her knees for hours, right through the morning, until her soul was emptied of thought, desire and fear.

The light had turned while she prayed, wheeling

round to cast a scorching lozenge of light into the dim interior through the doorway that could not be closed. Annette finally crossed herself, rolled from her knees and, when the blood-flow had returned to her feet, went out into the day. Prayer had left her so calm that tiredness had crept up on her once more, the legacy of unaccustomed toil and an uncomfortable night. Annette found a place where the sunlight was partially filtered by the shadow of a tree overhead and curled up in the dappled shade to doze.

She was awoken by something tickling her lips.

'You should not sleep with your head in the sun, child,' said a male voice. 'It will give you painful dreams.' She sat up hurriedly and the man who had been bending over her stepped back, discarding the grass-stalk with the heavy seed-head he had been deploying. Blinking, she realised that he was clad in black clerical garb and broad straw hat.

'Father ... Emil?' she murmured confusedly. The shadow had moved while she slept, exposing her head which now felt very fuzzy.

He nodded, smiling, and held out a hand to help her up, which he accomplished without visible strain. His hand was rough and warm. 'Claudette told me that you were here. What do you think of our little shrine?'

'Uh ... I have been praying all morning. It is very peaceful. But I am tired ... I fell asleep. I wanted to stay awake last night, but I was too tired by the walk – forgive me, Father.'

'No harm in that,' said Father Emil, strolling into the shrine. 'You need to rest as well as to pray. "Three nights at the shrine of St Veronique," you were told, I suppose? Well, you can keep vigil tonight and tomorrow. Did Claudette bring you food?'

'Yes, Father,' said Annette, following him within. Newly awakened, she was more comfortable in the gloom. The priest took off his hat, bowed towards the shrine and crossed himself.

'Ah, well, I have brought you these for tonight.' He unslung a bag from his shoulder and passed it to her; inside, a flask nestled up against more indistinct packages.

'Thank you,' she said. 'Father, have you heard of the Miracle of the Wolves?'

The priest looked at her quizzically. He had a lined face under untidy black hair salted with white, but the lines defined a map of good humour and his movements were vigorous. 'What has Claudette been telling you?'

'That the wolves come here to pray, some nights,' said she.

'Hmm. So they say. Anything is possible with God, child. But Claudette is a peasant girl, full of stories – and, I must admit, mischief, upon occasion. I would not believe everything she says.' He glanced at the altar. 'Do you know the story of St Veronique the Virgin?'

'Not properly, Father,' Annette admitted.

'The blessed Veronique lived in this area after Rome fell to the barbarians. She was a devout child and pledged herself to chastity, although she was held to be more beautiful than any other maiden within three days' journey. Then one day news of her beauty came to the ears of her local lord – some say he was a king, although I suppose that means little more than a brigand chieftain in those days. Now, he was a godless pagan who vowed to have the girl to wife – it's amazing how many of these fellows there are in history – and he came to take her by force. But Veronique prayed to the Virgin to make her so ugly that the chief would not want her any more, which is what happened; Veronique suddenly grew hair all over her face and body, so that everyone was terribly afraid and dis-

61

gusted. She ran away into the hills and did not come back until the lord had gone home, by which time all the hair had fallen out and she was fair once more.'

'What happened to her then?' Annette asked.

'I believe she spent the rest of her life as an anchoress, praying in the wilderness,' Father Emil said. 'Her relics were collected with great ceremony and placed beneath the altar you see here. The chapel was built later over the site. The point of the story, child, is that if we put our faith in God, no wile of the Devil can bring us real harm.'

'I see,' said Annette.

The priest smiled at her benignly. 'Now, before I go, would you like me to hear your confession?'

Annette bit her lip. 'Do you work for the Châtelaine Marguerite?' she asked huskily.

'I work for God, daughter,' he replied.

She nodded assent. There was no confessional box, so she knelt in front of the altar and he stood facing across her. She could not see his face from this angle, only his hands and his black-clad, rather stocky body. He spoke a few words in Latin, making the sign of the Cross, before she began.

She spoke reluctantly at first. Her unshriven sins were confined to the last few days. She confessed her anger at the young man by the gate and her periods of doubt in the efficacy of St Veronique. She confessed the paucity of her love for her husband, and the sin of being vainly self-conscious of her appearance when it rained. Then, with hesitation, she began to confess her feelings in the garden. She told how she had yielded to lust for both Gaspard and his lady, how she had forgotten her mission of purity, how she had wanted far more to happen than did. And as she spoke, she realised that the silence, the heavy weight of ritualised submission and the presence of a man listening to her tale were working to make her feel aroused once more.

She glanced up at him, and saw as he quickly crossed his hands in front of his groin. She hesitated. Her mouth was dry. He was so close she might touch him . . . anywhere. She began to speak again, though she knew she was compounding sin on top of sin, expanding on the events in the garden; how the Châtelaine had undressed her and touched her and how she had imagined Gaspard watching, his lust and frustration . . .

The priest stood like a statue, so still that he might not have been breathing, his hands rigid before him. He made no attempt to interrupt her story.

And then she described how she had felt an unnatural desire for Claudette, how she had almost swooned when they touched, how she had watched the other woman's hands and lips and breasts. Her thighs were slick and wet by the time she finished, a hot heartbeat pulsing between them. 'And I have committed the sin of lust, even in holy confession,' she concluded softly.

Father Emil's hands jerked slightly. He turned his back on her, facing the altar, grunted out a line in Latin and then spoke her absolution. He gave no penance. His voice was thick and strained. 'Saint Veronique bless you,' he whispered at last, turning. His hand brushed through her hair slowly, and then he fled from the chapel.

Annette winced in shame, blended in equal measure with aching frustration.

She began her vigil at sunset, having consumed none of the food but half of the flask of wine. It was a strong, dry vintage and it made her light-headed, but she began her prayers. Having emptied her burden of hopes and fears already before the silent altar she now alternated the rosary with periods of silence. When she began to lose consciousness she stood to her feet and remained upright, leaning from foot to foot, her hands knotted before her. She stayed awake until the owls had fallen silent and the insects ceased to creak and whine, until she had lost sense of time and self and place. She did not feel herself falling to the floor, but only a brief sensation of cold stone against her cheek before sleep closed over her head.

She dreamed that the chapel was full of wolves. A score of shadowy shapes pattering into the room on clawed feet poured like a canine flood around her and swirled before the altar. The harsh doggy scent of them filled the air; moonlight and candle-gleam glittered on their wet teeth and amber eyes, shimmering on their lolling velvet tongues and black serrated gums. They stepped over her, nosed her, pushed by her and then left, tacking out on their blunt claws.

She dreamed of darkness, endless and serene. She dreamed of warm, soft lips pressed against her own, and she woke with the touch of them still lingering.

A movement beyond the doorway might have been a fluttering skirt or the flap of a bird passing low. The candles were renewed and a loaf of bread and jug of milk stood near her head.

She spent the day alone, unvisited by servant or priest. Only when she went up the stream at noon to bathe in the biting flow of the stream did she see another living thing; as she climbed shivering from the water, a dust-coloured wolf rose from its crouch on a rock a little distance away and slipped back into the undergrowth.

At sunset, she was back at her vigil before the shrine. This was the last night; her last hope. If she could make up to the saint for all her earlier worldliness, perhaps she would be forgiven. The words slipped from her lips, a familiar blur of sound so well-worn they were almost without meaning, like the face stamped on an old coin now worn smooth. Her mind skidded off them again and again. She wrung her hands and began from the start: *'Pater noster . . .'*

There was a step behind her, the sound of a human

foot on the stone. Annette turned to find Claudette standing in the doorway, head low, watching her from dark eyes. Her hair was uncovered and unbound, wild as brambles.

'Are you ready?' Claudette asked in her deep, soft voice.

'For what?' faltered Annette.

'Tonight. The third night; your cure, if you want it. The miracle of St Veronique.'

Annette found her throat was tight. 'I don't think I'm worthy,' she whispered.

Claudette's lips curved in a smile, but her eyes were oh, so serious – nothing like her former countenance. 'Come with me,' she said. 'The miracle takes place outside, and I'm to be your guide. You don't have to be afraid, Annette.'

Annette swallowed, her hair creeping on her scalp. 'Outside?' she said.

'Trust me,' Claudette said. She pointed at the wooden cross nestling between Annette's breasts. 'Take that off and hang it on the wall with the others. It's your token.'

Fearfully, Annette obeyed. The white front of her robe was unbroken now except by the swell of her breasts. Claudette stepped forwards, untied a strip of cloth from around her wrist and held it up in one hand. 'The place of the miracle is secret,' she said. 'You'll have to go blindfolded. I will lead you. Do you still trust me?'

Annette slowly nodded, just once. She stood unprotesting as Claudette bound the cloth around her eyes, gently but securely. Claudette stepped away and there was a soft rustling. Annette felt her cold hand, now enfolded by Claudette's warm one, lifted and turned and – lips pressed to her palm. She shuddered, reached out as if falling to catch Claudette's arm, and encountered only soft, warm satin that flexed under her fingers.

'You're naked!' she breathed.

'Yes,' said Claudette, her voice gentler now. 'I don't need my clothes for this.' She took Annette's captured hand and laid it softly on her breast, the nipple large and tight against her palm. 'Does this frighten you?'

'Uh,' said Annette in a whisper, then, 'No. I'm not afraid.' She closed her hand tremulously on the softness of Claudette's flesh but could not encompass the ripe swell of the breast in her span. She heard Claudette smile – a strange perception – and then her hand was captive once more and she was being led out of the chapel. She forced herself to trust the other woman to lead her, moving close to her so that her feet might be set true on the path. Outside, pale light leached in through her blindfold; she raised her face to feel the moonlight. 'It's a harvest moon,' she said. She hoped for a reply, some friendly response, but Claudette kept quiet and steered her round the side of the building. Her feet found the path underfoot uneven but level and firm.

'There is a man here,' Claudette said, coming to a stop. Annette stiffened. 'He is your guide, too.'

'Hello, Annette,' came a warm voice. 'My name is Michel; I visited you in your house. Do you remember me?'

'I remember your voice,' Annette said hesitantly. 'I dreamed about you. You told me to come to the shrine.'

'That's right. I said you would be cured here.'

'Were you lying?' she demanded.

'No. Don't be afraid. You can be healed, if you want it, as I promised. But it is difficult, and it will change your life. You will not be the same as you were . . . or as other people. Listen to me, Annette: your sickness cannot be taken away, but it can be healed, it can be changed so that you are not crushed by it any longer. You will not have the blackness or the red rage. You will have other things to deal with, but you will be able

66

to control them. Other people have gone through this before you. Claudette. Myself.'

'What is wrong with me?' she moaned.

'It is simply one of the trials that God has seen fit to inflict upon us sinners,' the voice said. 'Now, will you come with us, Annette?'

'What if I refuse?'

The voice was endlessly patient; 'You will continue as you have done, and die of it. I'm sorry, Annette. It is the truth. You have to make a choice.'

Annette's hand tightened in Claudette's. 'I'll take your cure,' she moaned at last.

The man stepped towards her – on bare feet, from the little noise he made – and took her free hand. The kiss, now anticipated, still made her shiver. His chin was clean-shaven, but his skin not so soft as Claudette's had been. He folded her hand in his larger one, and between the two of them her guides led the blindfolded woman along the unseen and twisting mountain paths.

'Are you naked, too?' she whimpered when the silence seemed to stretch to breaking point. She heard him chuckle.

'No, I'm wearing hose,' he said. 'Does that help?'

Annette shrugged, the only gesture possible for her, but the exchange did help – she found she trusted the pair now to lead her, however far or steep their journey. She fell into a rhythm of step and pause, leaning on either arm beside her when the path twisted, losing track of time and all awareness of anything other than their footfalls and their breathing. It could not have been long, however, when they stopped, turned her and stood to flank her, still holding her hands.

'We're here,' said Claudette. A hand tugged loose her blindfold. Annette blinked.

They were standing in a hollow in the hillside, the sides of the bowl sweeping up all around them to the starlit sky. Light came from the waxing moon overhead

and the glowing heaps of three fires that had been
kindled on the bare earth. The three of them stood
exactly in the middle between the fires, Claudette on
her right hand, Michel on her left. Facing her in silence
was a gathering of people. Annette looked from face to
face. She saw Bernard de Montauban, and the Châtelaine Marguerite, and Gaspard, and Father Emil. Many
others too, men and women, young and old – a slender
youth with long fiery hair, a lithe girl with scarred
breasts, a stocky man with the dark eyes and beard and
skin of an Arab – perhaps thirty altogether, but no
children. Most were naked, or nearly so. Bernard sat
upright on a stone, with two young women lolling at
his feet, clad in a fur-trimmed sleeveless robe that was
belted about his waist. The Châtelaine reclined ele-
gantly at his right hand, her small, pale breasts still pert
and perfect as a girl's, her fingers nonchalantly buried
in the thick pubic hair of Father Emil, whose head
rested against her bare thigh. Gaspard stood behind
her, arms folded, his eyes mocking. He wore tight hose
that emphasised the muscular planes of his legs. None
of the faces were friendly, though all were expectant
and some looked pleased.

A half-dozen wolves sprawled or stood among the
human gathering.

Annette looked across at Claudette, who met her
gaze with an inscrutable sideways glance, then turned
briefly to look up at Michel. She did not recognise his
face, but she remembered the warm reassurance of that
smile on crooked lips and it made her feel better. She
faced her audience again. One of the wolves sank down
with a grunt into the lap of an iron-haired woman and
fixed her with its yellow eyes. Annette noticed that all
the humans around her had something in common,
whatever their age or gender; they were all fit and well
muscled, even the oldest, their bodies as toned as
acrobats or fencers.

68

The mutual examination was ended when Bernard stood up. He surveyed her with calm authority. 'Welcome, Annette,' he said, his tones relaxed and even. 'You know why you are here. You suffer from a malady that each one of us in this company has been tormented by, and each one of us has overcome . . . with help. The cure is certain, though not easy. It used to be painful and bloody. We are gentler these days, Annette. Now is your time to join us, if you so choose. You can be free. Do you understand what it is we are offering?'

Annette nodded wordlessly. She understood. Looking about her, she understood everything.

'Will you come with us?' Bernard enquired.

Annette felt Michel's hand tighten on hers. It had been warm; now it was colder than her own. Now this is the point where they have to kill me if I refuse, she thought. And Michel has been appointed to do it.

'Yes,' she said. The decision was neither easy nor difficult; it was simply as inevitable as the stars' progress across the heavens or the monthly tides of her courses. Bernard nodded, it seemed with satisfaction, and sat down again. The ranks of watchers stirred expectantly.

'Begin,' Bernard instructed.

Like dancers, Claudette and Michel moved to their places; she facing Annette, he standing behind. Claudette clasped Annette's face in her hands and with a smile leaned to kiss her lips hungrily, probing into the moist cavity of her mouth with a hot and twisting tongue. Annette gave a grunt of shock and would have fallen back, except that Michel's hands were on her shoulder-blades. A thrill of erotic pleasure stabbed her entrails; she moaned as his hands moved up under her arms to lightly caress her breasts, as Claudette's hands moved to throat and hips. Between them they undressed her, loosening the cord that held her robe about the neck and drawing it softly from her shoulders. Annette shut her eyes, opened them again to take in the rich glowing tumble of Claudette's hair as she stooped to cup and kiss each of Annette's breasts in turn, tugging gently on each exalting nipple with deadly teeth. Michel lifted the heavy burden of her hair and held it to one side as he began to kiss and nibble at the back of her neck. Fire and ice seemed to crash in her belly; she could not simultaneously cope with Claudette's ministrations to her firm white breasts and the way Michel was pressed up behind her, biting softly at her throat, his tongue describing spirals along the line of her chin and neck, his hands prowling her spine. The two torturers were unhurried, tender, ruthless in their command of her pleasure, almost making her forget the audience beyond as they tormented her acquiescent, yielding body. The robe slipped to the floor. She was naked between them. Claudette pressed her dark orbs against Annette's smaller ones, the collision of flesh and flesh electrifying, her thighs rubbing up against her. Claudette purred. Annette moaned.

Then Claudette fell to her knees in front of her prisoner, and Annette was exposed to the crowd. Michel pulled her up against him, her backside tucked hard against his groin, and slipped his hands round to her breasts again, partly to support and steady her, partly to lift and display those firm high treasures to a grinning, appreciative audience. Annette caught glimpses of people leaning forwards to watch, of the Châtelaine's hand moving rhythmically on the priest's swollen member, of Gaspard cupping and squeezing his own packet through his thin hose. But she stopped looking when Claudette tenderly prised apart her flushed and slippery lips and pressed her face into her oozing sex.

Annette writhed in Michel's grasp, her modesty torn in shreds, every eye in the place on her agony and need. His fingers closed round her delicate pink nipples, rolling and pinching them; her head thrashed back and forth on his shoulder in a delirium of outrage and lust. They tightened, and still it was not too much. Claudette's tongue was busy questing between her thighs, scouring them with hot kisses, her face crushed into the dark fuzz of hair and smeared with the freely-running juices of Annette's sopping, shameless cunt. Annette let her thighs be spread, let Claudette delve deeper, her tongue enter her vagina. Her clit was on fire, her tits two points of ice demanding more pressure, and she did not care any more if the audience saw her, if the Châtelaine's hand was a blur, if the scarred woman was writhing from thigh to thigh with eyes blazing; she did not care if they watched; she wanted them to watch as she came, she came, she came, grunting and thrusting without dignity into Claudette's' voracious mouth, thrashing her slender body against the rigid wall of Michel's strength until every last drop of her orgasm had been ripped out and lapped up on Claudette's tongue.

Then Claudette had slipped away to one side and Michel had released her, letting her sink slowly to her knees in front of him. He ran his fingers through her knotted hair and held her there with a hand to either side of her head, pinning her gently in place. Annette could not struggle. She felt Michel's erection rigid against the back of her skull, trapped beneath his clothes, and unthinkingly she pressed back against it, rolling her head from side to side. Michel made a small noise somewhere between a sigh and a groan and stroked the damp hair back from her forehead. She gawped mentally at the spectacle she must make; a married woman of the respectable merchant class, legs spread like a slut, pussy wet with her own juices and the saliva of a peasant strumpet, slumped panting in full view of two score of people who were entertaining themselves with the sight of her gaping gash.

71

'Gaspard,' came the Châtelaine's amused voice.

Annette looked up in time to see Gaspard stride down towards her, the arrogant swing of his hips emphasising the corresponding swing of the huge bulge in his brown hose. He reached her and smirked down into her flushed face as he undid the last few ties on his codpiece. Annette made one brief attempt to rise but Michel restrained her, his hands tightening in her hair. She was not to refuse this. Gaspard pulled his cock and balls out using both hands – he damned near had to, they were so big – and presented them for her inspection. They were dark and flushed with blood, plump as a donkey's, in a nest of wiry brown hair, and he dangled them in front of her like bait.

He's not even erect, Annette thought with confusion and a touch of chagrin – then he took his tool in his right hand, set his hips in a straddle and began to piss on her.

Annette burst into struggle but Michel was too strong and too well prepared for that, so when she cried out it was partly humiliation and partly the pain of her wrenched scalp. Gaspard laughed. The bright pungent stream of his urine splashed on her tits, on her aching nipples, on her belly and splayed thighs. Annette froze, let the terrible sensation of the hot, tickling, gushing stream soak into her. This was a shock unlike any she had anticipated, not painful, not dangerous – but nevertheless agonizingly cruel in its insidious gentle caress. Her belly seemed to melt. It felt unbelievably good. The male stink of it made her head swim. He had a copious, full bladder and took his time, sending rivulets of golden piss tumbling like mountain cataracts off her peaks and into her wooded valley. As the stream finally slowed he directed it up on her throat and then her face, splashing her eyelids and probing her lips. Annette took her courage in both hands and opened her mouth to the insistent stream, letting the last acrid drops gush over her tongue. Her lips grazed his loose, wet foreskin. She was rewarded by a flash of surprise on his face and a sudden stiffening of his cock. Gaspard let her mouth linger at his swelling glans for a few incredible seconds, then stepped back out of range, trying to hide his obvious reluctance. He did not bother to stow his tackle away, but smirked up past Annette at Michel and then reached out to cruelly squeeze the other man's turgid bulge over her shoulder. Michel bit down on a grunt. Gaspard, ambling back to his seat, seemed well satisfied with his vicarious revenge.

Annette could feel her heartbeat thudding between her thighs.

His Lady, the Châtelaine, was next in line, stepping between the seated assembly as delicately as a well-bred filly. Only a pink flush high over her breasts marred the pale satin of her skin, her features otherwise composed and calm. She paused in front of Annette and considered her. Her right hand was cupped and held at the same level as her perfect rosy nipple. She opened it to reveal a palmful of glistening semen – from Father Emil, Annette supposed – from which she scooped a pearlescent gobbet with one finger of her other hand, and conveyed it to Annette's parted lips. Annette accepted the cold offering with slight reluctance, letting it melt on her tongue as if it were the holy wafer, then swallowing the salty moisture with a shiver. She had no choice then but to humbly offer her mouth for another morsel. The Châtelaine fed her with unhurried delicacy, then pressed her spread palm forwards. Annette licked the last slick traces of spilt semen from her fingers. The Châtelaine nodded.

'Raise her up, Michel,' she said.

Annette found herself lifted to her unsteady feet once more. The Châtelaine slipped a slender hand into her hot crotch and Annette moaned with fear. Fingers spread her pulsing, unsated hole and delved within, causing new moisture to well up. The Châtelaine's face was a study in cool interest. Annette twisted on the rippling, teasing fingers and pressed her groin forwards hopelessly, unable to resist the hot waves of need that were breaking there.

'You are an eager little jade,' Marguerite murmured. 'Like a bitch on heat, my sweet Annette. Oh, my poor dear – do you need a good hard shafting?' She stepped back, smiling with a benevolence that was chilling to see. 'Bernard, my love,' she called, 'I believe your new pupil is ready to begin. Would you like to go first?'

Bernard slipped off his belt as he approached, though he did not shed his robe. Underneath, his body was hard as sculpted bronze, though the hair on his chest and curled at his loins was steely grey. His erect manhood was thick and stiff, marbled with blue veins. Annette, trembling with anticipation, met his gaze anxiously. His dark eyes glittered, pinning her with their easy authority. 'What is there to be afraid of, child?' he asked in that rich, reassuring tone.

She could not answer. He stooped, grasped her thighs and lifted her on to his hips, lowering her down over his rock-hard prick. Annette grasped his shoulders with a cry and wrapped her sundered legs around his rigid arse. She was tight from disuse but dripping with the juice of her wantonness, and though it felt as if he were splitting her apart she grasped him like she was drowning and he was rock she had to cling to. Michel's arms tightened around her in support; Bernard began to thrust into her, pushing her hips away and then ramming up into them, using Michel as a buttress against which to fuck her. He worked slowly, but struck deeper and deeper and without mercy. She was slammed between them as helplessly as flotsam on the sea, her back slapped against the smooth wall of Michel's chest, her cunt impaled on Bernard's terrible, implacable cock, the rhythm of his surging tides battering her. She came quickly, twice over, and then with a single grunt he spent his load inside her, his hands biting painfully into the flesh of her thighs. His face the whole time remained masklike, as impersonal and majestic as a god's, but when he lowered her to her feet he held her tenderly for a moment in the circle of his arms.

She whimpered as he left, wanting more. Her sex was burning.

It was as if Bernard's finishing was a signal to the remainder of the audience. They rose to their feet as he withdrew. Michel picked her up and walked back a few paces to where a number of blankets had been piled on the flat earth. He laid her down gently, kissed her lips and murmured, 'Be strong. Give way to everything.'

The circle closed.

She spun in the night; luminous, beautiful. She was the Earth, the centre of the circling planets, the focal point of the universe. She was a goddess, the idol of countless prayers, her supplicants kneeling in turn to worship her. Her flesh was the recipient of a thousand kisses, a thousand heartfelt groans, a thousand caresses. Oblations were poured out before her and upon her, the rich and fragrant scent of their liquid offerings perfuming the temple of her body. She shone. She received them all, turning none away.

They filled her, in every orifice. They soaked her in semen and sex-juices, pouring their essences one after another into and on to her. Her cunt was so filled with jism that it ran down her thighs and arse in silvery streams and her pubic hair was wringing wet, twisting into little curls. Her mouth grew bruised and slack with accepting their rigid cocks. Her breasts and belly were coated with a sheen of drying semen. One man wrapped her long hair around his penis and jerked off, clotting her scalp with pale droplets.

She came, over and over. She thought she would grow numb or start to hurt, but instead waxed drunk upon pleasure and shuddered into climax after climax.

Gaspard was one of the first to mount her, crushing her buttocks flat against the rough blankets, biting at her lips and moulding her breasts in his greedy hands. He was unsubtle and unimaginative, but he was huge and he rode her as if he wanted to break her. She screamed, clawed and struck at him, took everything he had to give and sobbed with frustration when he left. The Châtelaine silenced her tears by sinking down on her face, smothering her cries. Annette had never tasted a woman before, and drank in her wetness with desperation, her tongue lost among formless folds of smooth flesh and wiry hair, almost choking on the sweet, musky juices that flowed as Marguerite shuddered and wriggled into ecstasy. Annette learned the taste of another dozen women before the hour was past.

Michel, her guide, was by her the whole time, directing the next partaker into the field, turning her, comforting her, wiping her eyes, encouraging each coupling and each orgasm from the icy vantage-point of self-denial. She thought blurredly how unfair was his frustration and reached several times for his yearning member where it struggled in his trews, but he deflected her firmly each time.

When they had finished with her, the participants turned to each other for further play, rutting and writhing at the edge of her limited field of view. It seemed to Annette at one point that there were more wolves now than there had been to start with, but she was distracted by a couple straddling her head and fucking like dogs an inch from her face. Annette could see the thick root of the man's penis sliding in and out of the impossibly stretched hole of the woman, her juices coating his cock, his balls hanging down like ripe fruit and brushing her own forehead and nose. She stretched her head up to lick the woman's exposed clitoris, felt her start to spasm, kissed and licked her way from that burning point up along the slithering ridge of the penis to the wrinkled, tight pouch of the bollocks and back again. The woman climaxed loudly and the man followed in instants, slamming into her split lips and then withdrawing to let the last jets of his come splatter down on Annette's face. The woman finished by sitting back on Annette, anointing her with a heady mixture of her and her lover's fluids. Annette drank it like wine.

As soon as she was released this time, Michel rolled her over on to her front. Someone took her from behind, quick and slippery and panting, his balls slapping audibly against her pussy, and after he had finished another mounted her. Her first thought was that this man had an extraordinarily hairy chest and thighs – and then her second thought was a white streak of incredulity, but Michel held her down hard so that she could not wriggle round and look behind her. She buried her face in his leg, half laughing and half sobbing, and pure shock wrenched another orgasm from her.

It was not enough. She kept climaxing, but each peak left her unsatisfied. Something knotted in her chest, a fist of frustration. If, she thought, if only she could come hard enough . . .

Someone, tempted more by the amber rose of her unused arsehole than her sodden cleft, smeared her with her moisture and pushed into her tight opening. Annette, face down in Michel's arms, shrieked. Her husband had tried this with her before on several occasions but it still hurt; her whole body went hot and then cold with shock. She tried to flail about, but was pinioned and, without thinking, her mind a red jelly of

77

panic, she bit Michel hard on the upper arm. He yelped and knocked her away, and her sphincter took the invader up to the hilt. Suddenly it didn't hurt at all. Her rider moved, gently but inexorably, spreading her wide. The orgasm seemed to start at her anus and ripple up the entire length of her spine, thundering through every muscle in her body. She nearly collapsed. Her partner stiffened and filled her tight passage with his cream. As he withdrew, she fell on her belly.

'Is that really the way you prefer to do it?' Michel snarled. His teeth were pushing forwards, distorting his face, his eyes flashing with pain and anger. Then he looked closer at her and mastered himself. 'Right,' he said softly. He pulled her up and pressed her mouth against the bite-mark. 'Lick it,' he grunted.

Annette swallowed blood, tasting its metallic tang. It made her feel sick. She felt as though the world were spinning round her. The knot in her chest swelled. She began to gasp, sucking at Michel's torn skin; he had to push her away before she bit him again.

'You,' he said over her shoulder. 'Sodomise her again. She's going.' Then he reached down and freed his own smooth member from its prison. 'Don't you dare bite me this time, not if you want to live,' he hissed in awful warning, then pushed it, long and glistening and solid with frustration, into her mouth. Annette wrapped her lips around the rigid shaft and sucked it into her, drawing it as far down her throat as she could. His pubic hair scoured her nose as he moved within her. She did not need to breathe. Behind her, unseen, some unknown man shoved his fat cock into her arse again. The pain and the pleasure throbbed through her in waves as her muscles clenched and released. The fist in her chest became a flame. She was going to come again – but more than that. Her head filled with white fire. Her nails scored bloody streaks

78

down Michel's legs, even through the cloth. Her spine glowed and burst apart, her skin incandesced, her hips thrust against the earth, her arse opened, spread, unfurled like a flower. She felt Michel's red-hot penis jerk as he rammed it down her, felt the thick foam of his seed fill her throat and nose, tasted it as he pulled back, still ejaculating so that it flooded her mouth and tongue. She came – and it was agony, and it was a savage ecstasy that was worse than agony, as her soul and body exploded into a thousand pieces and flew back together in a maelstrom of knives and moonlight.

In that brilliant furnace of a moment, Annette tore through the veil of unreality to erupt into the world. The barrier before her mind, the haunting sense that she was somewhere else, that this was not happening to her, that nothing mattered, that her body did not belong to her – all that was destroyed utterly. She became, as she had never done before. She *was*, and she was herself. The clarity, the reality, the naked truth of her own presence filled her like a white light.

And she woke as if from a dream, the dream that you do not know is a dream until you realise it is gone. She lay sprawled on the blanket, her legs crumpled under her. Moonlight dazzled her weeping eyes. Michel pawed at her anxiously, nipped and licked along her dark muzzle. As clearly as if he had spoken, she understood his meaning: 'You must get up.' She struggled to comply, fanning her tail weakly, but her legs were as wobbly as those of a newborn foal. Her fur was damp. Michel and Claudette – she recognised them now by their scent more than anything else, for their forms were unfamiliar as yet – put their noses under her and pushed to help her rise. She had to lean against them for a few moments until she had regained her strength. The rest of the wolf-pack danced and circled around them impatiently, anxious now to be off on the hunt.

Annette put her head back to see the moon and whimpered with wonder. Claudette – very dark and long of pelt, still – licked at her muzzle. Michel bit her ear tenderly. Strength seemed to flow into her limbs. She took her first few hesitant steps; the pack greeted her with joy. Then they turned as one, gathered themselves for speed and poured out of the hollow into the night. Annette raised her voice with them and took up her place in the pack, running with the wolves.

The Temptation of St Gregory

Gregory kneeled before the plain wooden cross on the eastern wall of his cell and prayed that she would not return. He prayed with real fear, a cold knot in his gut, his eyes tight shut but tears squeezing from under the lids. 'Father have mercy. Against all the attacks of the Devil I have stood and will stand again in Your Name but, if it be Your will, let this cup pass from my lips.'

He did not look as if he should be afraid, this monk kneeling in his rock-hewn cell. He was a tall man and broad-shouldered with it, even if his long hair was grey now and his square face lined. The broad span of his hands, clasped here in devotion, and the hard ridges of his bare, muscular forearms testified to a previous career that was not spent in either fasting or meditation. Well-fed, he would have been formidable in any estimation; even now – gaunt and craggy-faced, the hollows deep about his eyes and under his cheekbones – he resembled an ageing warrior more than a monk. Which appearance was misleading, for Gregory truly was a man of God, sworn to poverty, chastity and prayer, and he had never been a warrior. His history –

extraordinary enough for a hermit – was that of a steward in the Palace at Constantinople. Those hands had wielded a whip in their time, and those bare feet had trodden upon marble and silk.

Gregory was afraid. More afraid than when he had stood before the Emperor and reported that his imperial daughter had been discovered in the act of congress with a slave; more afraid than when he had placed every last coin he owned at the feet of the Bishop and kneeled for the first time in his camel-hair robe to make his vows. He was afraid for his soul. He had overcome pride and greed and doubt in his time, denied his flesh every particle of comfort, starved until he saw visions ... and it appeared now that it was not enough. Around every corner a new trial waits, and even here in the desert there was no escape from temptation. Three days' ride from the nearest town, a day's walk from the nearest human soul – and that Father Rufinus, entombed in a cave with only a high slit left open to admit air and the occasional bowl of food – in a place where even the vultures did not circle, so rugged was the land and so empty of life; even here there was no hiding place from sin. The battleground between good and evil is the soul, not the market-place or the bed-chamber. God is never finished testing his servants.

While he prayed the sun sank and, with the oozing of the red sunset light into his chamber and the climbing of the shadows up the cliff-faces, she arrived. Gregory's voice faltered as her presence momentarily plunged the room into darkness; it was not a large window to his cell and she filled it before she pressed through into the room. She always arrived by the window, perhaps because climbing the stairs that spiralled the rock to his room would have been too mundane. The ruddy light broke in once more. Her feet, bare, were almost silent on the stone floor.

Gregory turned. He knew it was of no use ignoring

her; when he had tried to close his eyes upon her first visit, she had amused herself by riffling through his small store of scriptures, mockingly mispronouncing the Latin words.

The succubus smiled, though her mouth was so heavy that it seemed unsuited to the task; her lips, red as the stains of pomegranate juice, fell naturally into a lascivious pout. Her huge wings, folded now and arced high above her head, the black, velvety flesh and spines like those of some Queen of Bats, were visible for a moment before she shifted her stance and they became nothing but shadows behind her, a darkness against which her form seemed to glow.

'Gregory,' she murmured in a voice of silk. He crossed himself and crouched before the altar as if defending it with his life's blood, a martyr out of the old days of Empire. His eyes sought the floor, but he could not thrust her from his view and now he could smell her, a warm, musky scent like that of crimson flowers opening under moonlight.

She was sexuality incarnate, everything that Gregory had forsworn and denied himself. She was an ancient goddess come to earth, but a goddess of night and mystery, not some bright Olympian deity. Her skin was copper, her hair copper made molten and poured over jet, coiling in serpentine ropes across her skin so that it concealed her bare breasts but only just; enough to hide nearly everything but suggest all, the nipples threatening to peep out from behind their curtain at every moment. Her breasts were like large ripe fruit ready to be plucked, promising sweet juice and rich flesh. The full curve of her hips, the narrow span of her waist, the pool of her navel, the firm rounded lines of her legs – all were visible. She wore nothing but a small kilt of bronze pieces that hung at her groin and clashed like the ringing of tiny cymbals at the gate to her sacred temple; that and the gold snakes that spiralled up her forearms and lower legs, their cunningly moulded coils clasping her limbs and striving ever inwards to her torso.

She stepped across the room, moving like a dancer or a lioness. Her breasts swayed and bobbed under their own weight, hinting at dark nipples through the clinging fell of her hair. She trailed one hand across the top of the table, almost the only stick of furniture in that austere room, the better to emphasise the curves of her arm and her long fingers tipped with carnelian nails. She was a harlot; she was a goddess. Gregory, who had in the days before his conversion taken his women when and where he wanted – though perhaps fewer than most men of influence, because he had always been restrained by the stern sense of his dignity and position – felt his throat dry up and the blood surge to his loins. It was six years since he had lain upon the naked flesh of a woman; almost four since he had seen a female face at all. The Devil clearly knew his business.

'Get out of here,' Gregory said in a low growl. 'You won't get what you want from me.' There was no purpose in dismissing her more forcefully; he had tried exorcising the vision in the name of Christ upon her first visit, but she had merely smiled enigmatically and ignored the command. If God had permitted her to remain and test the monk further, who was he to argue?

'What *I* want?' the succubus asked, reaching the stone bench he used as a bed and seating herself gracefully upon it. She smoothed the threadbare blanket beside her. 'It is what *you* want that concerns me. I know exactly what that is, Gregory; that is why I am here.'

'You're here to tempt my soul into damnation,' he growled. 'Don't think I don't know that, demon.'

'I am here to give you what you need,' she said softly, looking at his lap.

The folds of rough cloth covered any betraying sign;

she could not possibly see what struggled beneath. Gregory cleared his throat. 'You talk like your master,' he said brutally, 'the Father of Lies. You know nothing of what I need. My need is Heaven. You are a serpent from the pit.'

She stretched herself slowly upon the bed, reclining upon her right side, her thighs rubbing one on top of the other. Gregory tried to look away.

'I am what you want,' she corrected gently. 'A thousand nights alone, Gregory, and I can smell your frustration on the wind from here to Alexandria. You're lying awake in the dark, unable to sleep, unable to pray, terrified to touch the serpent flesh in your own bed. The hardness of your pallet beneath you, the serpent trapped between flesh and stone. The orphaned memories returning to haunt you; slave girls kneeling at your feet, the Nubian maid you kept in your chamber, spying upon your mistress as she bathed ... Dreams that keep returning. Your seed spilt while you were sleeping. Do you think these things are secret?'

Gregory kneeled lower until his forehead nearly brushed the floor and groaned. 'I am a sinner; I have never denied it,' he said. 'But I have repented every moment and been forgiven by the ever-merciful Father. I am not fooled by the temptations of the flesh, demon; I have known them too well. You may be beautiful in outward form, but beneath a woman's skin lurks all the stinking corruption of the grave. You are a path to the worms and the fire.'

'And your flesh?' asked the succubus, her blood-coloured lips moving into a smile. 'Is it so holy?' The darkness around her that was, or might become, her wings seemed to deepen.

'My flesh is dust. My soul is in the hands of God. I yearn for Heaven, I strive for purity, but my flesh drags me earthwards. Who will release me from this body of death?' he shuddered.

She rocked her hips. The little skirt of metal pieces chinked and shifted, revealing flame-coloured fleece beneath. 'I can,' she offered. 'Lie with me once, Gregory, and I promise that you will never be troubled by your desires again. I will suck the lust from you like the juice from an orange. If that is what you want, I can make you a withered man, a eunuch for your God.'

Gregory raised his head and stared at her. 'Now you are tempting me with an escape from my sins,' he said bitterly. 'How truly you are said to be the subtlest beast of the field! Listen, snake, you cannot tempt me to sin that way. The body is a beast that must be tamed, mortified, denied. It must be brought to submission until the Last Day, when it will be raised in perfection.'

'You hate yourself,' she observed sadly.

'I know what matters,' he countered. His words were confident but his gaze skidded everywhere around her and his hands were clenched in his groin. 'The flesh is corrupt and will not last,' he said unevenly. 'My soul is immortal and may enter the Divine Presence. That is what is important. Your petty temptations are nothing compared to the ecstasy of eternal life!'

'Really?' she purred, rising from her reclining position. Her eyes – gold and luminescent, like the eyes of a cat, framed in dark lashes, burning with appetite – were narrowed and deadly. In two steps she was standing over him. Gregory shut his eyes. She took his head in her hands and pressed it forwards against her raised thigh, so that his cheek and lips brushed her satiny skin. He did not struggle, but began to recite the Lord's Prayer rapidly under his breath, his lips tickling her soft flesh. The smell of her – perfume and musk, the rich hot smell of a wanton woman – slipped down his throat.

'Lead us not into temptation, but deliver us from evil . . .'

She released his head and he raised his face to the

sky, eyes still closed, features tight with concentration. She bent over him. Her hair brushed his face and then his shoulders. She bent lower and the ripe globes of her breasts bumped softly against his brow, trailed down over cheek and nose. Gregory stopped speaking. Her breasts, soft, firm, alive with sensation, nestled in the hollows of his eyes. They were big enough to touch as they hung down, big enough to encompass the whole of his face. His nose had slipped into the warm cleft between them. He could not breath, except for the sweet smell of her skin. If he dared to open his eyes he could not see anything but the swell of her golden flesh dusted with tiny white hairs. She drew back to release his face and then turned from side to side, dragging the weight of each rounded fruit and the stiff point of each puckered nipple across his mouth. His lips were soft, the stubble upon his chin and cheeks rasping. She raked him with nipples hard as fingertips, then, pressing her two breasts together with her hands so that the nipples abutted, dropped them both together against his lips. The lips did not yield entirely, but his breath came hot and fast between them and the dampness made lips and nipples cling together.

'Am I not what you want above all else?' she murmured. 'Am I not the embodiment of beauty?'

'No,' he whispered, though his tongue brushed her flesh as he spoke. 'I have seen greater beauty.'

She pulled right back from him. Her eyes were stormy, her lips swollen with desire. 'Where?' she said.

Gregory reeled under her gaze. 'I have seen an angel,' he said hoarsely, 'and they are more beautiful than you. One stood outside my window in the dawn, less than a month ago. She shone with the glory of God. She was white and pure, like snow on mountain tops. All the glittering tawdry charms of Hell could not touch her divine beauty, because she was the image of Heaven. And I have woken in the night to see one at the foot of my bed. God has set angels to watch over me; how can I fall to your wickedness?'

The temptress drew herself up, her face dark and apprehensive. Suddenly her wings unfurled, their black leathery span filling the room. They clapped once, and she was gone.

It was some moments before Gregory could rise to his feet. He went over to the bed and would have sat down upon its hard surface, but shrank back – the cloth retained the scent of the monster where she had lain, and the smell – part flowers, part sex – was not calming. Gregory took up the knotted whip from the foot of the bed and kneeled shivering before the crucifix. Reluctantly, but with the knowledge of the inevitable, he pulled his coarse robe over his head. His lean, muscular body was marred by the obscene length of his erection, rising like the Tower of Babel from between his thighs and aspiring blasphemously to reach Heaven. The skin of his rigid cock was stretched taut and shiny, the swollen head purplish and dribbling in frustration from its leering slit of a mouth. Gregory prodded it with one fingertip, appalled at its vitality. It jumped under his touch. It was like a small devil living in his skin, a part of him yet alien and hostile.

Gregory brought the many-thonged whip up over his shoulder and deliberately laid a blow across his own back. The pain made tears spring to his eyes, but the monster only danced wickedly between his legs. Gregory realised that when Jerome next arrived with his provisions of bread and water, tomorrow or the day after, he would have to break his normal habit of silence and order the man to bring him a knife and bandages. He would have to undergo minuition – bleeding himself in order to weaken and quell the rebellious flesh. He brought the lash across to the other shoulder and down in one vicious movement. Red weals scarred his pale back. Again and again he endured the bite of the thongs, the stinging pain, until he was wet with sweat and weeping with contrition, and the devil had drooped its head once more.

It was dark by the time he ceased. Gregory climbed dizzily to his feet to light the one candle he allowed himself. His back was a crawling sheet of white-hot pain, like a thousand knife-cuts. He might have been bleeding but he was not concerned to check. As he found the tallow candle, fumbling in the gloom, he heard a rustle behind him and the room was flooded with a pearly light. His shadow jumped, weirdly shaped, upon the wall in front of him. He turned, heart thumping.

The angel was in his room. The light came from her wings, each perfect feather of which glowed with a glacial radiance, as pure as sunlight glancing off a snowdrift. Her skin was flawlessly pale, her long hair a silver only faintly touched by gold, her robe a water-fall of white linen that plunged to the floor and lay in folds that concealed her feet. She was as straight and slender as a willow-wand, an icon of maidenly perfection. The only touch of colour about her was the suggestion of pink at her lips and the intense blue of her eyes, deep as a summer's night, now turned upon Gregory with a look of compassion and unspoken wisdom that made his heart hurt.

The monk fell to his knees once more, crossed himself and then covered his shame with his hands, new tears blurring his eyes. He had no reason to think that an angel would be shocked by his naked flesh but he flinched nevertheless from despoiling her sight with such a crude reminder of human frailty, as Adam and Eve had hidden themselves in Eden, ashamed of their nakedness. 'Forgive me,' he murmured brokenly. The angelic light washed over his bare skin like a balm. A scent of indescribable loveliness had filled the room.

'Be not afraid, Gregory,' said the angel. Her voice was as gentle as the sigh of a breeze.

'Forgive me,' he repeated. 'A poor sinner who does not deserve such grace as is offered him, to see a messenger from the Lord Almighty with these poor eyes. I am . . . not worthy of your presence.'

'God's grace is always undeserved,' the angel reminded him gently. 'And be not so proud of your sins that you cannot be thankful, Gregory.'

'Praise God,' he amended swiftly, 'praise Him in the heights. Praise Him for His greatness and mercy.'

'Praise Him,' the angel agreed, 'and forget your sins, as He has forgiven them, and put them aside.' She stepped forwards and laid cool fingertips on Gregory's brow; a great wave of light seemed to sweep through him, leaving him dizzy with weakness. The pain of his torn back faded to a silken bliss. 'Tell me the desire of your heart, Gregory,' she instructed.

'To see the Lord,' Gregory choked, 'to be filled with His righteousness and holiness, so that there is no room for the grubby desires and cares of earth.'

'Then this shall be granted to you,' the angel said. A sweet smile suffused her face. 'Your body is a worn garment dusty from the road; a shabby half-tamed beast that has carried you for many miles. But the garment can be cast off and replaced, and the beast is not the rider. Today you will be transfigured, Gregory, as it is your great desire.'

A huge joy swelled in Gregory's chest, almost painful in its intensity. He clasped the angel's hand in both of his and showered it with tears and kisses of gratitude. His earlier self-loathing was forgotten, his lust disregarded as an insignificant thing. He did not spare his naked flesh a thought as the angel drew him to his feet; it was no longer of any importance. She laid a feather-light kiss upon his lips with her cool ones. He nearly staggered under the blow. He could feel a singing in his bones, a choir massed upon the edge of his hearing.

'I greet you with the kiss of love, Gregory,' she said.

'Praise the Lord who has made all good things,' he gasped.

She turned him towards the stone bed. 'You are weak with longing,' she said. 'Rest. I shall be with you until the moment of your joy.' She had to help him cover the few paces and lay himself upon the bed, and then she sat at the head of it, cradling his head and shoulders in his arms. She was effortlessly strong, despite her slender build. Gregory felt almost too weak to move. His limbs were full of light, a burning, cold shining that sucked away his volition, and a core of fire seemed to run through him from heart to bowels. He looked down the length of his lean frame and was surprised to see that he had a huge erection once more, a rigid quivering spire pointing upwards. The sight puzzled him more than anything else.

'Disregard it,' she said, turning his face up to look at her. 'It is only your body, a last cry of rebellion against your soul – and that is reaching to Heaven now.' She planted another kiss on his lips. For an endless spinning moment he was lost in a vision of light, his spirit soaring upwards as if to plunge into a great white sun. He came to his senses with the tremulous crystal chords of an unearthly music in his ears; he could hear the angelic choir quite clearly now. The angel who held him smiled tenderly and stroked a few grey hairs from his forehead. She was so beautiful he could hardly breathe.

A warmth enveloped his flesh. He looked down. The succubus was kneeling astride him, hands on his waist, and as he watched she impaled herself on his jerking prick and slid the entire length of it between her straddling thighs. Her own legs were tense with effort, her neck and back arched. Her ripe breasts slapped together as she began to move up and down on him, pulling almost all the way up on his cock before sinking back down until their hair meshed, so that he could

91

clearly see the swollen pink lips of her sex stretched around his thick member, the juices running from her and coating it in a slippery tide as she writhed on it. She moaned and twisted in unrestrained pleasure, devouring every inch. Her nipples were like black eyes staring at him. He was bemused to see that his own pelvis was rising to meet her, answering her hot wantonness with thrust after thrust into her wet, open parts.

Gregory turned his eyes anxiously to the angel.

'Ignore her,' she said soothingly. 'You are not your flesh. You are a soul filled with the light of God.' And Gregory felt the pure joy of the Lord fill him to every pore, until he felt as if he were incandescent with delight. He was hardly aware of the lewd grinding thrusts of his hips shoving into the demon's splayed pussy, so intense was the holy pleasure that filled him. His mind was filled with the face of the angel. She was as pure and beautiful as a lily, a white flower growing in the desert, a white bird soaring in the blue vault of the sky. The sound of singing drowned the desperate cries of the succubus as she fucked herself towards carnal ecstasy on his worthless flesh. There was nothing in him but wide spaces filled with flame. The angel was holding him, bent over him, cradling him from sin in the virginal fastness of her arms. She looked like the very Virgin herself. Gregory thought, with the last vestiges of clarity left to him, that she reminded him of a painting he had seen in a church in Constantinople of Mary suckling the Christ-child at her breast. He saw himself lying in her arms and a mute, helpless plea rose in his eyes.

She understood. With a smile of infinite comprehension and mercy, she parted her robes with one hand, revealing a small, white and perfect breast tipped with a little nipple of maidenly pink. Gregory gazed at it with holy awe. She tilted him towards her and his mouth closed over the cool, stiff point, his tongue enveloping the puckered surface. As his despised flesh below thrust and contracted towards its unholy apotheosis, Gregory began to suck upon the angel's breast. Ecstasy incomprehensible exploded in him. The fire and the light became a howling flame that tore him apart. His body poured pulse after pulse of acid seed into the hungry cunt of the demon, and his soul erupted forth.

The two winged beings stood in the cell, looking down upon the body of the monk. In his last spasms, his face had locked in an expression that could be read as numinous ecstasy.

'He was a poor fool,' said the dark one sadly. 'If he had only yielded to me, I would have taken his lust and left him with his life.' She furled her midnight wings around her as if for comfort.

The luminous one was not really looking at the empty shell before her; her vision was far away. 'He died in perfect joy,' she said, her voice empty of any emotion, wiping the corner of her tender mouth with one forefinger. 'He was a soul on fire, hurtling towards the white-hot furnace of his desire. He was a star falling into Heaven. His was bliss unspeakable, the culmination of every hope, the annihilation of being in utter fulfilment. He was . . . delicious.'

The other stared moodily at her sister. 'Give me leave to pity them,' she said. She leaned over and kissed her rose-petal lips softly. 'Until we meet again.' Then she was gone.

The white one did not react to the kiss, nor stir one feather of her cool purity. She was not of the kind to be moved by such things. She lingered a little time in the cell, motionless. When she had gone, only their mingled sweet scents remained as a witness to Father Gregory's passing.

The Fairest of Them All

*I*made the decision to bring my new stepdaughter under my wing the day before her father left to join the King at Stirling, when she arrived late and in disarray for his farewell banquet. It was not as if this was the first time she had displayed her rebellion, nor was it that her father took any real offence upon this occasion – his indifference to the behaviour of his youngest child was common knowledge in the household and I, the bride of a single summer, was perhaps the only one still surprised by it – yet it was the moment when I decided that his contemptuous disregard of the girl could not be matched with my own. I was not even old enough to have borne the child in my own belly yet, if anyone was to take her in hand, it would have to be myself, the loathed stepmother.

It was a windy autumn night, the draughts finding their way into that high stone hall making the flames dance in the sconces. But the company was loud and cheerful, almost everyone there looking forward to their sojourn in the royal court, to a break from the routine and isolation of life on the farm or within the dark and cold walls of the castle. The lairds of four glens, all subordinate to my lord Aillen, were there with their men ready to form his entourage. The presence of so many strange men, loud and boastful, was making the serving women flirtatious and nervous, and the hall echoed with laughter and shrieks.

Ursilla made her appearance during the second remove, stalking up the length of the Great Hall before every guest and member of the house, to the high table where we sat, and with us her vacant place. I was seated upon my husband Aillen's right side, scarred Connor his eldest son across him from me, black-bearded Donald the younger son (a year less upon this earth than myself) on my own dexter side. It must have taken some little courage for Ursilla to face us as she did, that I grant her. The whole hall fell silent as she approached, nobody daring to laugh, but every wary gaze upon her. Her dark hair was unbound and speckled with straw, her bodice loosened so that her girlish breasts all but peeped from behind it, her face flushed, her lips swollen, her eyes bright and defiant. If she had been carried into our presence impaled on a servant's knob she could not have announced herself more clearly or disgracefully. She tossed her head back as she met her father's gaze.

Aillen, deep in conversation with Connor upon the subject of stag-hunting, barely spared her a glance. 'You're late,' he snapped. 'Sit yourself down, girl.' His knife stabbed into the roast and gilded pigeon on the trencher before him. Ursilla visibly stiffened.

Donald was sneering openly at his sister, Connor more restrained but his eyes bright with a contemptuous interest that I found subtly disturbing. None of them looked shocked or ashamed, as they should have been even in front of such minor nobility that we guested that night.

I put my hand upon Aillen's (which was upon my knee at the time) and pressed it. 'It seems to me Ursilla

95

is not properly dressed for her father's table,' I said, my voice cold. 'Perhaps it would be better if she were to return to her room and repair her attire.'

'Hm,' Aillen grunted, his attention returning to his food. 'As you wish. Well: you heard your mother, girl.' He gestured with his knife at the doorway. That did it – Ursilla shot me a look of pure venom before picking up her skirts and hurrying from the hall. He glanced at her retreating form and added in a low voice to me, 'She is a sluttish one, that girl. Let her stew in her own company.'

As might be predicted, Ursilla did not reappear at all for the meal.

That night, alone with my husband in his chamber, I broached the subject of Ursilla once more as I kneeled in the centre of the bed, leaning over his broad shoulders from behind to run my fingers through the crisp black curls of hair upon his chest. He was built like a bull, that man, and I counted myself fortunate to have married him – not that anyone counted him unlucky to have found me, a wealthy and still beautiful young widow, for his second wife.

'Ursilla is a whorish wench, like her mother,' he pronounced as he pulled off his boots. 'Unmanageable – and unmarriageable. I have never cared for her or for what she does. While I'm away, you'll have the keeping of her, but don't expect much joy of that. If you can find her a husband you will have my blessings; if she falls down the well, it is no loss to me.'

I kissed him upon his strong neck, caressing his chest with my nails, feeling him shiver. 'She is a pretty lass,' I said. 'It seems a pity and a waste.'

'She is her mother's daughter,' said he shortly.

I knew the story of Aillen's first wife, caught in adultery and executed for it – beheaded, as befitted a noblewoman. Aillen, I imagined, had never been certain that Ursilla was of his own getting and had taken out his bitterness on the child ever since, though God knows she looked like him – pale of skin, dark of hair and eye, with black arched eyebrows.

'Well,' I murmured, seeking beneath Aillen's belt, 'let us see what her new mother can do.' And I left it at that, for the time.

In the morning Aillen's company departed, his sons riding at his either side, the clan banner fluttering and snapping overhead. With my husband and the other lairds went the greater part of the household: soldiers and freemen and servants all seething and churning in a clatter of hooves and carriage-wheels, the dogs barking, the harness jingling, geese and ducks squawking from their baskets, everyone confused and distracted and impatient. The barley harvest was safely in and only a small proportion of our people were to remain at the castle; serfs to tend the livestock, a body of servants mostly my own brought from Berwick, and a skeleton guard to defend us in the extraordinary event that we should come under attack. This last, however, was to be commanded by Callum, a man in whom Aillen placed absolute trust – and besides, my husband had been at peace with all his neighbours for nearly ten years. There was little to be feared over the coming winter except tedium and loneliness.

Aillen kissed me farewell, leaning from his roan stallion to press me against his bristling beard and hot lips. 'I will bring you back a bolt of silk from the royal court!' he promised.

Then he raised his hand in signal to his followers and rode forwards, disappearing through the palisade gate. I was left to gather my skirts and pick my way back across the dung-spattered yard to the stone tower-house. I was glad to get out of the damp Highland wind, though it was certainly no warmer within the walls. I contemplated the prospect of a winter without Aillen to warm my bed with real regret.

After giving orders for the serving of dinner, that night, I retired to my own chambers. Ursilla had made no appearance to wish her father a safe journey and I meant to deal with her at once. Once I had ascertained her whereabouts, I sent Janet, my maidservant, to fetch the straying girl.

She was ushered into my presence – Janet had one large and warning hand on her elbow – within a few minutes, this time at least in a reasonable state of dress. She paid me no curtsey but glared around the room suspiciously, her gaze at last settling in open insolence upon where I sat in my sewing chair. I suppose it was the first time she had ever been in these chambers – they had fallen into disuse over many years – but she would have seen nothing but the bed, tapestries and furniture proper to the lady of a house; except for the great bronze-framed mirror, all my more personal belongings were shut securely in the room beyond.

What she saw when she looked at me, I can guess – the cold, dark figure of the temptress who had enchanted her father, her straight body unsoftened by childbirth, her face unlined by the years proper to a second wife, her eyes the black, ungodly pools of a harlot.

I let her stand. Her eyes met mine with undisguised hostility, but she dropped her gaze soon enough. I saw her making the sign against the evil eye with her right hand that hung against her skirt.

'You did not come to wish your father farewell,' I said.

'I had lost a shoe,' she replied sulkily. 'I could not come out.'

I raised an eyebrow disapprovingly. 'Don't lie to me, Ursilla,' I said. 'You were in the scullery with your

98

bubs out, letting the cook's boy have a good feel of them.'

She pouted, her eyes flashing. 'What's it to you, then?' she demanded; 'You're not my mother.' I could hear the consternation in her voice, the unvoiced thought: *How did she know?*

'No,' I agreed. 'But I am your father's wife, and I have charge here until he returns. This is my household, Ursilla, and I have the authority over you – and I do not permit you to act in this way.'

She stared at the floor. 'My father doesn't care what I do,' she said.

I sighed a little. 'Maybe not, but I do. I see a fair young woman acting like a slut from the pigsty, and it offends me. I see a maid under my roof without honour or hope, and it hurts me.'

'And I,' replied she staring me in the eye, 'see a whore and a witch.'

Did she, now?

'You see a woman who gets what she wants,' I amended in an even tone. Her abuse did not rile me overmuch. I had expected worse. 'Because, unlike you, Ursilla, I know what I need and I know how to achieve it, and I have the self-discipline not to waste my energies on anything else. Unlike you.'

I leaned back in my chair.

'Look at the way you act, Ursilla. Is this really what you want? You said yourself your father does not care – not if you opened your legs to every man in Scotland. So why are you behaving this way? It is not as if you can be enjoying yourself, surely – I know who you have been lying with: the kennel-lad, the scullery-boy, a shepherd, a servant from the farm. Are they really such splendid stallions? Such fine and exciting lovers? I notice that you have never slept with any them more than once.'

Her soft young mouth was twisted tightly now.

'For example,' I continued mercilessly, 'I notice that you have granted your favours to some of the soldiers. Fearchar, I believe, and Thomas. Very young, both of them, and neither very comely.' Callow lads who couldn't believe their luck and wouldn't think of turning down the perfumed, pretty daughter of a laird, I could have added. 'And I wonder why you don't set your sights on a man like Callum, who might be worthy of you, and certainly is more likely to be worth the game.'

Ursilla tossed back her head, but she had blushed to the roots of her hair. Oh, Ursilla, I thought, though I let a silent pause creep into the room; you really rather like Callum, don't you? He is handsome and brave, and older than you – and perhaps wise enough to turn you down. You couldn't bear that, could you?

'You are disgracing yourself,' I said wearily. 'No one else. You are selling yourself short. Do you understand me, Ursilla? I am not worried for your father's honour or mine, but for your own.'

She looked at me, her breasts rising and falling sharply behind her bodice in a charmingly distracting manner. The colour stood high in her cheeks. 'I don't have to listen to you,' she said.

'You lack discipline, Ursilla,' I said. 'Discipline and self-respect. No one will honour you if you do not honour yourself.'

'You are a witch and a whore,' she repeated, starting to back off. 'You ensorcelled my father and I am not listening to you!'

The insult twisted my patience, already overspun. No lady in the land would listen to such accusations from her underling. I nodded to Janet, standing behind her. Janet had been my personal maidservant for a very long time and knew all my requirements. She was also a very strong and capable woman. As I stood to my feet, she grabbed Ursilla's arms from behind, before the rebellious girl had even noticed her proximity.

The young woman squealed with shock.

'You are acting like a child, Ursilla,' I said disapprovingly. 'A child who has never been taught what not to do. If you cannot discipline yourself, then others must do it for you. Janet, put her over the bed.'

Ursilla fought and shrieked – even tried to bite – but Janet threw her easily across the furs of my counterpane and pinned her there, face down, weight on her shoulders so that she could get no purchase to rise. I moved round to stand behind her and waited until she raised her head to take a breath.

'If you act like a child, you will be treated like one,' I said, my voice stern. I slipped a red satin slipper from my foot and threw her skirts up to expose her legs and bottom. She gasped and tried to kick out, but her legs only flailed helplessly and I kneeled beside them over the bed, out of their way but well within reach of her rising and falling arse.

She was beautiful. So pale, so fragile-looking that it took my breath away and almost shook my resolve. Her buttocks were perfect round globes that rose over the dark ravine of her sex like guardian hills, smooth and pearly as snow-covered winter peaks. Her satiny skin was so fine that I could trace the blue veins running under it. When she wriggled, glimpses of pink flesh appeared and disappeared among the lush dark hair that she could not hide. I laid a hand upon her left cheek and felt it spasm, the muscle rising under my hand to firm the rich flesh. She felt cool to the touch.

I began my task. The slipper descended with a stinging slap across the heart-shaped bottom, dividing the pain equally between each globe. Ursilla squealed, but only the first time. As the sharp blows came down she swallowed her outrage and merely moaned in her throat. She had plenty of pride, that girl, and would not scream under my punishment. Her back was rigid and she jerked with every blow, but she ceased her wild struggles. Her flawless buttocks began to glow a rosy red where my shoe struck. I paused in my blows to touch the flushed skin and was satisfied to feel that it was warm now under my fingers.

Ursilla moaned softly again as my hand stroked her swollen cheeks. That noise, wrenched out of something other than pain, made my heart turn over. Janet, flushed too, glanced up at me in surprise.

I recommenced the punishment, holding my breath, alternating each spank with the feather-light caress of my fingertips. She grew very still, her legs still thrust out stiffly but making no attempt now to wriggle or evade the slap. Indeed, she seemed to be holding her arse up high, as if to receive the blows better. Each impact made her buttocks quiver, her breath sigh out of her taut throat.

I tried an experimental tickle of the dark-furred pudenda peeking from between her thighs and found them as hot and swollen as her bum-cheeks. The touch made her part her rigid legs slightly, as if to afford me a better view of her shame. Her cleft was moist and aromatic, the tissues fat with stimulation. I thought I had never seen anything so beautiful as that sight; her coynt like a split fig framed by the white-and-rose mounds of her buttocks. Skin as white as snow, hair as black as coal and lips swollen red with blood.

I felt a terrible heat in my own flesh.

I could not resist the temptation to reach out for a fur pelisse that lay across the foot of the bed. It was a wrap that I wore about my shoulders when I ventured out of doors, sewn from the white fur of winter hares. The contrast of the pure white and the raven-black fur was heart-stopping. I folded the wrap in my hand and rubbed it against Ursilla's plump mound, trailing it up to her stinging, glorious cheeks and back again. She twitched and gasped. I almost forgot that the spanking was to continue, so absorbed did I become in the silken path of the fur gliding across her skin – almost, but not quite. I alternated the rich caresses of my fur-clad left hand with judicious, stinging slaps from the slipper in my right; enough to keep her on edge, tremulous and anticipatory of each blow. The white fur became damp as it soaked up the rapidly-increasing flow of juices from her sex, and then it began to stick together in little moist locks; much more and it would be unwearable. Ursilla was writhing now with a slow, rolling motion that matched and enhanced the unbearable soft touch of the pelisse, her secret innermost flesh distended and gaping, the smell of her desire like a perfume filling my head and drowning my senses.

I judged the moment and covered her mound with a firm and writhing grasp, almost entering her with the white pelt, as she threw her straining thighs wide and pushed down on my hand. She shuddered and shook, the flesh of her arse dancing, the heat of her body setting my whole arm afire. I am not sure I did not join in her incoherent gasps.

When she had ceased to sob, I pulled her skirt down and signalled Janet to release her. The girl did not look at me; she simply slid to the side of the bed and crouched at my feet, panting. I struggled to regain my composure, stroked her dark head once and then dismissed her gently, sending her back to her room. She slipped wordlessly from my chamber, her face crimson.

As soon as Ursilla had gone I sent Janet away, too, wanting to be alone. I had not anticipated such a fierce reaction to the punishment from my stepdaughter, nor from myself. Once alone, I confess that my first action was to sink my face into the wet and defiled fur.

It was nearly two days before I had occasion to discipline Ursilla again. In fact, she did her best to avoid me, although I maintained an eye on her in my own way. In the meantime I was kept more than busy by the many tasks that befall the lady of a household: overseeing the kitchens, visiting those who were sick and prescribing my own herbal remedies for their ailments, inspecting the produce as it was brought in from the fields, receiving petitions from tenants and dependants – a hundred and one duties to fill the damp, overcast days and cold nights. I decided that the understeward seemed to be tolerably honest in his book-keeping, but that I should inspect his accounts at midwinter in order to be sure. I sent an order to Carlisle for barrels of good French wine for the cellar and more spices for the kitchen. And I embarked on my plan to transform the Great Hall, sending men up on long ladders to knock the encrusted pigeon-nests from the rafters and ordering the old rushes – greasy, half-rotted and stinking – cleared from the flagstones so that they might be scrubbed before fresh herbs were strewn.

Ursilla pleaded sickness – an upset of the stomach – to avoid sitting with me at the high table, the first night. I acquiesced, but ordered that no food was to be sent up to her, and on the evening of the second day hunger drove her down to the hall. I was all but alone on the top table, only Callum and the castle priest – who stuttered abominably whenever he descended from Latin and gave every appearance of fear in my presence – to keep me company, and they would converse neither to myself nor each other unless I forced them to polite interchange. I had retreated into reverie, considering the banquet I intended to host at Christmas.

Ursilla showed up late, but I was pleased to see her at all and was inclined to be tolerant.

'You are feeling better, I hope?' I enquired.

She nodded, did not curtsey – which I should have reprimanded, but failed to – and sat down at the end of the long table on my right side, next to Father

Andrew and as far from me as she could manage. She muttered grace, broke her bread and began to devour the mutton stew before her with the speed of the starving.

I picked at my own plate, waiting until her appetite had slowed. The hall was quiet, those servants and soldiers eating in our company talking among themselves. Callum supped his beer through his red beard and watched his men. 'Ursilla,' I said, when I had had enough of my own thoughts, 'sit up here with me.'

The girl took a mutton-bone from her mouth and laid it by her trencher. 'I eat with good Christian folk,' she said in a low, clear voice, 'and not with you, lady.'

Father Andrew looked nervous. Callum leaned back with a grunt and looked at me, waiting for my reaction. A slow wave of silence washed down the hall.

'Ursilla,' said I, standing, 'you have the sense and judgment of a child, and for that I will forgive your rudeness, if you will apologise to me now.'

She bit her lip and set her shoulders.

'If not,' I warned, 'you will be punished. Like a child, if that is how you want to be treated. Is that clear?'

'God rot you,' she replied deliberately. I felt the indrawn breath of every witness in the hall. I turned away from her.

'Sergeant Callum –'

He was on his feet at once, blue eyes cool.

'Take the Lady Ursilla, put her over your knee and administer to her a sound spanking.'

He hesitated, nearly protested, the colour rising in his face. Our eyes locked. His discomfort was palpable, but my will is stronger than any vassal's. 'My Lady,' he growled, dropping his gaze and walking around me to Ursilla. I thought for a moment she would bolt, but she stood her ground, mouth trembling. I do not think she actually believed that I would do this to her in public. She had a lot to learn about many things.

'Tie her hands,' I added.

Callum loosened his knife-belt, caught up her hands behind her and swiftly strapped them together with the narrow length of leather. I admired his quick thinking and obvious skill. Ursilla gave one cry of outrage; 'You would not dare!'

Callum glanced back towards me. 'Do it,' said I.

He took his orders as a soldier should, put one foot up on the bench and dropped her neatly over his knee. His one hand steadied her by gripping her bonds while the other moved to the round upthrust promise of her arse.

'On the bare skin,' I instructed. Trained to obedience, his hesitation was hardly noticeable before he pulled up her skirts and laid them over her back. You might have heard a ghost walk through that hall. Every eye was upon the white glimmer of her raised and vulnerable buttocks, the helpless dark slash between them. A slow pulse beat between my thighs.

Callum began to measure the seconds with hard, echoing slaps. Father Andrew, seated only an arm's length away, closed his eyes and began to pray, his lips moving soundlessly. I will never forget that scene; the yellow candlelight gleaming on her pale skin and his red braided mane of hair, the rise and fall of the warrior's callused hand and the way it lingered after each blow, the jouncing quiver of her flesh, the sound of her gasping and crying out – the only noise in the castle to break the entranced silence between each slap. He had a good, firm hand, did Callum. I let him go to thirty blows before I called a halt, though she made no vocal plea for mercy.

'Take her up to my room,' I said, 'and return here directly.' I emphasised the last word. Callum swung his prisoner off his knee and on to her feet, turning to face me. His arousal was obvious even through the heavy fabric of his kilt and he wisely did not attempt to hide it.

'My Lady,' he said, his eyes fairly glittering. He pushed her out of the hall before him. Ursilla kept her tear-streaked face turned away from me.

I sat again and awaited my Sergeant's return. The hall slowly relaxed from the terrible tension and people began to talk again in soft voices. Faces were pale or flushed; there would be much activity between the blankets tonight, I knew.

Callum re-entered in good time, his erection under control once more. The face he turned to me was hot and dark with passion, which suited me well enough. He had been challenged, and shamed a little, and would not return to his old, lazy, condescending obedience. I have no use for a liegeman who is lukewarm in his affections; I want either devotion or dislike coupled with fear. My plans for Callum would have to wait, however, for the conclusion of my business with my stepdaughter.

Taking a formal leave of the diners – their salutations were loud and fervent – I picked up my skirts and mounted the long stairway to my room. Janet waited in her accustomed place outside the door.

'The Lady Ursilla is within,' she said, holding the portal open for me.

Nodding, I swept inside. Ursilla was kneeling on the bearskin beside my bed, her hands still tied behind her back, her face bowed so that her dark hair, knotted by exertion, fell in ropes before her face. I walked right up to her.

'Do you wish the punishment to continue?' I asked. 'Or are you ready to apologise for your rudeness?'

'Oh, yes,' she choked, leaning forwards, 'Oh, God, yes; I'm sorry.' She pressed her head against my thigh through the thick brocade of my skirt and began to sob. I laid my hand upon her dark head.

'I hate you,' she wept.

'No, you don't,' I said soothingly, stroking her hair. I let her wet my skirt with her tears for a little while. Then I took her chin in my hand and raised her stained face. 'Did Callum touch you?' I asked.

'No.' Her face crumpled again. 'Oh – I wanted him to!' Her humiliation and frustration washed over her anew. I was not entirely surprised by her response, but very pleased. Her skirts were rumpled up on the floor around her. Balancing myself with one hand on a bedpost, I slid my right foot under her skirt and nudged softly between her thighs. She opened to me with a groan of submission, spreading her knees helplessly. The heat of her flesh was startling – as was her wetness. She sank down on my satin-clad foot, her juices soaking through the slipper. I probed her gaping flesh, felt the rough scrape of her hair on my skin, felt her yield to my toes and try to encompass me, desperate for her raging, hungry flesh to be sated. She came almost at once, whimpering as she spent her torment in a flood of ecstasy and slick moisture. I watched her face twist and her breasts shake, saw her lose all control, and I delighted in her release.

I hoped after this that Ursilla would understand and in understanding change her ways, but old habits are like a mule we grow used to; it is frightening to put aside the old mount and harness a new stallion with unknown temper and wicked, rolling eyes, and to learn to ride this wild creature, no matter how fleet or handsome he might be.

I kept Ursilla with me when I could, making her work at everything from picking apples to sorting fleece. Idleness was not her problem, but it was the opportunity for her descent into the mire – and besides, it did her infinite good to hear me praise her when she pleased me.

And, oh, she did please me. In looks, she could not fail to charm; in temperament, her fiery spirit promised much – if only her pride could be harnessed with dignity and rebellion reforged into will. In the meantime, her need was to be mastered with love. My only doubt was whether this was a task that I should undertake myself, whether she was not too old for a mother's care, and I too young to provide it. I wondered if I might be able to find her a suitable husband, and considered speaking to Lord Malcolm of Eildon, a friend of my late husband's. My mistake was in mentioning this to Ursilla.

We were upon the glen road at the time, having been to visit the wife of one of our shepherds who was recovering from childbirth. I was riding my favoured palfrey; Ursilla was walking at my stirrup, as it was not my intention that she should be allowed such dignities until she had grown into that estate. Our conversation was polite and sparse, Ursilla speaking only in reply to my own enquiries and otherwise silent. When my musing aloud turned to her prospects for marriage, however, I saw her shoulders go up and her eyes flash as she turned up to me a face twisted with anger and fear.

'I will not marry your Lord Malcolm!' she shrieked. 'Nor anyone you choose to give me to!' She threw up her arms, her long sleeves flapping. 'This is my home; you can't throw me out!'

My mount shied sideways at this sudden explosion of shouting, fluttering fury and I was forced to wheel her in a tight circle to prevent her bolting. By the time the horse was obedient once more, Ursilla was a diminishing figure running down the track, her skirts hitched to her knees, her pale calves flashing. I stared after her but did not call. I certainly had no intention of riding her down. I let her precede me to the castle, holding my mount in on a tight rein, despite my own flustered anxiety. It would do me no good to be seen to be chasing her, whatever my instincts.

Of course, the consequence of this was that she arrived back within the stronghold a good way before I did. Her stamina, driven by panic though it was, was admirable. As I handed the reins of my palfrey to a groom, I asked where Ursilla had gone. Indoors, was the general response from those present. I bit my lip as I hurried within, brushing aside those servants who tried to attend upon me. No one in the Great Hall knew for sure where the young lady had disappeared to, so I strode to her rooms – but they were empty, as was the Solar, where I knew she sometimes retreated for privacy. Only when I returned, tense as a tethered hound, to my own rooms, did I find her. Janet was not in sight, but from within my chamber I heard a crash that made my heart jump.

The scene inside was one of chaos. Ursilla had taken up my boxes of jewellery and scents and thrown them to the floor, had upset the chairs and thrown open the coffers containing my dresses and hurled them about, tearing the rich trim from their necklines. The curtains of the bed were in shreds – by what means I did not realise until I saw the knife in her hand; she was slashing at my skirts, sobbing and grunting with the effort of ripping open the thick fabrics. I froze as I took the scene in. My glance went to the inner door, but that was still securely closed. My embroidery frame was collapsed, the bright threads spilled and tangled like the entrails of slaughtered birds.

I stepped into the room. She turned to face me, her visage a white smear in which her dark eyes glared, livid as bruises. She stepped back away from me, glancing about her, looking for some last thing to destroy. Something more to hurt me. Something precious. Her gaze seized upon the mirror; obviously expensive, obviously fragile – the decorated bronze

frame set with amber encased a sheet of real glass –
and she turned away in a swift, savage movement to
snatch it from its stand. I moved in quickly, but I would
not have got to her in time had she not frozen, staring
into the cloudy depths of the mirror, her hands gripping the frame. She had seen, unlucky girl, that that
room reflected within was naked of either her own
reflection or mine.

I gripped her paralysed wrist and twisted the knife
from her grasp, then I grabbed her shoulders and
turned her brutally to face me.

'Ursilla!' I snapped. She fell to the floor at my feet,
crouched on hands and knees. She was shaking convul-
sively and gasping so hard I believed she was about to
vomit. It was hard to recognise a young woman in this
savage, helpless, terrible creature.

'Look up!' I commanded, but she could not, turning
away from me a face frozen in a snarling rictus and
flinching from my touch. I bit my lip and clenched my
fists to stop them shaking. Then I unbound the soft,
woven belt from about my dress and knotted it around
her neck; I used it to drag her to her feet. And on the
end of that leash I marched her out of my room and
down the stairs into the bowels of the castle, past the
Great Hall, through the smoke-filled vault of the
kitchen and behind the ovens to the small buttery. She
lurched and choked on the end of the belt, keeping her
footing with difficulty. Servants scattered before us like
panicked hens. 'Get out of here!' I ordered, and they
fled.

When we were alone among the barrels of thin barley
beer and sour, elderly wine, I yanked Ursilla to her
knees once more and fastened the end of the lead to a
heavy table leg. Then I stripped her, ripping the clothes
from her back, laces and seams tearing under my
hands. I stole even her undershift from her, leaving her

naked on the stone floor, the belt around her neck her only garment.

'You,' I said, in tones of winter ice, 'will stay here until I come back for you. Do not move from this place. Do not speak. Do not touch that belt. You will learn obedience. Now.'

Carrying her clothes, I left her there. I gave instructions to the remains of the kitchen-staff that she was not to be approached or acknowledged. Then I retired to my room to effect what repairs I could to the wreckage.

I returned to Ursilla at the end of the day, long after the final meal, when all the servants had finished their work and the kitchen was empty. In the pitch dark, she must have had warning of my approach by the light of the candle-lantern I was bearing, but she did not raise her head as I entered the small room. She kneeled in the same position as I had left her, dark hair curtaining her face, but she had in the meantime found an old apron discarded nearby and contrived to wrap it round her as a shift in a vain attempt to conserve both her warmth and her modesty. She must have been quite cold in that room. The stained linen covered her breasts but barely brushed her naked pubic mound with its lower edge, and she crossed her hands over her pudenda as I stood over her. I found her shyness touching.

'Well, Ursilla,' I said softly. 'Does it please you to be treated like an animal, as you have acted like one?'

'I . . . I have to make water,' she replied. Her voice was cracked.

'I thought a bitch pissed wherever it pleased her,' said I.

She shivered. 'I wanted to wait. For you.'

I permitted myself a small smile, which she did not see because she still would not look up at me. 'Then, Ursilla, you have my permission to relieve yourself.'

She hesitated.

'Go on.'

She spread her thighs, gave a single little moan of relief, and let the piss flood out from her aching belly. It ran in steaming rivulets across the bare flagstones. The pleasure of that release was visible in the shudders that chased across her flesh; I could see the tension flow from her with the water.

'Thank you,' she whispered.

'Good,' I said. 'You may undo the rope now.' I watched her reach to the belt, but to my surprise she did not slip the noose from about her neck, but instead tugged free the knot at the table-leg, so that the loose end of the silken rope fell free and dangled down the length of her body. She made no move to escape the belt itself – indeed, I suspect she found it comforting now. My belly tightened. 'Come here,' I said hoarsely.

She came to me on hands and knees, across the length of the floor, her leash trailing, avoiding as best she could the puddles she had made. When she reached my feet she bowed her head low and kissed my right ankle, her warm breath tickling me shyly, the touch of her lips as soft as cobweb. The apron left her buttocks bare; they tipped up as she kneeled, pale as the soles of her tiny feet, almost glowing in the candlelight. I could not help but sigh under her supplicant caress, and leaned back against the barrel behind me.

Fearfully, with great hesitation and daring, she lifted the edge of my skirt further, and explored the curve of my calf with her lips, planting dozens of tiny, gentle kisses, breathless with trepidation, across the bare swell of skin. I permitted these familiarities graciously, even parting my legs a little to allow her greater ease of access. Not a word passed between us. No words could have fully expressed my surprise – my delight – my gratitude and glory. It was as if I had given birth to an angel. My heart felt as if it were trying to escape from my breast, my skin flushed with fire. I touched the dark and shining mass of her hair with my fingertips, not daring to grasp her in the savage caress I felt building within me, not daring to break that fearful miraculous moment of joy and mutual surrender. Her kisses burned my skin. I lifted the bunched weight of my skirt higher and higher, leading the way for her to my thighs and beyond. She whimpered softly as she kissed me. Her tongue described swirls of delight on my tenderest flesh, her face was in my hair, her lips were on my lips, her hot breath was on my soul. I opened to her. She crushed her face into the perfumed nest of my groin, gasping and nuzzling, her tongue a slippery finger of torment and need. She drank me down. She ate me up. I cried out and danced on her suckling, hungry mouth. I wrapped my fingers in her hair and crushed her closer, grinding on her writhing face, feeling her teeth and tongue and lips as I had never dared hope, feeling her wetness mingling with mine, feeling fire throbbing through my possessed and raging flesh –

And, oh, she held me to her lips like the Holy Grail itself as I was filled with the flames, and she drank the white liquid fire of heaven that poured through me down her open throat. In the cellar of a windswept castle, my skirts hitched to my waist, straddling the face of my stepdaughter – clasping her to that wet hole from which she had never emerged but now clove to as if trying to force her way back in – oh, there my heart was torn asunder.

I was foolish to mention marriage to her. I know that I am the guardian of her future, responsible for her prospects and her station. But, God forgive me, I do not think that I could bear to lose her.

Montague's Last Ride

Cecilia scraped butter on to the thin triangle of toast with her silver knife, then glanced down the length of the breakfast table at her husband. Rupert was absorbed in his copy of *The Times*, his dark head turned away, his fork hovering forgotten over a plate of lambs' kidneys. Cecilia smiled to herself, taking pleasure as she always did in the handsomeness of the man she had married, enjoying the contrast of his black moustache and tanned skin with the crisp white of his open shirt. He had been riding before breakfast and was still clad in tight breeches. The faintest scent of horses lingered in the air of the breakfast room.

Cecilia nibbled the corner of her toast and sighed gently. 'What are your plans for today, my dear?' she asked, looking out through the window beside her, across the broad balustraded veranda to the parkland beyond. The rich green of the grass and the darker foliage of the oaks shone under the morning light. It was going to be another beautiful summer's day.

Rupert laid down the newspaper and looked across at his wife. A smile warmed the cold blue of his eyes. 'I have to look at Home Farm,' he said, 'and then talk to the gamekeeper about the shooting in Hagg Wood. It will take most of the day, I'm afraid; I might have to miss tea. And this evening I promised to ride out to the Ambersons' for cards. I'll be back rather late, I should think. Will you be able to keep yourself occupied?'

Cecilia nodded. 'I plan to turn out the Blue Room,' she said. 'I thought the Chinese furniture would look best there, so I shall spend all day seeing to that.' She pouted, without any real unhappiness, purely for the prettiness of the effect. 'There is still so much to unpack. I don't know when we shall ever get to the conclusion of our own furniture, never mind sort out what was here when we arrived.'

'Ah, the burden of inheritance,' smiled the new Lord of Massingham Hall. 'Just be sure not to throw out too many of the family heirlooms, my love.'

'I shall certainly discard that hideous moth-eaten chaise longue from the Bamboo Bedroom,' she warned.

He nodded. 'Get Ramson to move it up to one of the servant's rooms,' he advised. 'But don't work too hard, Cecilia. I don't want you to be exhausted when I return.' His smile brought a glitter to his eyes. Cecilia blushed faintly and looked down at her plate. It was fortunate that there were no servants currently in the room.

'Of course, dear,' she murmured. 'But I did have a very relaxing day yesterday, talking to Lady Amberson. I'm sure I won't have to sleep too early tonight.'

'I'm glad to hear that,' her husband said softly. His gaze clung to her, to the curving slenderness of her pale figure under the cream silk of her dress. Her blushes only made her dimpled face prettier, betraying as they did to him her pleasure, her anticipation, her trepidation at what her husband might demand of her. Though wed nearly a year, there was no complacency between them yet.

'Actually, I had a very interesting conversation,' she

116

said, her hands fluttering like pink birds on the snowy linen of the table's edge. 'Lady Amberson knows a great deal about the history of the area and your family. She told me all about the mausoleum at the bottom of the lawn.'

Both of them looked out at this point through the open window to where, just visible in a sheltering copse of cypresses, a small white building glimmered among the green.

'Ah,' said Rupert. 'One of my ancestors, I assume?'

'Oh, yes,' Cecilia said with dreamy enthusiasm. 'And a terribly romantic one. The Wicked Lord Montague.'

'Wicked?' he asked, teasingly.

'Oh, terribly, even for his time. He was hanged as a witch in the seventeenth century.'

'Good grief. I had no idea any of my relations were so interesting.'

'Oh, I'm sure you would have been proud of him,' Cecilia laughed. 'He was dreadfully handsome and very brave, and said to be passionate about two things: horses and women. He had the finest stable in the county and rode to hounds every day he could. And in between rides he would spend his time seducing, well, just about anyone in a skirt. No woman was too inaccessible or too much of a challenge . . . nuns, countesses, brides, shepherd-girls. He said once that he would come back from Hell itself for the chance to bed a beautiful woman. And it was rumoured – well, more than that, in the end – it was said that he had made a pact with the Devil; sold his immortal soul for one boon . . .'

'Which was?'

'That any woman who looked into his eyes would be consumed with lust for him.'

'Good call.'

'It was his downfall in the end. He infuriated every husband for sixty miles around, rich and poor, and made too many enemies at Court. Eventually he was reported to the magistrates, and there was a very hurried, furtive trial – it was said afterwards that the judge had been cuckolded by him, too – and they hanged him at the crossroads upon the common. But there was trouble outside the court-room, because the women present starting wailing and calling for mercy for him. So Lord Montague was tried blindfolded, unable even to see his accusers, and they put his eyes out with hot irons before hanging him, as soon as sentence was passed. They were afraid of his "magical" stare.'

'Fascinating,' Rupert said dryly.

'Apparently, they were quite justified,' she continued. 'Even though he was a convicted witch and a servant of the Devil, when he was executed many of the local women in the crowd wept openly for him. And several tried to run forwards and hang upon his feet after he had dropped – to break his neck, you see, and give him a quick death instead of letting him strangle slowly. The constable's men had to hold them back with pikes.'

Rupert raised one dark eyebrow. 'I admit their devotion was touching,' he said. 'And the wicked Montague was brought back for burial at Massingham Hall?'

Cecilia nodded. 'He had already had his own tomb built, and not on consecrated ground either. Besides, he was nobility and it would not have done to leave him swinging. I had a look through the iron gate yesterday,' she added. 'You can see inside quite clearly. The interior is completely plain, with no carvings or crucifixes at all. I think he must have been a dreadful pagan at least. There is just this big stone sarcophagus with not even his name on, just the one word "*Resurgam*".'

'"I will rise again",' her husband mused. 'I wonder if that was a joke.'

Cecilia stifled a coy smile.

'Well,' said Rupert, shaking his head, 'it sounds like he made a very unwise bargain to me. Really quite rash, not to mention indiscriminating.'

'Oh, I think it rather wonderful,' Cecilia disagreed, her pink lips forming a moist 'O' that quickened Rupert's pulse. 'Just think, he might have had anything the Devil cared to grant; riches, power, the friendship of the King. But he wanted more than anything to be adored by women, desired by them, to have as many as he could take. He wanted them all; rich and poor, plump and thin, pretty and plain – the female body meant more than the rest of the world to him. I find that so . . . elemental.'

'It certainly sounds like he has charmed you, at any rate,' Rupert observed. His voice had dropped to a low, ominous purr.

Cecilia blushed again and could not meet her husband's eyes. 'It's very romantic,' she protested weakly.

'My dear, you don't fool me for a moment,' he said. 'I can tell by your face, and your voice, and your manner that you find this ancestor of mine more than romantic. Your imagination has got the better of you again, my lovely wife. You are quite aroused by the thought of this wicked Lord Montague, are you not?'

Cecilia's head drooped modestly on her slender neck. The loose sweeps of her honey-brown hair hid her eyes, but did not disguise from his view her flushed cheeks or parted lips. 'If you say so, my love,' she whispered.

Rupert stood. His own arousal would have been quite obvious through the tight riding breeches, if she had dared to look. 'I do say so,' he told her. His blue eyes were bright and hard, his smile mocking. 'And what do you think I should do about a wife of mine who is wet and pliant at the mere thought of this long-dead rake?' He reached to the side of the table, where his riding crop had been laid carelessly when he came in for breakfast. 'Get up,' he ordered her in a low voice.

Cecilia's head lifted in alarm; 'What about the servants?' she gasped.

'You had better hope they do not come in,' Rupert said coldly. 'Now stand. Bend over the chair seat.'

Shivering, Cecilia obeyed. Rupert stepped up behind her and lifted her long dress over her back with the crop. White silk drawers were revealed, edged with lace, but he pulled these down to her knees with one swift, ruthless motion. Cecilia gasped and buried her face in the padded back of the chair.

Rupert drew the stiff rod of the riding-crop up the inside of her right thigh from knee to cleft. Cecilia twitched involuntarily, the white globes of her buttocks shuddering. The crop was slapped warningly between her legs, from thigh to thigh.

'Further apart,' said Rupert. His voice was thick.

She spread her legs hesitantly, baring the tender puckered skin of her naked arsehole, the shadowy fuzz of her secret hair, the pink petals of her flesh. Rupert, his breath rising sharply in his throat, surveyed his wife with utter satisfaction. He tapped her puffy sex-lips with the end of the crop, heard her whimper nervously, and felt his own rod harden to iron, straining against his breeches. He laid his free hand firmly over the rigid bulge of the constrained weapon. At the end of the springy crop there was a small loop of stiff leather. He twisted this between her legs, probing her, spreading the petals of the blushing flower. It slipped in and out easily; withdrawn, it brought with it a trail of clear moisture. Cecilia groaned almost inaudibly. Rupert ran the loop from front to back of her slit, spreading the wetness of her willing compliance generously. The scent of her was like perfume.

'Slut,' he said.

Her arse writhed, offering itself to the whip. The leather was darkened now, soaked with her juices.

'Whore,' he breathed, leaning over her, gripping his own flesh as if it would tear free from him. Very gently, he began to beat a tattoo on her spread sex with the end of the crop, working across the pubis and the swollen cunt, pausing now and then to administer a stinging blow to either white buttock. Cecilia whimpered and shook; the leather slapped and splashed on her wetness; his rhythm was unrelenting and expert, driving her masterfully to her crisis. With a stifled, wailing cry she opened to the pleasure that the whip was hammering into her flesh, then collapsed into the chair. Dropping the crop, Rupert pulled his tormented cock from his breeches with both hands and sprayed great gouts of pearly jism on to her splayed and quivering arse-cheeks.

As soon as he had recovered, he pulled her silken drawers back up over her bespattered globes. She would carry the stain and the stink of him round with her all day; that thought was a warm knot of pleasure in his gut. He helped her to her feet and kissed her hot forehead. Her lips quested feverishly for his, but he restrained her and pushed her gently away.

'We have a busy day,' he reminded her, his smile mocking but not unkind. 'Tonight, my dearest. Be patient. And try not to think of my wicked ancestors – I am just as wicked as you could wish and, what is more, am alive so that you might have the benefit.'

With a final sip of tea he left the breakfast room, slapping his riding crop cheerfully against his boot and whistling to himself.

Cecilia stood, dazed and frustrated, before the windows overlooking the park. Pleasured but far from satiated, her hot and swollen flesh tormented her now. It would be a whole day before Rupert came to her bed and filled her needy body with his hardness. She should, she knew, attempt to think of other things. Indeed, what else was there for it but to find some distraction? The thought of the Blue Room, with its faded screens and damp, overstuffed bed, was not attractive at the moment. She looked down at the swell and fall of the sward before the windows, wondering if one of the gardeners might have passed by unnoticed while Rupert was playing with her. The thought, in her present aroused condition, was more titillating than alarming. The Hall's herd of white cattle was visible, grazing in the far distance across the park, but she did not really see them. Her gaze drifted back to the cypresses and the old mausoleum. A sigh escaped her lips.

Cecilia found the great iron ring of household keys where she had first seen it, in the bureau in the Smoking Room – Rupert's study, now. The panelled room smelled of pipe tobacco and furniture wax. She stood over the desk and sifted through the keys. Only four looked large enough and old enough to be candidates for the gate to the tomb, but she took the whole ring. She made her way around the side of the Hall, through the walled vegetable garden and past the greenhouse with its neglected vines, down to the ha-ha that divided the lawn from the park. She crossed that ditch by the narrow bridge under the yew tree, shutting the gate behind her. It would not do to let the cattle on to the lawn.

Already the sun was fierce and there was a sticky, humid feeling to the air which made the heat worse. No clouds relieved the monotony of the blue sky. It was going to be a scorching day.

The mausoleum of Lord Montague was a little way from the ha-ha: a small, plain building constructed of brick covered over with white plaster that now was stained and crumbling. Only the surrounding trees and the thick ivy that grew up the rear seemed to protect it from the elements. In the front wall was a single gate of wrought and scrolled iron. By peering in through the bars, one might make out the interior; the pale table-like tomb standing in a drift of ancient leaves, the cracked greying plaster of the ceiling, and the single carved word on the tombstone.

Resurgam.

Cecilia tried one key after another in the lock on the gate. In all honesty she expected to find that even if one did fit, the gate would be rusted solid and beyond her powers to open – it was over two centuries old, after all. However, it appeared that the previous owners of Massingham Hall had maintained their ancestral memorials with due respect, for the third key she tried did, with a little coaxing, turn in the lock. The gate moved reluctantly, grating on its hinges, but with neither the squeals of protesting metal nor the showers of rust that might have been anticipated.

Within, the mausoleum was cool, a welcome relief from the sweaty heat outside. Empty of all features except the marble-topped tomb, it filled up at once with the echoes that Cecilia brought with her. She stood on the threshold for a few moments until her eyes adjusted to the dimness, then wondered why she had come at all, for there was nothing to see in this single bare room. The drifted leaves near the doorway turned to dust underfoot. She trod carefully and approached the tomb with a sensation of mingled melancholy and disappointment. Her fingertips brushed the cold marble. She walked all around the tomb once, slowly, but found no new feature. She thought of Lord Montague lying beneath the slab, perhaps within arm's reach; thought of his body mouldering silently in the darkness, and then idly imagined how he would feel lying motionless, staring at the unseen marble with empty sockets while soft legless things swarmed and gnawed within his entrails and black scuttling beetles burrowed in his skull. The morbid sensuality of it appealed to her; she envisaged no discomfort but only the slow tickling squirm of dissolution. Then she sighed at her own foolishness. Montague had been dead too long; there was likely nothing left of him by now but dust and a few fragments of bone.

She laid both palms on the marble slab. It was so cool on her hot skin.

'My poor Lord Montague,' she murmured, 'lying here all alone in a cold bed. No warm body to hold you close. I'll bet you never had to do that when you were alive.'

She slid her hands forwards on the cool stone and stretched her torso across the slab, feeling the chill soak into her arms and breasts and belly like water. For a moment she felt dizzy. The rock was icy against her cheek and brow. The hot ache between her legs was unabated, however, and she would not be able to soothe that by lying there. Reluctantly, after reclining a few moments, she pushed herself back to her feet once more. Then she discovered that, standing, her crotch was directly on a level with the top of the slab. Where she stood now the corner of the stone pressed into her groin, and she could rub her swollen, needy sex against its cold thrust. Dreamily, she lifted her skirt before her and spread it upon the tomb-top so that her damp silk underwear was all that separated her from the rigid marble. She began to press herself forwards, rubbing herself off on the white rock, while the hot waves of her passion, held back so precariously, began swiftly to rise. She imagined Lord Montague stirring in his tomb, sensing her, smelling her; pictured him lifting his withered arms towards her, his black and corrupt penis swelling, stiffening – and with that thought she came, her suppressed whimper echoing in the tiny room like the shriek of some small animal.

When her senses had fully returned she found that sweat had broken out across her brow and lip and that her legs were trembling beneath her. The climax had been far fiercer than she had anticipated, with a backwash of unconsciousness that verged on the startling. Straightening her skirt, Cecilia moved uncertainly from the mausoleum, shocked by the weakness of her limbs. She pulled the gate shut behind her, looking across the lawn to the looming bulk of the Hall, wondering if anyone had seen her exit from the tomb. Nothing stirred in the bright sunlight.

Halfway back to the Hall, she realised that she had left the ring of keys dangling in the unlocked gate to the tomb. She turned with some reluctance to go back, then paused. The dark gateway to the tomb gaped at her across the grass, the bars almost invisible against the blackness, but in that darkness behind the iron something paler moved. She blinked – and it was gone. She found her heart was jumping in her breast. There was no suggestion of motion about the tomb any more; no sign of life. Yet somehow Cecilia did not care to return to that gate just now, but backed away thinking that if Rupert missed the keys she could send one of the servants. Or perhaps simply fetch them tomorrow.

She walked uneasily back to the stolid comfort of the great house.

After a cool bath she felt a great deal better and spent the rest of the day as she had planned, directing the servants in moving furniture into and out of the Blue Room. There was only one incident that gave her any cause for dismay, and that was when late in the afternoon she glanced out of one of the windows. The Blue Room was high up in the East Wing of the Hall, overlooking the park behind the building, though from a different angle to that of the Breakfast Room. When Cecilia looked down idly from that vantage point she thought she caught a movement by the ha-ha, and was sure she could see the dark shape of someone loitering in the shadows under the yew tree. She sent one of the housemaids down to look out of the scullery door, but the girl toiled back upstairs to report that there was no one outside at all. In the time the maid had been away, Cecilia had kept an eye on the yew tree; the shadow had not moved, but she had grown less certain that it was the figure of a man. With the negative reconnaissance she turned away from the window and tried to dismiss the strange feeling that had settled in her stomach.

She ate alone at supper in the big, draughty dining room and did not look out of any of the windows. After her meal she read magazines by the fire until it was time to retire to bed. Her own room was in the West Wing on the ground floor, one door down the corridor from her husband's. She went into his chamber briefly, sat before his mirror and sniffed at the bottle of hair-oil, hoping to find the familiar smell comforting. It was not that she felt nervous or unhappy, but it was an odd, dislocated hiatus, as if she were slightly drunk or somehow detached from herself. She felt as if she were expecting something to happen. The humid weather had continued into the evening, pregnant with the threat of thunder, and it made her head feel thick, her blood pound slowly in her veins. The house creaked as floorboards swelled and settled. The servants had been gloomy and irritable all day.

Unwilling to wait up longer for Rupert, who might despite all promises be out until nearly dawn, Cecilia at last retreated to her own room. This chamber had large French windows that opened out on to the veranda. It looked south and east across the parkland, a lovely room in the morning and filled now with all her own ornaments and pictures so that she felt quite at home here even after so few weeks. Cecilia changed into a long white cotton nightdress and crossed to the windows. It was so warm that it was tempting to leave them open while she slept, but she knew night air was supposed to be unhealthy, so after gazing out into the park for a little while she pulled them to. The moon was rising, the park a grey sweep in which the black blotches of trees were indistinct landmarks. She thought she could just make out the pale brush-stroke of the mausoleum on the moonlit canvas, but it was difficult to be sure. A tawny owl hooted in the distance. Drawing the curtains, Cecilia slid into bed and sank into a heavy sleep.

She awoke from the middle of a dream; a cloying, unfocused erotic embrace in which Rupert was in her, his hips grinding upon her own, his tongue in her mouth and also, impossibly, suckling savagely at both her breasts. She moaned as she came awake, angry that she had not reached the climax she was so desperate for and snatching in frustration as the fading shreds of the dream. But she knew at once that she would not be able to retrieve it. She stared at the unseen ceiling, letting her breath slow. The fur between her legs was a swamp of hot moisture. The sheet was rucked down around her hips, knotted around her legs. Cecilia wondered why she had woken. The room was in absolute darkness. The only sounds were her own movements and the only glimmer of light the paler square of the curtains over the moonlit window. They were stirring in the warm air. Cecilia turned her head towards the drapes and thought, The window is open. But I closed it before I went to bed.

With that thought came the conviction that there was someone in the room with her.

She held her breath. There was no sound, not the slightest whisper. Nevertheless the conviction did not weaken.

'Rupert?' she said.

There was no reply.

When she could not bear the silence any longer, Cecilia kneeled up in the bed, freed her legs from the sheet and groped on the bedside table for the matches she knew were there. Familiarity allowed her to find the ornate brass oil-lamp quickly and she pressed the trembling flame to the wick. Only when it had caught and she had adjusted the glass did she allow herself to look around.

Lord Montague stood near the foot of her bed. Cecilia forgot to breathe.

She could see that he had once been more than handsome; he wore the rags of his beauty as he wore the torn trousers and the loose, yellowed linen shirt. His hair was dark and fell to his shoulders like a gleaming shadow; his cheekbones were high, his shoulders broad over a lithe body and narrow hips. But his burial clothes did little to hide the terrible wiry thinness of his limbs, or the discoloured skin stretched tight as parchment over jutting collarbones, or the long narrow hands with their yellowed nails. And – *he had no eyes*. Blackened pits gaped at her, turning his face into a mask.

For a moment that could not be measured – for both breath and heartbeat seemed to have deserted Cecilia – they faced each other down the length of the bed, both perfectly motionless. Then she opened her mouth and gave a terrible choking gasp. But at that moment he began to walk towards her, and the cry she might have uttered died in her throat. A clutch of cold like a strait-jacket gripped her entire body and she could not stir from where she kneeled. The action of walking transformed the figure of Lord Montague from a simple corpse, an object of disgust, to something much worse. The horror of it hit her like glory; he was beyond mere revulsion.

He did not move like a living man – he was too stiff, unused to the motion. His bare feet clicked on the polished wooden floor. Cecilia shut her eyes briefly, but opened them when he stopped before her. Her next shuddering breath brought the sweet carrion stink of him to her nostrils. She noted without thought that beneath the stained cravat knotted about his throat the bruises could still be glimpsed, torn and livid. He inclined his head towards her.

Slowly she reached out with one hand and touched his chest, just where skin and cloth met at the deep neckline of his shirt. He was cold and his skin slightly damp to the touch, like old leather left out in the rain. There was no rise and fall to his ribs. Cecilia whimpered deep in her throat and very gently Lord Montague raised one hand to brush and then cup her cheek. She shut her eyes against the chill, rough texture of his brittle fingers. Her own hand slid down the front of his shirt, felt the tightness of the abdominal skin and the suggestion of writhing movement beneath. A dark wave of dizziness threatened to drown her. Rising above it like a woman fighting a rough sea, she opened her eyes wide, raised her head and did not flinch even when his face descended upon hers and their lips met.

He stank of death. He tasted of death. Breathing deeply, she could not support herself any longer; all the strength seemed to have soaked from her. She sank helplessly down from her kneeling position, back against the pillows, and watched dreamily as his hands, slow but deft, traced the outline of her breasts. One by one he undid the little white bows down the front of her nightdress and then exposed her plump breasts. His hands were so cold; her nipples leaped at once under their icy caress and became hard as pebbles, her breasts heaving under his touch. He cupped her in his skeletal grasp and bent to tug one stiff pink nipple lightly in his teeth. She moaned and writhed under the horror and the pleasure. Her hips moved in blind circles. She brushed his dark hair with one hand, felt something wriggle away from her palm and did not care. His touch was torment.

'Oh, God!' she gasped as he pulled and rolled her screaming flesh between the leathery bones of his fingers. The coldness within her was giving way to a terrible burning, melting heat; her groin was all liquid fire and desperate need. When he released her, she began to sob dryly.

His hands went to her nightdress and the fabric tore like wet paper under them. He bared her down the entire length of her body, seemed to contemplate the sight, and then traced that line across her soft skin with his fingertips, nails scoring pink lines on her. His touch reached her pubic mound, the rough hair of her secret flesh. Cecilia swallowed her last gasp, froze, and then opened her thighs to him. His fingers slipped into wetness. Her eyes pleaded.

Lord Montague hesitated there for only a second or two. His head turned back and forth as if he were looking at her, though his empty sockets mocked that thought. Then he stooped forwards, slipped his thin arms under her shoulders and thighs, and lifted her. No grunt of exertion escaped him, and his thin limbs were stronger than iron. Cecilia's rounded, pale body dangled effortlessly in his desiccated grasp. She did not struggle, but let her head loll against the sharp angles of his shoulder. He turned and strode out through the glass doors into the darkness.

Cecilia hardly felt the night air upon her naked skin. Her head reeled with her own desire, with the cloying smell of decay, with shock and confusion. She was not fully aware of their progress across the lawn and down into the park, the hiss of his feet on the grass, the shriek of a startled night-bird; she only became more conscious when her bearer passed under the lintel of his mausoleum. There should have been inky blackness within those four walls, but a pale phosphorescence lit the scene; enough to show her the great marble slab cast on to the floor and the box of the sarcophagus gaping. Lord Montague stepped easily over the small wall into his tomb, held her there briefly in his arms, then bent and laid her gently upon the rotted fabric that lined the stone casing. Something scuttled near her head but she paid it no attention. She lifted her arms to her ancient lover.

He stooped to her. The rotted cloth of his trousers ripped under her nails. She felt the cold, hard length of his embrace along her entire body, his thighs parting hers, the icy length of his slippery member pushing up between her hot inner lips. She opened to him eagerly, tasted his tongue and moaned under the exquisite pleasure of his entrance into her living flesh. His cock was of extraordinary thickness and the initial pain made her gasp, but it only heightened her subsequent ecstasy as he bore down into her. She wrapped her legs around his thrusting hips and, as the rhythm built, groaned aloud with pleasure, clawing at his back. His flesh disintegrated under her nails and she felt the bare bones of his spine against her fingertips, but it did not slow him or give him pause in his terrible struggle. The appetite that had driven him back from the grave overmastered everything. Not death, not damnation, not the collapse of his earthly flesh could stop him, could hold him back from a final possession of her sweet, wild, heaving body. And she rose to match that appetite and each thrust, the darkest desires of her maddened heart finding their apotheosis in her inflamed clitoris and convulsing quim. Slippery with sweat and vaginal juices and the liquescence of his dissolution they rutted to their unnatural climax. Lord Montague stiffened at last and, spasming, poured his black essence into the cup of her yawning cunt, just as

Cecilia tore her throat raw shrieking her orgasm into the echoing chamber of the tomb.

Black waves of unconsciousness claimed her at once. She did not hear the sound of men stumbling through the open door, nor see the glow of lamplight upon the plaster. She did not see Rupert lean over the lip of the tomb and freeze, staring down with unbelieving horror at the sight of his wife, naked and unmoving, her legs splayed and pussy agape, clasping in her embrace the rotted and blackened remains of a crumbled skeleton.

Bodyguard

*A*t the end of the ninth day they came over a rocky hillock just like any other, stubbled with grey stunted thorn trees, and suddenly the Harran Valley was below them: the white scar of the South Road, the hesitant green of the long grasses that flanked the small river – and the sand-coloured blocks of the Inn at Harran squatting between the boulders in the entrance to a minor ravine. Jhearl gave a sigh of relief and turned smiling to her companion, saying, 'Oh, Ambele – there it is! We're here. Thank the gods.'

The other woman, her visage set in sombre planes under the ritual cicatrices that defined the lines of her face, did not smile. She watched the dust-clouds blow up the road below them and moved her spear thoughtfully from one hand to the other. It was a long spear, taller even than she was, with a broad bronze head honed to a wicked sharpness. Her dark hands gripped the shaft lightly, with easy familiarity.

'And thanks to you,' Jhearl added swiftly. 'I would have died out there if it hadn't been for you. I'll see that you are well paid.'

The mercenary nodded, stony-faced, before indicating a possible path down the valley wall and setting off again. Jhearl watched her with a mixture of bemusement and relief as she followed. Ambele was unlike anyone else she had ever met. In the days since they had been thrown together, she felt that she had come to comprehend the Kledish woman very little better; quiet, patient, always watchful, the grief of her recent loss bottled up and only audible in the keening songs she moaned to the moon each night, rocking on her heels as she squatted with her back to their meagre camp-fire. Jhearl wished that she understood better, that they had been able to talk as they walked through the desert fringe, but though they shared enough of the same language Ambele had clung to silence, breaking it only for practical instruction and warning. Probably it was enough, Jhearl thought, that they had walked together at all.

She placed her own feet in the prints left by Ambele's bare soles down the sandy, treacherous slope, though she had to stretch her stride to do so. Her feet hurt badly, the remnants of her white silk slippers held together now only by strips of cloth torn from her skirt. Nevertheless she smiled as they scrambled down the slope and the words fell bright and easy from her as they had not done in a hundred miles; 'Food, and new clothes, and clean water to bathe in,' she promised. 'Fresh melon, and kid stewed in milk, and a skin of wine. And I will be able to comb out my hair at last. Ah – the dust!' Ambele said nothing.

It seemed to Jhearl that they could hardly have offered a greater contrast, as two women, unless by some miracle they had been washed of the dust that coated them and Jhearl had been restored to her previous station upon a white mule with scarlet harness. Ambele was dark and glossy as a chestnut bud, as supple and lean and dangerous as a hunting bow, her black hair captured in a thousand knotted strands like the cords of a whip, her long torso encased in a padded leather breast-plate, her hips swathed in the pelt of a leopard that Jhearl did not doubt she had killed herself. She herself on the other hand was, beneath the dust and her ragged yellow dress, pale and prettily rounded, rather short of stature even for a woman of Celephais, with soft limbs that had never known a need for harder muscle. She almost had to trot to keep up with her companion's tireless stride and the pain of their journey had marked her badly, she feared. But now at its end, grazed knees and blistered feet and cracked lips forgotten, she held her head up and moved with a sunny confidence that Ambele was unused to, and she sensed the mercenary's curious sidelong glances at her.

They reached the road as the last brilliant light of the afternoon left it and began to retreat up the far side of the valley. There were no other travellers in sight, but as they approached the Inn at Harran they noticed the hoofprints and dung on the road, the smell of wood-smoke and the sound of a cockerel calling. Here in this narrow valley on the fringe of the barren hills there was life, for here there was water and commerce both.

As they drew up to the outer wall of the inn a dog rushed out and began barking at them, a grey creature as ragged as they. Ambele dropped her spear-point and levelled it at the dog's head and it backed off, hackles raised. Jhearl remembered the night she had woken to see her protector standing taut above her, while silently in the moonlight the shadowy forms of four hyaenas stalked around them, eyes glinting in the faint glow of the camp-fire embers. Ambele had held her post all night, facing off any beast that dared close in too far – she had bloodied one of them that was insufficiently cautious – until dawn had caused the disappointed animals to break off and depart. Jhearl smiled at the cowed dog.

There were large wooden doors to the gateway of the

Inn at Harran, but they stood open and beyond the wall was the courtyard, in which stood the buildings of the inn proper – store-rooms, a stable, the goat-byre, and the two-storied bulk of the inn itself. Tales of this place had not exaggerated its prosperity and it looked both well kept and welcoming. There were people in the courtyard; the first the two women had seen since the terrible night that had thrown them together. An old woman squatted stripping beans from their pods into a copper bowl, a boy clad in a dirty striped robe swung his legs from his perch on a mounting block, and two stout men, both merchants by the look of their attire and their shrewd, appraising expressions, sat on a carpet in the shade of one wall and talked over the bubbling pipe between them. All the inhabitants raised their heads to stare at the two newcomers. Jhearl tilted her chin in the air and strode airily through the court-yard towards the building right at the back, stifling her limp. Her hips even swayed. Ambele, less relaxed and glancing about her, stalked at the smaller woman's heels.

At the door a short man stepped out to meet them, wiping his hands on his jellaba. The dog ran up to stand at his side and the two, man and cur, eyed the women warily.

'You are the innkeeper?' Jhearl asked.

He admitted as much with a curt nod.

'I require a room,' she said; 'the best you have in this place.'

He raised his bushy eyebrows. 'That would cost you three pieces of silver.'

Jhearl smiled, fixing him steadily with her eyes and said, 'That's no problem to me, innkeeper; I have money. The caravan I was travelling with was set upon by a pack of ghouls, but I escaped with more than my life.'

'Ghouls?' the innkeeper said warily. 'Where?'

'One night out from the Bindar Well. We were camped and they came under cover of darkness. All our party were slain, except myself and this Kledish woman –' she nodded over her shoulder '– who was also travelling in the party. I have employed her as my guide and my bodyguard, to bring me to this haven.'

As she spoke, Jhearl saw in her mind's eye the dull glow of the camp-fire, the dark figures struggling over it, the flash of steel in the torchlight. She remembered again the rock pressed into her face, the weight of Ambele on her pinning her to the earth, the salty taste of her hand clamped over her mouth, the pain of the other woman's fingers tightening on her arm as figure after figure around the distant fire slumped to the ground until there were none left standing but the naked dog-faced ghouls first capering triumphantly and then hunching over the corpses of the fallen. Though she herself had lost no one in the skirmish but two slaves and her mule, Jhearl still felt cold at the memory. Her shudder was not dissembled.

The innkeeper's eyes were wide now. 'You survived the attack? I have never heard of such luck.'

'We were not by the camp-fire when the attack came,' Jhearl said haughtily. She had gone out on to the darkened hillside to relieve her bladder in private and her path had crossed Ambele's on the way back. She remembered how she had jumped at the first sight of that black figure climbing between the boulders, thinking she had been followed by one of the men from the caravan.

'And you have walked a long road,' the innkeeper said, 'if you came from Bindar Well on foot.'

'We came across the hills,' Jhearl agreed wearily. 'I did not think it wise to use the road any more, alone and with only one guard.'

He nodded, his manner easing visibly now. 'There is a good room free,' he said, 'if you will show me your

137

money in advance.' He indicated the interior of the building and Jhearl stepped forwards with a gracious smile. In fact, she was stung by her need to justify herself in public to a rustic innkeeper, and ashamed of her ragged clothes and dirty cast – but she would not have shown her self-disgust for anything in the world.

'Will your guard sleep in the common room?' the innkeeper asked. Ambele stood like a rock in the courtyard.

Jhearl raised her arched brows. A lone woman lying in the straw of the common lodging would not dare to sleep all night. 'She'll share the room with me,' she instructed.

'Very good,' said the innkeeper, and led the way into the shadowy depths of the building.

The room was, to Jhearl's relief, quite acceptable, though by her tastes rather bare. A shuttered window let slants of yellow evening light in to stripe the stone-flagged floor. The wooden bed, its fleece mattress covered with a blue woollen blanket, looked roomy and clean. Jhearl told the innkeeper to turn his back while she lifted her torn skirt and fished from beneath it the purse strapped to her thigh. 'Thank you, lady,' the man said as he accepted her coins.

Ambele threw her water-skin into a corner and crossed to look out of the window.

'Have you a bathing-tub in this place?' Jhearl asked. 'I want to rid myself of that part of the desert which I am still carrying.'

'I'll have a bath brought in to your room,' the innkeeper promised, quite servile now that he had seen the size of her purse. Jhearl's practice was to travel nowhere without enough coin to buy herself out of trouble – a habit left over from days when respect was a rarer gift than gold.

'Find me clean clothes, too, if you would, and a comb. And for her.'

'Of course. I will have your meals sent to this room as well.'

Jhearl shook her head at this; she had had enough of silence and near-solitude. 'No; if you have a bar-room that is fit for a woman to eat in, then we will dine there.'

'As you prefer, lady,' the innkeeper said, turning to leave.

She hesitated briefly and then said, before she lost her chance, 'The inn does not seem over-crowded. Do you have many guests at this time?'

He shrugged one shoulder. 'Not tonight. At this time of the year it is not steady trade – but in a week's time we might be full, if a big caravan comes through. You can never be sure.'

'Ah. There is no one here from Kuranes' army then?'

'No, lady.' He paused as if awaiting her next question, but when she glanced away he retreated and closed the door.

Jhearl went and sat upon the bed. It felt soft enough to fulfil her every need that night – though by now she knew she could sleep upon bare rock. She sighed to herself and looked over at Ambele, who was gazing motionless out of the window. The stillness of the Kledish woman was something that Jhearl had not yet grown used to, that ability to suspend all animation and become a part of the desert background whenever no movement was necessary. Jhearl was aware that she was actually rather nervous of the tall woman. Her strangeness; her silence; her closed-off, guarded glance that betrayed no emotion. Jhearl was used to reading people and knowing how to act for them – she knew exactly what any man wanted within minutes, she prided herself – but Ambele was a mystery.

'Does this place suit you, then?' she asked softly.

'Well enough.' Ambele's leather armour creaked as

she turned. 'It is good to sleep tonight without listening for danger.'

'Where will you go from here?' Jhearl enquired, a little shyly.

Her hireling shrugged. 'I do not know. I brought you here; you are alive. Now I have to find my own people. One cloud does not last long in the sky. But they are a long way from here, south, at this time. I will join a new caravan at this place.'

'Well, while I am here, I will pay for your lodging,' Jhearl said. 'It is only fair. I brought you to this inn.' She had a reputation in Celephais; beggars considered her heartless, servants demanding. Her generosity was never unearned, but to those who served her loyally she was unstinting.

Ambele tilted her proud head back and looked at her narrowly. 'You are meeting someone here?' she asked.

'Yes,' said Jhearl with caution. 'A friend.' She was startled at this, almost the first question Ambele had asked of her. There might have been more to come, but instead both women turned towards the door as they heard the rumble of thunder in the passageway beyond. It rose to a grumbling roar and then the door was knocked upon and opened. A middle-aged woman, needle-eyed and brisk, ushered in two men rolling a huge wooden half-tub, exactly like the bottom part of a wine-press. This was tipped noisily on to its base in the open centre of the room. Jhearl was impressed by its size, and by the speed with which other servants hurried in with buckets of water to fill it. The old woman folded on to the wooden clothes-chest two rough towels that had been draped over her arm, and placed on top of them a lamp, a bunch of twiggy green herbage and a jar of soap. The last person to enter the room was a little slave girl who carefully laid out a selection of dresses upon the bed. Jhearl nodded. The hiss of water slopping into the tub ceased and the old woman rounded up her underlings with a clap of her hands before following them out, all without saying a word to the paying guests.

Jhearl eyed the tub with pleasure and dipped her fingers into the water. It was clear and tepid, delightful after the heat of the day. 'See that no one else enters the room,' she told Ambele, then as the other woman went and stood against the door she loosed her clothing and let the filthy dress slide to the floor. She kicked free of the silk rags and stepped into the tub, sinking gratefully into the cool embrace of the waters. She could not stretch out flat, but she found she could sit comfortably enough with all but her knees – pink and a little scarred now – and shoulders submerged, the little wavelets lapping about the swell of her plump breasts. She let out a sigh of relief, reached up to her hair and pulled it free of the knot it had been in for over a week now. It fell to her shoulders like tarnished sunlight. She ducked briefly under the surface to let the waters wash her hot scalp and rose streaming water and gold. She pushed her wet hair back from her face and looked over at the doorway.

Ambele, her back against the door and her spear propped nearby, was undoing the strapping that held her armour on, absorbed in the knots. She glanced up in time for their gazes to meet and Jhearl, to her own astonishment, looked quickly away. She felt suddenly self-conscious about being naked in front of another, a sensation quite titillating in its novelty. The cool water had made her nipples tighten and now they broke the surface like little pebbles. Jhearl turned away, hiding her confusion in the action of reaching for the jar of soap. Her mind was suddenly racing.

It was fine and expensive soap, scented with rosepetals. Jhearl scooped a handful from the stone jar and began to rub it into her skin. The wet slipperiness of it on her flesh was pleasant, as was the sensation of her

141

own fingers expertly rubbing the sore muscles beneath. She massaged around her neck and collar-bones, into her armpits and down the gently curved line of her belly. Her flesh was both hot and cold, firm and soft, depending on where her fingers explored. She lathered up both hands and massaged her breasts in a double grasp, hefting the cool weight of them, feeling the cold jewellery slip through her fingers. She rubbed each toe individually and then had to kneel up in the tub in order to reach down between her thighs, and from behind between the plump curves of her buttocks, to soap the hot folds of her sex. She found that despite the cool water she was slippery there even before the addition of soap. She rubbed her pubic mound slowly, stirring the trimmed golden fleece, and glanced deliberately over at Ambele.

The dark woman stood watching, her muscular arms folded over a thin, stained shirt. Her face was impassive, but her eyes did not flinch away when Jhearl turned. She did not partake of that studied carelessness that women affect when they are naked together, looking quickly elsewhere as if to say, 'Breasts? – no, I hadn't noticed. Why should I? They don't mean anything to me.' Ambele might have been fascinated, or she might have been contemptuously indifferent, but she was not pretending that she did not see.

Jhearl sank back into her pool and unhurriedly soaped face and hair, swirling them clean before arising again with a gasp. Then she reached out for a handful of the twiggy herbs that had been brought with the bath and began to scour her arms and legs with them. The crushed leaves gave up a bitter green scent. The dirt was stripped from her now and her skin felt like it was singing. She was almost finished.

'Would you scrub my back?' she asked Ambele.

Without a word, the mercenary took the herbs from her dripping hand and kneeled behind her. Jhearl straightened her back, felt a slop of cold soap hit it and then Ambele's long, strong fingers start to rub it in. The first jolt of desire tripped through her like a hot coal jumping from a fire. She had to bite her lip to keep from making a noise that would betray her. Jhearl was familiar with sex; to her it was a skilled craft, complex and nowadays even pleasurable – but the sick dizziness of desire was something she thought she had forgotten long ago.

Ambele's hands moved up to her tight shoulders and massaged soap into the base of her neck.

'Uh,' Jhearl breathed. 'That's good.'

The twiggy claws of the scrubbing-brush raked her spine, stabbing her with pleasure, stripping the ache from her bruised flesh. When she had finished that, Ambele dropped the leaves aside and put both hands lightly on Jhearl's shoulders. 'What do these mean?' she asked, leaning close, her warm breath tickling the bather's ear as she reached down over Jhearl's shoulder with one hand and flipped the silver ring that pierced her right nipple. Jhearl fought a shudder. All the skin across her breasts tightened and her nipples lifted, out-thrust and swollen.

'They don't mean anything,' she managed to say. Desire was so strong in her it felt like fear, constricting her throat. 'I wear them for decoration. And because it feels good.'

'Oh?' Ambele said. There was a new edge of amusement in her voice. She caught the silver ring between thumb and forefinger and tugged gently, drawing the nipple out with threads of fire. Jhearl gave a tiny whimper.

Ambele chuckled, a rich unexpected sound that made a pulse jump in Jhearl's groin. And then she was gone and a waft of cold air had taken her place. Jhearl turned quickly to see her bodyguard standing again, holding out one of the towels towards her. Dizzy with colliding emotions, Jhearl stood and took the towel. She wrapped it around herself and stepped from the tub. Ambele's gaze was cool and open.

'Do you wish to bathe?' Jhearl asked. Ambele looked dubiously at the now scented and cloudy water.

'A river is better,' she said. 'But you must never waste water.' So saying, she pulled the shirt over her head and unfurled the leopard-skin from about her waist. Jhearl dried the last moisture from her face and neck, feeling her blood thump in her throat. Ambele, her skin the same colour as her breast-plate had been, hardly looked naked; there was no vulnerability about her as she stepped into the pool and sank to her knees, just grace and confidence. She cupped her hands to sluice water over her face and back, her palms flashing pale against her thighs as she stooped.

'Shall I soap your back?' Jhearl offered, her throat dry.

Ambele cast her a surprised glance, but shrugged one shoulder, striped where the water had cut the pale dust on her skin, and settled down deeper into the water. Jhearl tucked her towel in under her armpit, took up a handful of cold soap and began to rub the scented glop into Ambele's muscular shoulders. Ambele relaxed after the first touch and leaned forwards against her thighs, letting Jhearl's small but expert hands knead the tension from her.

'You are good at that,' she murmured at length.

'Practice,' said Jhearl, moving down to the biceps. There was hardly any fat on Ambele at all, her muscles hard and sharply defined under the hairless skin. Jhearl wanted to bite the smooth ridges beneath her hands. She moved around the side of the tub until she was facing Ambele as she worked on each arm in turn, then, gently, without a break in her rhythm, shifted her touch to the top of the breastbone, to the pectorals. She dropped a new fingerful of soap between Ambele's

144

breasts and began to massage that across the deep ravine. Her eyes lifted briefly to meet Ambele's; the Kledish woman was staring at her, wary but unresisting. Jhearl demurely dropped her gaze and ran both hands over the soft peaks, working up a lather with dextrous fingers. She felt the big nipples harden under her palms and encouraged them with circular caresses, the slippery flesh sliding and quivering under her grasp.

Ambele let out a pent breath with a sigh.

'Good?' asked Jhearl in a low voice.

'Good,' Ambele admitted, almost reluctantly. She leaned back against the side of the tub and watched Jhearl work. The towel wrapped about her employer's torso had slipped, freeing her round breasts. The silver rings in her pierced nipples danced, flashing, as those pale orbs jounced and quivered.

Jhearl rolled the other woman's nipples between thumb and forefinger and Ambele gave a sound like a purr. Suddenly she seemed to submit to the pleasure; her eyes shut and she tilted her head back, her shoulders sagging. Jhearl pressed her advantage further, tugging and pinching gently, raking paths through the soap with teasing fingertips.

'May my husband's ghost forgive me,' Ambele said sadly, 'but you are better than him at this.'

'You were married?' Jhearl asked. She wanted to press those breasts together and take the twin nipples in her hot mouth. She wanted to delve under the water to the weed-lined grotto beneath.

'He died at the Bindar Well,' Ambele said softly. 'The other man with us was his brother.'

'Oh,' said Jhearl with genuine sadness. 'I'm sorry.' She leaned forwards and kissed Ambele softly upon the lips. Ambele's eyes flew open; brown gazed into blue.

At that moment there was a loud knock upon the

145

door. Jhearl jerked to her feet and grabbed her towel around her.

'Lady,' came a male voice from the other side, 'Your food is ready when you want it served.'

'Good,' said Jhearl dizzily. 'Of course. I will be a few minutes.' She heard a heaving splash behind her.

'Lady,' the voice repeated, quieter now as if in confidence, 'There is a man here who asks if you are Jhearl of Celephais . . .'

Jhearl moved to the door and stared at the blank wood. 'I am,' she said in a low voice, barely enough to carry through the barrier.

'He has been here several days. He says he has been waiting with a message for you. He says the message is from an old friend of yours.'

'Ah.' Jhearl lifted her head, frowning. 'You may tell him that I shall be pleased to speak to him when I dine,' she instructed.

'As you wish, Lady. A table is prepared for you.'

Heavy footsteps retreated down the corridor. Jhearl stared at the whorls and knots in the wood for a few moments more, as if trying to read their strange script. Nyan was not here, then. She felt let down, though some concern leavened the dough. But he had sent a messenger. That was good; better than no word at all.

She turned back into the room. Ambele was standing with her back to her, rubbing the thick sheaf of her hair through a towel. She had already wrapped a white cloth around her, tying it over one shoulder. It sheathed her from shoulder to ankle, clinging damply where it touched across her hard, flat buttocks, a cool white tubular barrier to eye and hand. Jhearl bit her lip against her sharp pang of disappointment.

'Let's go and eat, now,' she said softly. 'We are both hungry.' That was an understatement; for over a week now they had subsisted on what game Ambele had been able to spear – small rodents, mostly – together with stringy desert tubers and a handful of dried dates that she had carried in her purse, all of it cooked roughly over an open fire or not at all. Only the desert heat had smothered Jhearl's hunger-pangs, and now that she had cooled it was hard to ignore them.

Ambele's face was closed once more when she turned, a blank mask from the deep places of Kled. It was as if a spell had been broken and the enchantment which had animated her and warmed them both had faded under the evening shadows.

They dressed swiftly, Jhearl pulling on a soft, blue dress with full sleeves, Ambele belting the white cloth – no doubt originally intended as a shawl – over her hips and slipping a long open tunic over it. This left her arms bare; against her skin the undyed wool seemed to glow. The clothes were plain but clean, which was sufficient.

'You don't need to bring your spear,' Jhearl said as she opened the door.

Ambele shrugged her head sideways and put the weapon back against the wall. She had already checked the long knife belted at her left hip.

Dinner at the Inn at Harran turned out to be served – at least for those respected guests of means – outdoors, under a trellis draped with vines at the side of the inn. Thick rugs were scattered over the ground; Jhearl chose a small one to one side and seated herself gracefully. The evening stars peeped between the leaves overhead, but scented oil lamps on copper plates in the centre of each rug cast a warm light over the fabrics and kept the night-insects at bay. There were a few people already coming to dine. Jhearl nodded almost imperceptibly to the two merchants, but declined when they offered her a seat beside them. She already had business.

Ambele prowled restlessly, looking behind each entwined pillar before she would consent to sit. But the food arrived quickly and drove all thoughts of restlessness from every mind; spit-roasted mutton, fresh figs, bowls of curd, flat bread spiced with cardamom seeds and almonds coated in sugar-paste. The wine was bright and fresh, not of a sophisticated quality but very suited to the setting. The small boy from the courtyard came out and began to play upon a double-stemmed flute. Guests thickened upon the rugs. Jhearl had to force herself to eat slowly. That part of her mind which was not upon the food turned over the prospect of Nyan's messenger anxiously.

She had not finished her meal before the innkeeper led a man out from the doorway and pointed across the other guests towards her. The stranger made his way over. Jhearl wiped her mouth delicately.

'Lady Jhearl?' said the man, squatting down upon the rug so that he did not loom over the seated woman. Ambele rose warily to her feet.

'Yes?' said Jhearl. He was a broad man with bright blue eyes in a weathered face, handsome in a rough way, hair long and tied back at the nape of his neck, dressed in trousers and hide jerkin rather than robes. A city-dweller without a doubt, miles out of his own territory. But not a soldier.

'Lady –' he smiled, his eyes keen; '– I am glad you have reached this inn; I was expecting you days ago.'

'I had problems on the way,' Jhearl said, not smiling yet.

The man noticed her coolness and looked abashed. 'My name is Rosh,' he said quickly. 'I was sent here by a friend of yours.' And swiftly and smoothly her turned his palm over and displayed for the briefest of moments the silver token of Prince Nyan.

'He told me he would be here,' Jhearl said. 'What has happened to him?'

Rosh cleared his throat. 'Can we talk privately?' he asked. 'Not here.'

Jhearl's head was buzzing from the wine and the food, but she remembered still that she was alone among strangers. 'Over there,' she said, indicating with her head a darker space beyond the trellised courtyard, behind the wall of vine leaves. It was still within sight of light and help should she need it.

Rosh's eyes were hard. 'Fine,' he nodded.

They both stood, Jhearl a little unsteadily, to her surprise. Ambele caught her gaze, her eyes questioning. 'Wait here,' Jhearl said, waving at the carpet beneath her feet. She followed Rosh into the blue evening, aware, but unconcerned that everyone in the yard was watching her go.

Beyond the lamplight the night was cool and calming, and not so dark as she expected. Jhearl could make out the bulk of the stables and the pale wall of the courtyard. A goat bleated from the shadows.

'My lord did intend to meet you here,' Rosh said, putting a hand on Jhearl's arm to steady her. He drew her deeper into the gloom. 'But he was delayed on King Kuranes' business. Things are happening that demand his attention. High affairs of state.' They were close to the boundary wall now, in the darkest part of the yard. She could smell the leather of Rosh's jacket better than she could see his face. His voice was low; she had to move closer to hear his words.

'He says that he will be delayed until the Festival of the Moon. He says that you must wait for him – here.' With these last words Rosh pushed her against the wall, palmed the knife from his sleeve and drove it towards her heart.

It did not strike home, not that time. Jhearl, pushed backwards, stumbled over rubble and fell to the side. At the same moment Rosh gave a grunt and lurched forwards, then jerked back. The knife-blade skidded across Jhearl's ribs under her left arm and then clattered to the floor. Rosh shuddered all over and fell to the ground; another figure crouched over him.

Jhearl shrieked. The cut stung like fire and blood ran down her side. But Rosh did not move again. There came the sound of people running, and against the light wobbling and growing in the distance Jhearl saw Ambele straighten up and pull her foot-long blade from Rosh's back.

'Are you hurt?' Ambele demanded.

Jhearl did not reply. The innkeeper and several guests came hurrying up, clutching lamps, shedding light upon the confused scene and upon their own shocked, avid faces. Rosh's body sprawled in the dust; there was surprisingly little blood visible but his bowels had opened in death and the smell was offensive. Jhearl stood up, clutching her ribs, and turned away.

'What happened?' demanded the innkeeper. His gaze settled on Ambele. 'You killed him!'

'I'm her bodyguard,' Ambele growled. The knife still glistened stickily in her hand.

Jhearl swallowed her heart and said squeakily, 'Open his coat.' No one moved. 'Look inside his coat,' she repeated.

Warily, the innkeeper signalled a servant to comply. The leather jacket opened to reveal, sewed under the armhole, a braid of human hair with two blue glass buttons knotted into the end.

'Do you know what that means?' Jhearl asked.

The innkeeper nodded. 'He was an assassin,' he said wonderingly.

'Are you hurt?' Ambele asked again.

'Scratched,' said Jhearl, shaking her head. Her voice was at last under control again. 'Take me back to our room, Ambele.'

The mercenary slipped one arm around her shoulders in support and began to lead her away. 'Why did he try to kill you?' the innkeeper asked their backs.

'I have no idea,' Jhearl muttered.

Back in their chamber Ambele sat her employer on the bed, pulled down her dress to expose the wound, wiped away the worst of the blood with the blue fabric, examined the cut and then applied a strip of damp lizard-skin that she had taken out from her pouch and unwound. Jhearl was too stunned to protest; she even held the scratchy poultice in place. The wound was quite shallow and had mostly ceased to bleed by now; she had been very lucky.

'Do you want to lie down?' Ambele asked from where she kneeled on the floor at Jhearl's side. She shook her head. Ambele looked sombrely at her as she hitched her torn dress back up over her shoulder. She felt wretched.

'Who sent the assassin after you?' Ambele asked. 'Was it this man?' She produced the slim silver token, as long as one of her fingers, which she must, Jhearl realised, have taken off Rosh's corpse.

She shook her head. 'That is the seal of Prince Nyan of Celephais. He has always treated me with great courtesy.'

'That was the man you came here to see? Your friend?'

'A . . . client. He sent me a letter to meet him here. He is away from the city a great deal.' Jhearl sniffed; when she shut her eyes she could feel the moisture welling up beneath the lids.

'Ah,' said Ambele, dropping the token in her lap. 'So you are a spy?'

Jhearl laughed weakly. 'I am a prostitute, Ambele. A very expensive one, yes. I have the finest house on the Street of Pillars and I only favour the very richest, the finest men in the city. Nobility. Heroes. They vie for my attention, send me the most lavish gifts they can buy, beg me to accompany them to banquets. I am the ultimate status symbol in Celephais.' She giggled help-

151

lessly. She could feel Ambele staring at her. 'But I am a whore, that's all. I stay out of politics.'

Ambele got to her feet and stared down at her. Jhearl braced herself.

'So who would hire an assassin from Dylath-Leen to kill you?' Ambele persisted.

Jhearl groaned and rubbed her hand over her face. 'Nyan's wife,' she admitted. 'She is not pleased with her husband's patronage of me. She must have taken one of his tokens and written me the letter. Better to do it out of the city.' There was she knew always the possibility that it was Nyan who had done this, for reasons best known to himself – jealousy perhaps – but she did not want to think about that now. It would have to be faced later.

'I see,' Ambele murmured. 'So what will you do?'

'I don't know. I can't accuse her in court. I can't just refuse to see Nyan again, not if I value my livelihood; he is one of the most powerful men in the Kingdom. I might tell him that she has done this – but he might take that as a terrible insult ... or, worse, punish her, and then my life would not be worth a copper. I have to go back to the city. I can't run away. I need to think about this. I don't know what to do. I have never had someone try to k-kill me before.'

Jhearl was starting to shake now and her voice cracked into incoherence. Nothing in her experience – not the casual abuses inherent in her profession, not the ruthless indifference of those who had tried to use her in the past, not the gibbering loathsomeness of the feasting ghouls at the Bindar Well – none of these had prepared her for the prospect of someone who desperately, purposively wanted her dead. She had never cultivated enemies, preferring a peaceful and stressless existence; this malice was so personal that it shocked her. She clutched her own ribs with trembling hands, her teeth juddering.

Ambele watched for a moment, face tight, then suddenly sat down on the bed beside her employer, put her arms around her and pulled her tight to her breast. Jhearl buried her face in Ambele's shoulder, feeling the strong arms grip her. The mercenary's skin felt hot against her own; she smelled of roses and desert sand. Nothing was said. Ambele simply held the smaller woman until the shaking eased, her cheek pressed to Jhearl's golden hair, their breasts squashed together. Jhearl felt dizzy with relief, weak with gratitude that she did not have to bear this alone, but even as her limbs calmed her heart thudded painfully in her chest. She turned her face so that her lips were at Ambele's throat; she could feel the Kledish woman's pulse slow and strong. Gently Jhearl sat back and raised her head, Ambele's grip loosened – and then Jhearl kissed her again, on the lips, on her full, hot lips, as softly as the brush of a bird's wing but long and lingering and full of aching hope.

Ambele started, very gently, but did not pull away. It was Jhearl who at last broke off and looked questioningly into the other's eyes. She saw doubt there and uncertainty. She knew in a sickening moment that the mercenary would not respond. And at that same moment Ambele reached up one hand to Jhearl's cheek and pulled her into another kiss.

There was hunger in this second embrace; hunger on both sides as well as hesitation and a certain gentle clumsiness. Neither woman was in totally familiar territory. Their tongues met in a wet, cautious dance and their hands moved slowly across landscapes that seemed at once well known and wildly alien. Skin was far softer than either pair of hands was used to caressing and yielded in unexpected places. Jhearl bit her partner's lower lip gently, begging and receiving a mirrored response. Ambele tugged the blue dress down once more so that she could slip a finger into the silver

153

nipple ring and tug, causing Jhearl to groan into her mouth and arch her back.

They peeled each other clean of clothes without hurry, oddly shy where they had not been before, touching each new exposed stretch of skin as if it were a nervous creature that needed to be reassured by stroking. Their breasts internestled, cupping each other as they pressed close to kiss, then Jhearl kneeled up on the bed and rubbed her breasts over Ambele's, nipple prodding nipple, pink against brown, like little fingertips exploring each other's softness. Ambele cupped her partner's breasts and bent her head to them, taking each silver ring between her teeth in turn and tugging, twisting her tongue over and under and through the loops. She left Jhearl's pink buds fat and swollen and glistening with her saliva when she came up for air.

'Oh, gods!' Jhearl whispered, blue eyes wide and filled with tears of pleasure. She offered her breasts again shamelessly, cupping and lifting them.

'You like this?' Ambele murmured low in her throat, taking each proffered ring in her fingers and pulling them straight.

'Yes, gods, yes, Ambele!' Jhearl gasped, then dropped her hands so that the full weight of each breast hung from their piercing, stretching the pink flesh alarmingly. Ambele was startled; she released the pressure quickly, lowering each orb; then, when she saw the look of regret on Jhearl's face, thumbed each in compensation. She twisted one ring gently, exploring the new possibilities it offered and nearly driving Jhearl over the edge; the pale woman slumped into her arms, writhing, the sweat springing out all over her back.

'You want me to hurt you?' Ambele murmured.

Jhearl shook her head then bit her throat in reply before backing away, thighs splayed, arse spread, head lowered so that she could lick Ambele's breasts and belly and finally her pubic mound. Her uplifted arse was displayed in a perfect quivering heart-shape. Her breath came in hot, damp gusts through Ambele's fleece, but did not remain long – there was only enough time to make Ambele gasp and wriggle, before the tall woman grabbed the soft sweep of yellow hair laid up her lap and dragged Jhearl back up to nuzzle her dark breasts anew. Jhearl whimpered in pleasure; her grateful tongue was savage and her mouth a devouring wetness that made Ambele shake with joy.

Their lips met again.

Gently Jhearl lowered one hand between Ambele's thighs, her fingers brushing the soft skin and stirring the thick curls of hair. Both women froze in position, knee to knee, their eyes locked, their lips inches apart. Only Jhearl's hand moved, invisible, her fingers tickling the soft lips of Ambele's sex, stroking, parting them, sliding softly inside the velvety folds to find the slippery dampness within. Ambele seemed to stop breathing, her lips softly parted above as below, her hands cupping Jhearl's breasts, the silver rings snared over her thumbs.

Jhearl's fingers described a serpentine dance in the wetness that encompassed them, releasing a scent musky and sharp like may-blossom, probing and then recklessly penetrating, sliding into her hot muscular hole one digit at a time; then two, then three; all together, twisting and wriggling, spreading her wider, Jhearl's thumb still sliding and shuddering over the nub of the unseen clit, working the wetness from well to hill.

Ambele spread her thighs further, her lips working silently, her pelvis making little thrusting motions against Jhearl's rhythmic invasion. One hand deserted a silver ring to reach out and stroke the gold fluff between Jhearl's legs; the blonde woman faltered momentarily, her eyes glazing over. But the mercenary was not intent upon penetration, only on caressing and teasing the fleecy mound. Jhearl found her rhythm again, and this time Ambele matched it in slow counterpoint, pinching her tormentor's pink labia together over her stiffened clit.

They both began to gasp, uttering little breathy moans, their lips bumping and brushing helplessly together, tongues reaching out to entwine, everything slippery, ungraceful, undignified – the fragility of their fingertip-embrace an agony in the face of their mutual need, a torment that was becoming ecstasy.

'Ah – yes – harder – gods, yes!' Jhearl hissed.

Ambele's fingernail-grip on the nipple-ring tightened to the point of cruelty. Jhearl stopped talking and broke into a bubbling wail, her twisting hand becoming a fist, a club, a spear, as she lost all control and fell from the dizzying peak of her orgasm, smashing into fragments upon the jagged rocks of pleasure below. Ambele hung on for a few more precious seconds, desperate neither to hurt her lover nor to cease hurting her until it was no longer necessary. Then without warning her eyes rolled up under their lids, her head snapped back and she climaxed, sobbing under her breath in her own language. Jhearl, still massaging her bucking pubis with a cramped hand slippery to the wrist, leaned forwards to plant blind, drunken kisses upon her throat and jaw as she came.

Shuddering with spent tension, Ambele sagged forwards into Jhearl's arms. The two women slipped together full-length upon the bed, thighs intertwined, arms around each other, their heartbeats jumping together beneath hot, slick skin. They held each other until the last ripples of ecstasy had died to calm. Tears had wet Ambele's scarred cheeks. Jhearl slipped one cradling arm free and licked the salty juices from her own shaking fingers, and then the two women kissed again, softly.

Ambele laid a heavy caressing hand from her

employer's ribcage to her crotch, measuring the heat, the hunger, the wet and gasping need of her.

'You're careless,' she murmured gently. 'Look; that cut on your side has opened again.'

Jhearl just laughed. She could hardly feel the sting. But Ambele slithered down the bed, straddled her thighs and bent her head to the shallow wound, licking the blood delicately from her pale skin.

Jhearl, pinned beneath her weight, gave a long sigh and closed her eyes in purest pleasure. She had employed many bodyguards in her lifetime, but none before had taken their duty of care to quite such intimate lengths.

Sacrifices

My subjects, when they dare approach my temple, do so only at sunset. They toil up the track beside the stream either alone or one treading narrowly behind the other, for there is no room on the path for two to walk abreast and the only alternative would be to walk in the water, which they fear to touch because it is sacred. They bring me corn and wine and chickens, whose necks they wring upon the temple floor. Sometimes they slaughter a goat for me and burn it on the flat rock at the entrance. Once or twice, I remember, they offered children. That was in very bad years, when the olive crop failed and the only harvest from the sea was raiders.

I am a merciful goddess, however, and those years are few.

My house, to their eyes, is a narrow cave in the yellow rock, from whose entrance the cold stream trickles even in the height of summer. It is a long walk from their nearest village, and they do not come very often. And they are afraid of me. They keep their eyes fixed upon the ground, upon their worn leather sandals, and they do not bear torches into the darkness of the cave's interior. There they work in the pitch black, offering up their small sacrifices, before hurrying away, never looking back. They know how terrible is my divine beauty. Some even approach with their eyes squeezed closed.

They never see me standing at the back of the temple, before the door which they could not find. I accept their sacrifices graciously but I do not disclose myself; the sight would be too much for them. Behind the inner door is the chamber within which dwell my sisters, Stheno and Euryale, but they do not often venture out. There is our bed. No mortal has seen this place.

I spend much time in my house, weaving at the great loom or conversing with my sisters. But sometimes a restlessness comes upon me and I choose to walk the dry, pine-cloaked hills, or follow the small streams down to the sea. Sometimes I walk into the villages of my subjects, or join the crowds gathered for religious festivals. I feel a curiosity about these people, and am amused by their strange, ignorant ways and their rough practices. I like to watch the dancing, though I do not join in.

Of course, such mingling takes preparation on my part. I cannot hide my divine glory as my sisters can – that is the work of the jealous Owl Queen – so I must resort to mundane subterfuge. I bind my long black hair, which is my greatest pride, so that it no longer undulates and hisses about my head in a cloud like living thunder. And I go up among the rocks above my house to a cave where the wild bees make their pendent nests. I have learned to take the waxen comb and melt it by lamp-flame, fashioning it into a mask that might pass for mere mortal beauty. When I tie that over my own features I may walk among men, unremarked except for the stillness of my expression and the fact that I am a stranger – a woman arriving alone and leaving wordless. The men of these parts are not like

159

the truly civilised folk who confine their wives within the walls of the house for all their days – they are rude peasants for the most part, even their kings, and, among them, all must work if all are to eat. But they do not let their women walk alone. When I join a crowd, always I am noticed, and watched, and coveted by their men. My figure is fair beyond any mortal maiden's.

This pleases me.

When I slip away from the celebration, or leave the press of the market, very often a man follows me. If I like his form, if his face is unmarked and his manner not too reminiscent of the beasts, I will let him follow me into the groves. Or sometimes I come upon a young shepherd with his flock in the hills, and I amuse myself by dalliance with him. Mortal flesh is hot to the touch and coarse, filled with swiftly changing tides of blood and strength. They smell like goats, and they have no more stamina in their love-making than in the pitifully brief span of their lives, but some few of them have a strange sweetness that moves me upon occasion; the briefness of their flowering only accentuates their beauty. They are like morning glories that wither upon the vine; but who is to say they are less fair for all that?

I, who have loved the Earth Shaker himself, delight in the childish simplicity of a tremulous, eager, mortal man.

The problem, my curse, of course is the mask. In the dusk, or under moonlight, my foolish lovers may not notice its artificiality – but the wax is thin and may easily be broken during our embraces. It melts when it comes into contact with hot, flushed flesh. The cords tear free. Then my glory is revealed and, like Semele before the Thunderer, they are struck down and destroyed. This has caused me much distress and frustration, just as the Owl Queen desired, I suppose; and the pitiful remains of my lovers are scattered about the countryside here, in quiet valleys and secluded copses, bedded down in the pine-needles or in isolated meadows. Sometimes I go back to visit those to whom some fond memory clings, and I gain a melancholy pleasure from their beauty preserved so terribly; they remain like flotsam cast up on the sands when the great wave of my desire has been spent, clean and smooth as sea-worn shells.

One whom I still visit frequently is the body of a shepherd youth. He was named Hermias, if I remember rightly; tall and well-knit for a shepherd, I imagine that he may even have been the son of some petty king or noble, for it is their practice that even the highest must work to put food upon their tables. He had eyes of the deepest cornflower blue and the first curls of his manhood's beard upon his cheeks. Ah; he was a delight. His skin was soft as a girl's, his hands quick and eager and strong, his lips hot upon me. He stands now on a shaded hillside above a stream, leaning back against a tree, his hands on the bark behind him, his head drooping with exhaustion. His skin is cold now and glimmers white through the gloom under the trees, the black rings of his hair now pale as bone, never stirring in the breeze. Tree-bark is growing over his fingers. On his face is still frozen the first suggestion of the shock and terror that gripped him when I raised my face from his thighs and met his eyes – and the mask slipped. Even the tiny beads of sweat on his forehead have been perfectly captured. His phallus is a perfect curve, like a white bow strung for battle. I remember it growing cold in my mouth, how it knocked against my teeth as I withdrew. I even wept a little for him, for I was not yet satiated. I regret his loss. I come to caress the hard lines of his chest sometimes, and sigh for his unexplored perfection.

Ivy has grown around his feet now, and tendrils coil up the muscular planes of his thighs. One small strand clasps tightly to the plump arc of his phallus, tiny roots clinging on the marble. His testes peep from a nest of green leaves and his hard buttocks are crisscrossed with the questing lines of the plant. His lower parts thus clothed, he resembles a satyr; leaf-bearing rather than goat-skinned, he is a better genius of the woodland than is the reality.

But even like this their loveliness is transient. They are blurred by the wind and grow green with algae. Their features crumble and melt with the decades. Hermias will wear away in time. I endure, alone.

It pains me that I live like this, here in the far West, among a half-barbarian people. Once my altar stood in the precincts of the temple of the Owl Queen herself and I was her attendant, the guardian of her door. But I dishonoured her holy sanctuary and she has cast me out, and taken from me the divine power to dissemble. Like all the great gods she is vindictive; there would be no forgiveness from her even if I were to stoop low enough to beg it – which I shall not.

I am still a goddess.

The Earth Shaker came to me when I was in her temple. I was alone, my glory veiled, within the inner sanctuary. As I remember, I was tending the offerings upon her great altar-stone – harvest offerings of wine and fruit and grain, and an amphora of finest olive oil. My back was to the door and I did not hear him enter, but he spoke my name. No mortal would have been able to see me. I turned, and recognised him at once, and felt my heart stop within my breast.

He stood in the centre of the hall, dressed simply in a plain chiton; a chlamys of eggshell-blue trailed from his arm across the marble flagstones. He brought with him a smell of sea air and the faint sound of horns blowing. I had never seen the Earth Shaker this close before, but I knew it was he for I had in the past wandered to the shore and spoken with his daughters as they played among the rocks. They were wild-spirited maidens, very different from my silent sisters, and I enjoyed their light speech of the sea and of distant lands. But one day their laughing and splashing ceased even as I spoke to them, and they slipped silently back into the depths with looks of fear. I turned then to see that I was being watched from the sands; a stallion stood fetlock-deep in the waves, a horse blue-grey as the ocean under a storm sky, unbridled, his mane tangled and long. He raised his head and snorted, and the white gulls wheeling overhead all cried in alarm. I recognised at once who he was and fled back to the sanctuary of my Owl Queen's house. I knew there was no fondness between them and that she would protect me.

Here in manly guise, the Earth Shaker was a man in the prime of his maturity, broad-shouldered and deep of chest, his hair and beard flowing in disordered locks. I saw that the lines of a habitual frown lingered between his piercing eyes, though he was not frowning now. He smiled. The cloak slid from his arm to the floor.

I turned my back on him then and laid my hands upon the altar, my heart in my mouth. I heard him speak my name again, his voice very deep and soft, like the murmur of the sea. I could have called upon the Owl Queen; I should have. She would have heard my cry, there in her own temple, and she would have rescued me. But I held my silence. I heard him walk up the length of the hall to me, and I said nothing.

Why? I know why. Because her rescue would have been indistinguishable from her wrath; I would have spent eternity as a nightingale or an owlet. Unravished, yes, but . . . no longer a goddess.

I was the guardian of the temple. They used to sacrifice poisonous snakes to me.

And because . . . because my virtue as the virgin

companion of the inviolate goddess was a tedium and a burden. I desired other things.

Because I wanted the Earth Shaker.

Not that for a moment I expected devotion from him. He is no different from his Olympian brother. They are brutal and grasping, no more given to selflessness than the thunderbolt or the salt ocean. What they want, they take, unless one has the power to flee them or trick them. I would get no more from him, I knew, than a moment's lust. But he was one of the great lords; and his majesty awed me; and his desire flattered me.

Strangely, since my disgrace he has continued to visit me in my new house, upon occasion. We share my carved bed and my sisters stand at the foot, speechless, in witness.

I remember the coldness of the altar stone beneath my palms. I remember the wick of the lamp spitting a little. He came up behind me, slid his large hands about my waist and pulled me back against him. I could smell the sea. One of his hands rested against my stomach and I felt my belly knot inside me. We stood for a long time like that; his face bowed to my neck, his arms surrounding me. I felt very small in his embrace. His lips were hot on my throat. His long hair washed over me with a shock like the cold salt-wave, making me shudder. I was so tense that even his firm grasp did not cause me to yield against his body; he must have thought me afraid.

Gently, his paired hands moved on my frame, never releasing me. The thin cloth of my peplos was no barrier to him. He cupped and lifted my breasts, moulding them in hands that had killed titans, squeezing and pressing them together. I did not move. My head drooped to one side. He whispered my name once more, his voice slurred with pleasure. My flesh responded to his every touch; to the tickle of his fingertips across my hardening nipples, to the firm pressure of his palm flat upon my navel and my mons, to the caress that was half stroking, half pinching; I wanted to writhe against him, to make him touch me anew – but I could not move. Here was the power that destroyed cities and wrecked ships, concentrated on my shaking, gasping form with terrifying purpose.

His hands dropped to my hips and he pulled me back against his groin. I could feel his erection, hard as rock; it jabbed my soft flesh. The heat between my thighs was molten. I moaned a little. He pressed hard against me, fingers biting into my skin fiercely enough to bruise, and rubbed his thick member up and down. His teeth closed on my earlobe; I could feel his breath coming fast and shallow.

Then he pushed me away. The gap between us was like the void of Tartarus, filled with loss; I would have turned, but his hands, still on my hips, pinned me in place. One palm went to my right buttock, comforting my torment. My throat was so dry I could not speak. He stooped to gather the long skirt of my peplos, drew it up in handfuls to my waist. The brush of air upon my skin told me I was naked, my arse exposed, and the skin across my rounded behind tightened. He touched me again, one hand holding my dress up while the other explored the softness of my flawless flesh before delving smoothly into the cleft between. He found the diamond of flesh that cannot be hidden, cannot be concealed, however I might stand or twist – and the liquid warmth within it. I jerked and started when his fingers opened the folds of my sanctum. He laughed softly at me. Still holding me against the altar, he withdrew his hand from my slippery petals and replaced it with the blunt spearhead of his phallus. It was the first time I had felt such a thing upon my naked skin. It was hot and thick; he did not try to pierce me straight away but slid it up and down my furrow, teasing me, slathering it with my juices.

I found my voice. I cried out and turned suddenly to face him, breaking his grasp and knocking his member aside.

I could see by the look on his face that he expected me to try and flee then; he grabbed me hard at the waist. But I furled my arms about his neck and offered my lips to his instead. My mouth yielded to his invasion. His kiss was wild as a gale, and tasted of salt. He crushed me against him, his trident pinned between us, pressed achingly against my mons; and his hands were rough now. He tore the clasps of my peplos so that he could bare my breasts and seize them in his mouth. Then, breaking off from his devouring kisses that were almost bites upon my nipples, he reached past me and swept with his broad arm everything that was on the altar, all the votive gifts to the Owl Queen, to the floor. He lifted me and laid me upon the broad stone, then mounted above me. He parted my legs.

Olympus: but there has never been, there could not be anything to match that fearful mingling of our bodies. Not even the Foamborn and the Warlord can have coupled with such savage delight. He was like a stallion upon a mare, a ship under full sail upon the sea, a spear piercing my entrails. His phallus felt as thick as a branch and as hard as bronze; it ploughed into me like the ram of a ship cutting the waves. I melted, I flowed, I engulfed him. He rode me upon the sacred altar of the Owl Queen. I cried and twisted under him, and he shouted above me, lips drawn back from bared teeth. I tore at his back and kissed his throat and lifted my hips so that he could thrust deeper and deeper yet, slapping me back against the marble. My black hair was spilt in a wave across the white stone. Tears ran from my eyes and I sobbed, pleading shamelessly with him for more, for faster, for deeper, for harder – for the completion of my ruination – until he covered my mouth with his and stopped my breath and I felt myself turn to light. The fire of my ecstasy roared around him, and he became incandescent also, both blazing in divine flame that lit the temple from end to end.

Even a mortal would have seen our glory and been blinded by it, if any had been present.

He held me for a time while the numinous glow faded, and then he left me. I lay motionless, dress torn, legs splayed, breasts marked pink by tooth and nail, lips swollen – and my eyes full of awe. When I had recovered myself enough to sit up, from my puffy sexual bowl a libation of our mingled moistures poured out upon the altar.

It did not occur to me until later that he had engineered everything in order to insult the Owl Queen. They had been enemies ever since she defeated him in the contest for the fealty of Athens.

Bitch. She did not forgive me for desecrating her altar. When she found out, my own was broken. Her curse was cruel.

I have never borne him a child. I wonder at that; I have never heard of his seed failing to come to harvest elsewhere.

In my house, I weave these things upon my loom. My sisters spin for me. My yarn is dried grasses and cobwebs, wool found snagged upon the thorns and our long hairs, black and ash-grey and white. I weave the Owl Queen, cold and terrible with eyes that seem to glitter, accoutred with helmet and aegis. I weave the Earth Shaker, proud as a bull. I weave myself and my sisters – and I weave the pale, forsaken monuments that are left of those whom I have loved.

Sometimes, though, I have used my curse deliberately, and it has not been chance that froze a man for an alabaster eternity. I am the goddess of this place, lowly as that station may be, and it is not fitting to skulk in the shadows as if I were ashamed. But it also pleases me to be merciful and to show pity to my subjects. One year when I walked upon the shingles of their narrow shore, there came around the headland a great ship of fifty oars, filled with men. I heard the horns blowing the alarm in the town upon the hill, and saw that the people were running back to the walls to defend their homes from these pirates. I met them where the road bends round through the olive-trees, stepping out to greet them and drawing the folds of the chlamys from my head. They had anticipated ambush, I think, but not like this. Not one of them got the chance even to loose a spear. Forty men died on that path, forty sun-hardened warriors with bronze helmets and shields of bull-hide, vanquished silently and almost instantly. The doves in the canopy overhead did not even notice the slaughter, so quiet was it, and their songs and jostlings went on undisturbed. I stepped between the motionless ranks of men, admired the chasings on their armour, fingered a fluttering tunic which had some fine embroidered edging, and then made my way back through the vineyards to my house among the untended hills. As the sun went down that night, I stood upon the great flat rock and danced my victory.

What my subjects did with those warriors I do not know; smashed them to make rubble for some road, I suppose. Most of the pale bodies I leave in my wake stay undisturbed, either lost in the wilderlands or shunned out of piety and fear. I have seen them treated by the peasants with wonder and even fear. There is one in a grove of cypresses by the river, not far from the royal palace of their little king, which is well known and often visited by the womenfolk. Perhaps they mistake my old lover for Priapus. They bring offerings of fruit and garlands of flowers, and make requests for happy marriages and many children.

Yesterday I witnessed one of their rites by chance. I

found it touching, in a strange way. They were led by the king's daughter; I could tell that by her retinue of handmaidens and their rich dress. The troop came down to the river bearing baskets of linen to wash and I concealed myself among the bushes only just in time, seeing no reason to reveal myself to such a giggling, light-hearted party. The princess was most fair, in the unremarkable way of mortal women – rounded, pale limbs unmarked by labour and dark hair tied high with a golden filet, her eyes outlined heavily in black. She supervised the washing of the soiled clothes, doing little work herself, and then gave gracious permission for bathing to take place. The girls discarded their dresses and splashed about in the shallow river, throwing water at each other and shrieking. Then they sat upon the banks and dressed each other's hair, drying their limbs in the sun, careless and self-absorbed as nymphs. I waited in the shadows, idly amused, so motionless that a mouse ran over my foot and did not see me.

Then the king's daughter grew restless, pulled on her peplos over skin still damp, and led the whole crowd, with much stifled laughter and sideways glances, into the cypress grove. I followed, unseen. All their real attention was on the marble form of the idol within the trees. At the sight of him, even my heart stirred.

I have forgotten his name, or even if he told it to me. He is old; his upturned face has worn away a little, blunting his nose and smoothing his hair. He kneels, knees braced apart, hands splayed on his thighs. There is a bare patch of earth about him where the women of the town have walked. His phallus rises straight as a spear, white as the moon. It too has been worn by much touching and anointing. It is slender and smooth; not ugly or massive so much as to frighten a virgin, but quite virile enough to bring a blush to her face. The handmaidens of the royal court, none of them older than their princess, giggled and sighed and hid their faces in modest hands at the sight of such a shocking thing. Then without exception they came forwards to touch him, to pay their respects. Some were nervous and only stroked his shoulder; some tickled his straining member teasingly; one of the older ones, greatly daring, fondled his hard pouch and kissed his unyielding lips before swaggering away, swinging her hips for the benefit of her companions.

The king's daughter stood with hands on hips, watching these flirtations. Her lips were parted and her colour high; she was the only one of the maidens who was not laughing. I watched her closely, my interest piqued. She signalled to her entourage and gave them some order, and reluctantly they all retreated to the edge of the clearing and sat upon the grass in little groups, their backs to the princess and the image.

The conversation of mortals flutters like leaves in the wind; unless they are praying it is difficult to follow their words, they make only wittering noises that are hard to concentrate upon. But she prayed, when she was sure that her companions had stopped looking over their shoulders. She leaned forwards to the stone image, put her pink lips to his ear and whispered a heartfelt plea. I heard those words clearly enough. She wanted a gold-crowned hero, a king's son who would love her and make her his wife – and soon. The sincerity of her desire made my nape prickle. She was ready for bedding, that maiden; her words were only confirmed by the unconcealed curves of her young body showing through the half-transparent folds of her wet, clinging peplos. Her eyes smouldered as she stepped back from him and bit her lower lip.

Then she kneeled, as many had kneeled before her, and laid one hand on his rigid shaft. She stroked it cautiously, as if it might come to life under her touch – and I could almost believe it would, if stone were able

170

to be tempted as flesh is. She circled the snake's head with one finger, blushed, then leaned down and pressed her lips to it in a long, devout kiss. He looked whiter than the snows of Olympus against her rosy skin. I saw the very tip of her pink tongue lick his alabaster wand.

She sat back and looked around her, silently daring any of her entourage to have been spying, but they were obediently turned away, awaiting her orders. Hesitantly she took from the folds of her peplos a small stone jar. When she broke the wax seal I smelled a waft of expensive perfume, such as is used after bathing upon the skins of great princes and queens. She wished to make an offering. I licked my dry lips. She slipped her painted fingers into the jar and drew out a scoop of slippery white unguent, then very slowly applied it to the phallus before her. The scent filled the grove; the handmaidens stirred and whispered. She trailed her fingers up and down the elegant shaft, spreading it from wrinkled balls to smooth prick-end. As she gained confidence she used both hands and found a firm, rhythmic grip. I watched entranced as she massaged the erection – gods, it was already so stiff and vertical that it could not have responded in any way except to erupt in spurts of silver sand, and I could almost imagine that happening, so lifelike was his form and so intimate, so apposite their pose.

A handmaiden stifled a nervous giggle.

The king's daughter paused, looked down at herself and shifted her posture. Something between her legs was causing her discomfort; she wriggled her creamy buttocks as if to accommodate some alien presence. Then, looking about her from beneath her lashes, cheeks burning with shame and some other, more imperative emotion, she rose to her feet, pulled her peplos up around her thighs, straddled the image's hips and, one hand on the back of his neck to balance

171

herself, sank slowly down over his slippery stone member until it touched the doors of her secret underworld.

I had to admire her strength and her determination. Unable to drop straight down the entire length of the rod, she had to brace herself on straining thighs and cling to her obdurate partner's neck as she introduced the bulb of his phallus to the wet lips of her virgin hole. Her eyes closed in concentration and her face creased with effort; she did not wish to hurt herself, yet her every instinct was to take the shaft as far as she could within her. She rocked back and forth, letting the cold stone stir the hot hearth of her fires, mingling the chrism with her own juices. Her peplos slipped from her shoulder and one rose-tipped breast slid into view; she did not notice, or care, that it was quivering shamelessly in full sight of the gods and anyone else who might look at her. She did not cry out but her breath was ragged, and the faces of her handmaidens, who still did not dare look round, were growing pink.

My own breathing had almost stopped. Her head lolled from side to side, she arched her back and thrust her buttocks out, rolled her hips and pawed at his face. She seemed unable to slide the phallus more than an inch or so into her, despite its slenderness; something was blocking the path. She worked the hard prod from side to side, stretching her pink inner lips unbearably, spasms chasing visibly through her limbs. Her face, prettily blushing before, was flushing darker. Her breasts strained up as if towards her unfeeling lover's face. I was entranced. She was reaching her crisis; the agony of pleasure was upon her and she could not stop. Her eyes, half open now, were unseeing, her mouth slack, her face suffused with a pain that was not pain. I saw the spasm come upon her, as clearly as if I had felt it in my own flesh. She impaled herself deeper and deeper on the glistening stake between her thighs, thrusting it into the cavern that begged to be filled. I knew her agony; my own hot wetness was slicking my thighs.

She threw back her head, mouthed a silent scream, and rammed the phallus to the hilt within her. Every part of her shook; her breasts wobbled wildly. Then her legs gave way and she collapsed, straddling his hips, staked upon his spear.

I was filled with awe. To offer up her maidenhead to her god was to make the most terrible, costly, precious sacrifice. That her god was a false one who could never know of her devotion – that was a tragedy that moved me as the prayers of the most fervent worshippers could not.

She withdrew panting from him, her pleasure and her pain still unvoiced, and readjusted her dress. She left a little blood upon the stone. Then, after silently contemplating him for a time, she cleared her throat, and ordered her entourage to their feet. They turned to look at her; some puzzled, some concerned, some embarrassed. They could not be sure what had happened, but most would have guessed. She snapped her fingers, head held high – an imperious expression on her face – and ordered them from the clearing. The fluttering cloud of maidens disappeared from my view.

On the great loom in my chamber that scene is emerging now from the jumbled weft, threads of colour spiralling in to fuse and make the image of a mortal maiden loving a statue. It burns in my mind, and there under my hands it takes shape and grows. It kicks inside me, like a child wanting to be born.

All these strands come together; the anger of the Owl Queen, the Earth-Shaker's scheming, a youth's pleasure, a maiden's need, a broken mask. My desire. These are spun by fate like strands of carded wool, to make the threads of a design that will be a wonder to those that see it. What skill, they will say, what artistry, to produce such a bold image from these little shreds of fleece.

The image troubles me, and I brood upon it as I sit upon the flat rock near my house, warming myself in the sunlight. I do not dance now. She worships a false god who will not hear her. When the world is filled with divinities, how is it that they turn so easily to ones of their own imagining?

I am uneasy.

A man is coming up the path towards me – but I will not hide, this time. He carries a bronze shield, I think. He must have polished it; the disc catches the light and shines like the sun.

Toil and Trouble

The curse was written not in blood but in chalk, scrawled on the wooden door of their courtyard; 7-3d-1fl-1x.

The family gathered; Marlam Silversmith brooding like a thundercloud, Sermil his mother loud and bitter, his younger brother Oris stiff and clench-fisted, the servants conferring nervously. Only Elgith said nothing, had no measure of outrage and patriotic resentment to add to the hoard. She followed her mother-in-law out to the gate, looked at the marks and silently tailed her indoors again. It was not her right to express indignation. She was not from the city and its occupation by the Empire's soldiers was not a personal affront to her, though this privilege was claimed by every other member of the household.

'They will bankrupt us!' Sermil complained to her eldest son; 'You know how the price of food has been – we will starve!' Marlam, typically, said nothing. He had a closed, secretive face and was not a man inclined to share his worries.

'Where will they sleep?' Sermil demanded relentlessly: 'Will they put us out of our own beds?'

Marlam looked round at his brother. 'Clear the stable,' he ordered. 'They can sleep there.' His three horses had been requisitioned during the siege and had doubtless lined the stomachs of many a soldier, so their lightless quarters now stood vacant. Oris raised his thin shoulders and scowled but did as he was told, leading off two servants to begin the shovelling-out.

'See to the shrine,' Marlam told his mother darkly, and strode away towards his workshop.

Sermil, unable to command her own son, turned her frustration as usual upon the house servants and her son's wife – lowest of the low in the household hierarchy. Elgith braced herself before the rain of abusive contempt and tried not to hear.

'Now go and hide the wine under the boards in the back cellar, you lazy slut,' Sermil finished. 'If they find that I hate to think what they will do. Heathens. Filth. You know what they did to the Bishop.'

Seven soldiers of the 3rd Phalanx. One file-leader. One auxiliary adviser.

The prospect of a gang of drunken soldiers in possession of the house was alarming, and Elgith set to her task willingly enough. She was a hard worker, for all Sermil's complaints, and only her sullen attitude marred her demeanour. Elgith made it her habit to get her work done blamelessly, keep out of the way of the rest of the family as much as she might and speak as little as she could. There were those outsiders who thought that she and Marlam were a well-matched pair.

When she emerged from the cellar, the statue of the Windlord was missing from its prime place in the shrine, though the other gods, blank-eyed and bland of feature, were undisturbed. The Empire of the Shining Mask could find a place for lesser gods, for the Tradelord and the Harvestmother and the dozens of other deities that the free peoples of the lands had worshipped since time first dawned. The Empire tolerated anything, good or ill, fair or foul, so long as the rule of the Effulgent God was unchallenged; the only virtue it demanded was obedience. But the Windlord – he was the restless, undisciplined soul of the free people and would bow to no one, and he would not be tolerated in the city by its new masters. They had destroyed his temple on the top of the cliff; it had been their first action upon taking the city. Ranks of battle-bloodied soldiers, their bronze armour and spear-points flashing in the sun, had advanced in protective cordons about the yellow-robed priests of the Effulgent God. The air had whined with battling spirits and stunk of protective magics. When the great altar of the Windlord was overthrown, horns blew across the battered city, and all the populace fell silent to watch a shape wheel across the sky from the tip of the mountain; a winged bull, the Windlord's child, had descended upon the temple, trumpeting with rage. But the soldiers of the Empire had released from its cage a screeching wyvern, dripping with venom and uncleanliness, which had slain the sky-bull and then rampaged unchecked across the city, slaughtering any not bearing the mark of the Shining Mask until it had eaten its fill. Only then had the soldiers and priests moved to recage their monster. The warning from the Empire was clear: we have terrible weapons in our armoury – don't force us to use them.

Now, no doubt, Marlam's little silver statue of the Windlord was, like hundreds of similar idols across the city, hidden in a safe and secret place, to await the time of its revenge.

Elgith went down to the market to try and find fresh eggs. There was pitifully little on the stalls, and that overpriced. War and conquest had driven the farmers from their fields; occupation blunted the city's instinct for trade. Hoarding was now the fashion. The chalk curse had appeared all over the city on every house greater than a hovel. Until new barracks could be built, soldiers of the occupying army were to be billeted among the populace. All the noble palaces at the top of the cliff had been seized for officers' quarters and command stations, but the cluttered dwellings of the merchant quarter, where houses were built back into the rock and on top of each other in a cascade down the face of the ravine, were to take the bulk of the rank and file. Marlam Silversmith, a middling dealer and worker in precious metals, was to bear his share of the burden.

The price for meddling with the chalk-marks upon your door was to have your thumbs struck off; you and your household, if you would not confess. The Empire did not tolerate insurrection.

'The Windlord has abandoned us,' people whispered in the secrecy of their own chambers. But, 'Ah, we are still alive, praise the gods,' they muttered in the market place, glancing at the knots of soldiers on every street corner. They would look uneasily up at the sky before speaking the mildest discontent; it was difficult to feel secure any more while in an open space under the eye of the sun. Yet they lived, and their city stood – all but the stones of the Windlord's temple, even now being dismantled. Though there were brutalities, it was a contained and disciplined cruelty that brooded over the city. The way of the Shining Mask was conquest and assimilation, not destruction. These soldiers were here to stay, not to pillage; when they retired, they would be granted parcels of land here, and when they married it would be to local women. They would breed the next generation of loyal citizens; that too was a part of their duty.

The curse bore its bitter fruit a day after the chalk – marks appeared. Elgith was in the kitchen alone, washing the platters from their evening meal, when she heard the noise in the courtyard. She ran to a window to peer out between the shutters. She saw Oris gesticulating with his thin arms at a tall man in a yellow cloak, though she could not hear what was being said. Beyond them a knot of Empire soldiers leaned on their spears, looking bored, and to one side a stocky, tanned man in civilian clothes stood with arms folded and stared about him with interest. Low sunlight caught at something in his hair that glinted. There were no horses in evidence; the Empire's army moved on foot, unlike the mounted warriors of the free people.

One of the soldiers was despatched into the stable at a word from his officer. Elgith heard Sermil come into the kitchen behind her, nagging one of the servants she had in tow.

'They're here,' Elgith said quietly. Sermil pushed her aside at the window.

'Yah!' the older woman exclaimed in disgust. 'Get your husband, Elgith!'

She threaded her way through the twisting corridors of the house to Marlam's workshop, not needing a candle although the passages, cut into the rock of the hillside, were almost completely dark, for she knew all the ways of the house well enough by now. Marlam's trade of course demanded light, and the workshop was one of the few favoured rooms to be built from wood and out at the side of the building, under the master bedchamber, overlooking the sheer drop to the rooftops of the streets below. Marlam was sitting before one of the great windows, drawing out a design for a new chalice with painstaking care.

'Husband,' she whispered, pausing in the doorway. Marlam ignored her until the end of a line and then turned his face towards her, eyes dark and cold as ever under the grizzled fringe of his hair, expression as blank as those of the gods he had sculpted. 'The

179

soldiers are here,' she said, unable to keep the apology out of her voice.

He put the charcoal stick down with a snap. Elgith shrank to the side of the door as he passed her, turning her face away. She would have preferred to linger in the workshop alone, but she did not dare to be seen shirking.

They reached the main hall and found that the soldiers were already there – or at least the tall officer and the man with the brass rings knotted in his unkempt brown hair, the latter of whom was leaning against the great elm boards of the long table while the soldier paced slowly up and down the room. Elgith, huddled with the rest of the household in the kitchen doorway, stared over Sermil's shoulder as her husband entered the room.

'Marlam!' Oris said with audible relief, turning to his brother.

'Marlam Silversmith? You are the master of the house, I presume?' said the brown stranger. 'Your hospitality is much appreciated by the Emperor, blessed be his name. This is Fileleader Soron Shal –' he indicated the officer, who turned briefly from looking out of the window into the courtyard, glanced once at Marlam as if to fix his face in memory and then turned away again without the slightest acknowledgment '– and I am Tarkelion Dirskis. I have the honour to be attached to the Empire's legions as a specialist adviser in siege engineering.'

Marlam looked at him, jaw set.

The fileleader said something in the Empire's choppy language and Tarkelion Dirskis nodded. 'I think some food and drink would be appropriate at this point,' he said. 'We must celebrate our arrival at your warm hearth.' He raised one eyebrow ironically.

Marlam looked over at the kitchen doorway. 'Get food for them,' he commanded. 'And for the soldiers.'

Reluctantly, as if breaking free from the hypnotic gaze of a serpent, the others moved to obey. Elgith pulled down a ham from a hook and began to carve it, glancing back into the dining hall whenever she dared. Marlam walked stiffly out of the front door and stood upon the step, staring into the red sky.

Tarkelion Dirskis pulled out one of the chairs and sat down at the table, putting his feet up on another and pulling an eating knife from inside his tunic. Elgith studied him covertly. He was a man of only middle height – Elgith would have been as tall, eye-to-eye, for she was not short for a woman – but broad of shoulder, broad of face and broad of hands. These moved deftly and his eyes were equally quick and keen, lined with casual good humour in a coppery face. His beard was a half-hearted stubble. He did not look anything like his compatriot of the Empire who joined him at the table, but then the Empire took its soldiers from across the width of a continent and counted them all equal so long as they were loyal. Fileleader Soron Shal was far more striking in appearance: muscular with an easy litheness, pale, with cheekbones that might have been carved with a knife. But it was his eyes that were extraordinary, their irises nearly white surrounded by black rings, visible even indoors under lamplight. A glance from him was like a slap in the face. His hair, caught high at the back of his head, fell past his shoulders in a black sweep so straight and glossy it looked like water. But both men wore the sigil of the Shining Mask upon their tunics and on bronze amulets strung around their necks.

Elgith wondered if Marlam would stoop to crafting these symbols for the new inhabitants of the city, or for those old ones who chose to embrace the Empire. There was bound to be a market.

The kitchen was soon an ant-hill of activity. The two house-servants were busy reheating what scraps they could find and stretching the stew with pared veg-etables and fat pork. Sermil bustled about cursing under her breath and frying slices of coarse bread in dripping. Elgith finished slicing the ham and began to prepare the spiced fermented sauce that accompanied every meal she had eaten since coming to the city. Only Oris stood idle, digging bitterly with his knife-point into the wood of the chopping-block. No one dared raise their voice or shut the door between them and their guests. Those two sat quietly throughout the preparation, talking between themselves in low tones and the foreign argot of the invaders, Tarkelion Dirskis cleaning under his nails with the point of his knife.

When the stew was ready one of the yard-men was summoned to carry it across to the stable, accompanied nervously by an old maid-servant with two pitchers of sour beer; younger women could not be risked in the presence of the soldiers. Elgith poured better beer into pot flagons for the higher-ranking occupiers and placed them on a tray.

At this point Sermil pressed up to her side, smelling rankly of old clothes and rotten teeth. 'You can serve,' she hissed spitefully. 'You never know, they might come from your home town.'

Elgith glared back at her, wanting to spit into that sneering face, but did not dare protest. The servants watched knowingly. She picked up the tray and a loaf of bread and carried it through to the table.

Both men fell silent at her entry and turned their heads idly to watch her. Elgith did not look at them. She glanced towards the front door, which was ajar, but Marlam was blocking the narrow slice of the open-ing from outside, only his back visible from the room. Elgith placed her burden down on the corner of the table between the two men, forced to stand where one was on either side of her, each within an easy arm's length. The tray rattled in her unsteady grasp. She could feel their silent inspection, but she gave no sign that she was anything but alone in the room. Straightening, face still averted, she made it back to the sanctuary of the kitchen. Only then did she realise that she had been holding her breath.

The kitchen, still full of people, was as silent as the other room, faces turned towards her watchfully or away in deliberate lack of interest. Sermil stood with her hands on her hips, expression caustic, and Elgith matched her gaze with open contempt. She balanced a line of platters down her left arm, seized two wooden bowls and two skewers in her right hand and marched back to the dining table.

The diners were engaged with cutting up the loaf and trying the beer when she arrived. She laid the dishes before them, the meat steaming in its sauce.

'Thank you,' said Tarkelion Dirskis softly.

She made the supremely foolish move of glancing at him. He smiled at her – and he had one of those smiles that lights up a face and makes dark eyes shine. Instinctively she smiled back, only a flicker, the curve of a lip which she damped down instantly. But it was too late. She had sprung the trap. As she put the last of the bowls down he slid his arm around her waist and pulled her, not roughly but quite firmly, into his lap.

Elgith gave one muted gasp and went rigid. The world shrank down to a tiny sphere that included only her, bolt upright with her back to one man's chest, and the other man sitting facing her. Panic soured her throat; she was an expert in male humiliation and this scene was familiar in its ugliness.

Soron Shal smiled.

'Hello, Copperhead,' Tarkelion Dirskis murmured in her ear. He smelled travel-worn and slightly, pleasantly, of male sweat. His thighs under hers were very hard. 'You don't come from this city, do you?'

Elgith shuddered. 'No,' she breathed, her breath so

shallow she felt faint. Her heart was racing; he must be able to feel it, his arm was around her ribs and his left hand up under her right breast.

'Hmm?' he said. 'Where from?' His voice was still full of his smile, though the mockery was subdued.

Soron Shal began to pick absently at his food, but his eyes never left her; he was clearly enjoying the floor-show immensely.

'Ah,' she said, 'Raurinel.' It was an independent kingdom – and a Protectorate of the Empire of the Shining Mask.

'Really? One of our beloved allies ... How did you get here, then?' her tormentor asked. His breath was warm on her neck.

Elgith tried to muster her thoughts. 'I – my father was a silver-trader. We travelled. He died of fever while we were here.' Her palms, clenched to either side, were slippery.

'Ah. Peace to him. He was blessed with a lovely daughter.' The teasing was quite gentle, as if he were not doing this entirely to discomfort her. 'This smells good,' he added, his free hand indicating the plates. 'Did you cook it?'

'Hh,' she nodded.

'And what's this?' He pointed at a pale, wet dish full of small lumps.

'That's, um, *himmir*; flour dumplings in spiced sauce. You eat them with a skewer. There.'

'Well, let's try them,' Tarkelion Dirskis said, taking up one of the Y-pronged wooden skewers and spearing a dumpling. He conveyed it over Elgith's shoulder to his mouth. 'Very nice,' he commented after swallowing. 'You like them? Have one.'

He raised the next little dumpling to her lips. Elgith tried to shy away from the sloppy morsel, then realised that struggling would be even more humiliating. She tongued it from the skewer clumsily and it tasted like

184

glue in her dry mouth. The white sauce had dribbled down her lower lip and chin; she had to reach up and catch the smear, sucking it from her finger. Her heart thumped then and the arm around her tightened, pulling her harder into Tarkelion Dirskis' lap. She could feel his arousal.

She saw Soron Shal's smile widen to a grin. He shook his head in amusement. His teeth were unnaturally sharp.

'Now that's a sight for sore eyes,' Tarkelion Dirskis breathed, his lips brushing her burning cheek. He was not only jesting, nor simply trying to shame her. The physical evidence of his sincerity was pressing painfully into her backside. Elgith had to strangle the impulse to wriggle. And then into their small and deadly world broke the figure of Marlam, fists clenched as he stood before them and stared.

Cold lead filled Elgith's stomach. She could see only Marlam's eyes, flat and dark as chips of stone.

'What do you want?' Tarkelion Dirskis asked, dragging his attention from the woman on his lap. Soron Shal made a small but significant movement, invisible from where Marlam stood, that put his hand on his sheathed belt-knife.

'That is my wife,' said Marlam. His face was still closed, his voice low. It was a narrow, lined face devoid of any warmth, even hatred, the hair grizzled and lank. Elgith saw the scene with an outsider's vision and wondered at the contrasts.

Tarkelion Dirskis certainly sounded surprised; 'Really? I would have thought you were too old for her.' He looked again at Elgith. The blood was running from her pointed face and the freckles that dusted her skin stood out against her paleness. 'Very pretty, your wife,' he mused. 'Well, you tell me, Copperhead; shall I put you down?'

Elgith shut her eyes so that she could not see Marlam and whispered, 'Please.'

He sighed in her ear and then, to her utter astonishment, he released her – though his movements were slow. She could hardly believe it was that easy. She stood up and took a step away from him, her legs feeling like pieces of cut rope about to fall. When she looked back he was still watching her, his disappointment clear, no longer smiling. Marlam just stood and glared. Then, with a short dismissive movement, the siege engineer dropped his attention back to the food before him.

Marlam turned after Elgith.

'The fileleader has asked me to state,' Tarkelion Dirskis said clearly, 'that the accommodation for his men is adequate. We will be expecting better, however. Your best room will have to do. I like a view from my bedchamber, personally.'

Elgith fled into the kitchen through the brittle silence. She did not hear Marlam's reply because, as she got into the other room, Sermil pulled her into a corner, hissed 'Whore!' and grabbed and savagely twisted a handful of the bright hair at her temple. Tears of pain sprang to Elgith's eyes but she gasped only silently. Sermil yanked her daughter-in-law to the ground. 'Little trull!' she whispered to the willowy girl, then released her and stepped back.

Marlam was standing in the doorway regarding the scene. He closed the door behind him and Elgith staggered to her feet, panic rising. Everyone in the room waited for Marlam to move.

'Our guests have decided to take the best room in the house,' he announced. 'Elgith and I will be moving into your room from tonight, Oris. You will be sleeping down here in the hall. You had better make preparations.' His gaze lingered on his wife.

Oris stepped forwards, protesting, 'What do you

think I am? A –' but, before he could complete his sentence, Marlam brought up one fist to his angry face, faster than anyone could follow, and knocked him across the room.

'I think you forget what *I* am,' he told his brother.

Oris could only cup his broken nose in one palm and try to staunch the flow of blood.

Preparations were made, as instructed. While Sermil tended to Oris, Elgith silently cleaned up the cooking utensils, sprinkled sawdust on the bloody patch of floor and eventually stepped nervously into the dining hall to retrieve the last of the crockery there. The Empire men had gone, leaving the door swinging open upon the blue night. She gathered up the empty plates and took them back in to wash. She felt cold now. Retribution had been delayed, but it would fall.

The two women worked to rearrange the rooms, taking Oris' kit from the windowless back chamber, down the stairs into the hall and leaving it by the hearth. His bed was too difficult to move so they made up a heap of sheepskins and blankets on the hearthstones. Then they shifted everything from the master bedchamber that they could into Oris' room, leaving only the bare bed, the piss-bucket and one chest that was too heavy for them to lift. It was hard work and took hours. Sermil grumbled throughout and sometimes wept angrily. They took down even the woven hangings that draped the walls and left the faded woodwork naked. The room seemed bigger when they had finished, the corners uncluttered by boxes or pots. It retained no reminder of Marlam. Elgith rather liked the place.

They were installing an extra pallet-bed below the shuttered window when the room's new occupants returned from the tavern or wherever it was they had been, booted feet thumping up the steps and clattering on the floorboards. Sermil threw back her head and stalked out, bristling like an offended cat. Elgith slunk at her heels – but was stalled, as she had expected, by a hand on her arm.

Both men smelled of beer. She did not look up at them, though that refuge had long been overthrown. She was surprised that they had come back alone. Tarkelion Dirskis, glib and charming and mundanely handsome, was the kind of man she thought would never have to sleep by himself. Soron Shal was different, his beauty so marked it was almost discomforting.

'We want,' said the military adviser, 'a drink before we retire. Something stronger than beer. I'm sure your delightful husband has some hidden about the place.' Elgith nodded and he released her arm. 'Nice room,' he added. Soron Shal laughed and threw his swordbelt on the bed.

She hurried from the nice room down to the kitchen and unlocked the cellar door. The ground floor was deserted now, the servants having retired to their beds, so she jumped when she heard a footfall behind her and whirled about. Marlam stood in the doorway, arms dangling loose by his sides. He rubbed fingers and thumbs together caressingly, a familiar habit that made her shudder inside. 'What are you doing?' he asked.

'The fileleader wants some drink. There's a bottle of apple brandy in the cellar, isn't there?'

He considered. 'Go on,' he said. 'Don't take too long.'

She found the small stone bottle by the light of her candle-stub and climbed back up to the kitchen wiping off the cobwebs. Marlam had waited for her in the dark. He watched her find two small horn cups suitable for the liqueur then followed her back up the stairs. She felt sick under his gaze, tense as a thread pulled against a knot, her legs and stomach weak. The stairs seemed unbearably steep. When they reached the landing, Marlam stopped. Their new room was just there at the head of the stairs.

'Hurry up,' he said to her.

She walked away down the passage to the door of the master bedchamber, feeling him watch her. His gaze was like chains on her skin – rusted chains from an oubliette full of rotting bones. She reached the door and turned to look at his waiting figure. She knew that she should leave the bottle and cups, knock and walk away. Her husband was waiting for her.

Instead she knocked, held her breath, and when the door was opened slipped into the room.

Tarkelion Dirskis was holding the door ajar; he looked at her with an expression of surprise and pleasure. Elgith stepped out of the line of sight of the corridor and mouthed, 'Shut the door!', at which he looked just as pleased, but more surprised. However, he shut the door obligingly and for good measure slid across the latch so that it could not be opened from the other side. Elgith put the bottle and cups on the floor and raked her hands through her hair, her head swimming.

'This is an unexpected pleasure, Copperhead,' he hazarded. She noticed that he had stripped down to shirt and hose, his feet bare on the wooden boards. Elgith looked around the room and saw Soron Shal reclining on the larger bed, hands behind his head, watching them with a look of sardonic amusement. He had gone further and discarded even his shirt. His chest was perfectly hairless, and the sign of the Shining Mask gleamed at his throat.

Her heart was racing. They had the undisguised predatory innocence of lions; her instinct was to turn and run. But there are worse things.

'I want to stay here tonight,' she said. Her voice was hoarse and high. She forced herself to meet the tanned man's eyes. 'With you.'

'I'm delighted to hear it,' Tarkelion Dirskis replied. 'Won't your husband have something to say about it, though?'

'No. Forget him,' she instructed with audible desperation. She looked quickly aside at Soron Shal but found no help there and was forced to stumble on; 'There's no problem. You can ... do what you like. Have me.' Despite her words, when Tarkelion Dirskis took a step towards her at that moment she backed off. The movement brought her up against the wooden pillar in the centre of the room.

'Actually,' he said quietly, 'since you walked into my bedchamber after midnight I had rather taken that for granted.' The remains of his smile still lingered at his mouth but had drained from his eyes as he added, 'I would like, however, to know what is going on.'

Elgith cast about her, searching vainly for sanctuary in the bare room, but in the end was forced to admit, 'Marlam ... my husband enjoys hurting me.'

A cat squalled in the courtyard below.

'And you, I take it, don't enjoy being hurt?' His tone was grave, but Soron Shal gave a quiet derisive snort that made Elgith start; she had assumed until now that he could not follow their conversation.

'If I liked it, Marlam wouldn't do it,' she said through twisted lips.

'I see.'

'He likes to find something to punish me for,' she muttered, the words crawling from her throat like slugs. 'He will really go at me for sitting on your lap. I ...'

She stopped. She had not come here for sympathy. They were probably getting off on the thought themselves.

'So why don't you leave him?' Tarkelion Dirskis asked.

She twisted her hands together at her throat and

faltered; 'I haven't any family here. I've no one to go to. Raurinel is too far for me to travel alone and the only way the Guild helped when my father died was to pass me on to Marlam.' Her voice was shaking, but it was hard, too. 'His first wife had killed herself. I will not end up like that.'

'I see,' he said again. 'So you thought I was a better risk?'

'Better than the devil I know. If he touches me again I will take a knife to the bastard, and then he'll either have to finish me off properly or ...' She bit her lip then to stop it wobbling.

Tarkelion Dirskis rubbed the back of his neck thoughtfully and looked over at Soron Shal before turning upon Elgith with a shrug. 'Well,' he said, 'I certainly have no objections to your staying here; and I'm sure the army has none either.' He advanced on her again and this time she had nowhere to back away to. Instead she averted her face.

'Thank you,' she whispered to the gods.

'I wouldn't say that,' said Tarkelion Dirskis, misunderstanding. 'You will be earning your keep, after all.' He put one hand to her throat and jaw. His touch was warm, though the fingers were callused. 'Stop shaking, girl,' he added gently; 'I'm not a bloody monster.'

She squared her shoulders against the pillar and tried to face him, but her eyes kept squeezing shut. He cupped her face in both hands and lifted it. 'Come on, look at me. This was your idea, don't forget. It's not that bad. Now, what's your name?'

'Elgith,' she whispered.

'Elgith. That's better. Nice name. God's ballocks, girl – green eyes and copper hair; where did you get those? You're rare enough for the Emperor himself.'

She concentrated on staying upright and fixed her eyes on the low ceiling beyond him as his hands explored her throat and breasts, the layers and fastenings of her clothing. She wore a pale linen shirt under the tight constriction of her front-laced bodice, and a long woollen skirt to her ankles beneath that. He slipped the bow and pulled the laces of her bodice from the top eyelets with a small rasping noise, enough to loosen her shoulder-straps and allow him to tug the blouse down from her bare shoulders. Hair stood up on the nape of Elgith's neck. His movements were neither rough nor deferential, merely business-like, though his touch lingered in the cleft of her freckle-starred breastbone. He was not in any hurry. Slipping one hand after another under the linen, he eased her breasts up into the light where he might admire them. Supported now rather than flattened by her stiffened corset, they jutted plumply, pale as small moons, and he covered them with warm palms. Elgith stared at the wooden groining overhead and bit her lip again. It did not feel unpleasant, not in itself, this kneading and caressing of her exposed flesh; only when she remembered that it was a stranger's hands upon her did her skin crawl.

Still cupping her breasts, pinching her small nipples tight between thumbs and forefingers, he pressed the length of his body against hers. It felt almost as hard as the wooden pillar at her back. His still-hidden cock nudged her thigh through the intervening layers of cloth, stabbing bluntly at her skirted groin; he dropped his face to her neck, breathing the scent of her hair and skin. She heard him groan into her throat: 'Ah, yes . . .'

He smelled warm and beery and sweet, his breath hot on her throat. Elgith felt a tiny answering warmth move within her, like the tickle of thaw-water on ice.

He sought up under the bottom edge of her bodice, found the drawstring of her skirt and pulled it free. Her skirt, plain and respectable, tugged loose easily then and he let it fall at her feet, followed it up with two layers of underskirts that had plumped and muffled the long lines of her legs, and then pushed his fingertips through the bright copper wire of her pubic hair. She quivered and this made him laugh in his throat. He slid down on one knee, hands on her hips, the better to examine his new toy – and found the lines of bruises, green and purple, across the insides of her thighs. Elgith stared down at the top of his head, at the complicated knots binding the brass rings into his hair, hating the tokens of her victimisation, hating him for being a witness to them – just for a moment. Then he leaned in to her, his lips soft on the vulnerable crease between thigh and pubic mound, his tongue exploring her tickling flesh. She raised her eyes defiantly across the room and saw Soron Shal, propped up one side, his face set in calm concentration, his hose open, his right hand busy at his crotch. He was pulling upon the long curve of his penis, squeezing the smooth shaft, dropping his palm to cup and caress his balls; without hurry, without apparent passion. Elgith had never seen such meditative perfection. She thought of Marlam standing outside the door, sick with rage, while one soldier of the hated Empire buried his face in her muff and the other watched and masturbated. A soft warmth burst within her, like a flower opening.

When Tarkelion Dirskis spread her labia with his fingers and sank his lips and tongue into her cleft, she did not try to stifle her wriggle of pleasure. Instead, she eased herself open, allowing him greater access to the taste of her wetness. A flush drowned her freckles. She was very aware of herself, clothed only between hip and breastbone, her figure constrained by the tightness of a bodice from which her breasts overflowed, unconcealed; it must make a fine sight for Soron Shal, whose hand was moving faster now as Tarkelion Dirskis ground his face back and forth, deeper into her flesh. Elgith sank her fingers into the military adviser's dark hair and pulled him closer still; she saw his eyebrows flash in surprise, felt his tongue boring eagerly into her. Marlam was waiting outside the door, she told herself; helpless, humiliated, full of a hatred for her that was entirely impotent.

Orgasm hit Elgith like a whiplash, coming from nowhere, leaving her shocked and shaking and hot. Her upthrust breasts wobbled shamefully as she writhed on the face of the enemy. But as soon as she had stilled he pulled away from her, rose to his feet – blocking her view of Soron Shal on the bed beyond – and cleared his throat.

'You're full of surprises,' he said thickly. His chin was slick with her juices and he smelled of her, onion-sharp; Elgith felt confusedly that this was wrong and she nuzzled into the stubble of his beard, trying to lick him clean of the alien scent. Tarkelion Dirskis gave one groan of helpless shock and his hands at last freed his own desperate member from his hose, guiding it into her as he partly lifted her, partly crushed her against the pillar. They were well-matched for height; she barely had to straddle to admit him access. The feeling of his hands on her buttocks, his thick cock splitting her swollen flesh, stretching her tight, aching quim, was better than she could have dared hoped. It rekindled her arousal and brought her back to a new plateau of desire. He was so very strong; she let him support the whole of her weight, lifting her from the ground with each swift thrust, digging his fingers into her splayed arse-cheeks, gasping into her neck and hair. She lurched towards orgasm again – but his desire was too great and he climaxed before she could, shuddering upwards into her and then holding as motionless as a statue, hardly breathing. Elgith clung to him, not daring to voice her own frustration.

Without unsheathing himself, he lifted her weight on to his hips, turned and carried her the few paces to the pallet-bed, where he laid her back upon the wool-filled mattress and paused for a moment, his knees beneath her thighs, to look down at her. He stroked her mound with one hand. Elgith was still flushed and panting; she watched her possessor from beneath lowered lashes, wondering what he planned next. There was no sign of his erection flagging; he still filled her, but he showed no inclination to renew his exertions just yet. Elgith dared to steal a glance over at the other bed and saw that Soron Shal was now sitting at its edge, thighs parted, a mottled flush upon his sweat-sheened chest. The soldier scratched lazily at the back of his neck, his smile reeking of satisfaction.

'Charming,' he said – or, rather, that was what it sounded like to Elgith.

Tarkelion Dirskis laid one finger accurately upon her exposed clitoris and began to stir. She whimpered. Without taking his eyes from her face he asked a question, low and husky, in the Empire language. Soron Shal gave a considered, expansive, reply.

'I think,' said Tarkelion Dirskis to her, pulling slowly free and stretching out at full length by her side, 'that there are depths to you that will take long, careful exploration.' His voice was low in her ear, sending a shiver down her spine. 'Some tasks are worth spending a lot of time on. Hmm? I also think Soron Shal would very much like you to wrap those lips around his hard cock.'

Elgith glanced sharply over at the other man, uneasy. There was something in Soron Shal's sardonic coolness that she mistrusted. 'He ... has already spent,' she protested.

'Ah, I think you'll find he is a man of unusual talents,' Tarkelion Dirskis murmured. He ceased caressing her throbbing crotch and gestured with sticky fingers. Soron Shal eased himself to his feet and walked over and, as he did so, Tarkelion Dirskis rolled on to his knees and pulled Elgith into his lap, her back to his chest, facing the soldier as she had done at the table earlier in the day. She was given a very good look at what was coming for her; a smooth, almost elegant curve of flesh, still plump with blood but far less veined and ridged than the siege engineers' thick member, and swinging beneath that a hairless, velvety pouch bigger than her clenched fist. Elgith's eyes widened.

Tarkelion Dirskis wrapped both arms around her and stroked the lower part of her belly, tickling her pubic mound.

'He's hung like a ram,' Elgith whispered, awe-struck. The man at her back chuckled; Soron Shal raised one brow and then stroked two fingers down the length of his shaft in an inflammatory caress. There was quivering tension in his erection still and it leaped at his touch; the swollen purplish glans peeking past his foreskin.

'You've already made him come once,' Tarkelion Dirskis said in her ear. 'Clean him up.'

Elgith leaned forwards. There were glistening snail-trails of semen spattered across the soldier's belly and pendent in his glossy pubic hair. She tongued these delicately from his skin; they were cool despite the heat of his flesh beneath, and bitter on her palate. Soron Shal held very still under her ministrations, but his member jerked and nudged her jaw.

'Suck him,' Tarkelion Dirskis instructed.

Elgith shied away. 'I won't be any good at this,' she confessed; 'I've never – Marlam didn't like me to – '

Soron Shal snorted.

'It'll come with practice,' Tarkelion Dirskis promised; he reached out and to Elgith's shock took the struggling cock in a firm, familiar grip. 'Here.' He pulled the foreskin back and eased Elgith forwards, guiding her mouth down over the fat cock-head before she had time to protest. 'That's it. Good girl.' Soron Shal groaned and put a hand on either side of her head. His cock

196

was absolutely rigid in her mouth now, like a length of hot iron sheathed in velvet.

'Suck it. Lick it. Take it all the way to the back of your throat. Gently, now – no teeth. Use your tongue and your lips. That's right, Copperhead.' Tarkelion Dirskis matched her pace as he spoke, cupping and stroking Soron Shal's huge balls rhythmically, reaching forwards between his braced thighs to gently torture the spot behind the soldier's scrotum. Their victim heaved and writhed with pleasure, teeth bared, belly hard as a board, sliding his long wet member in and out between Elgith's pursed lips. Her eyes watered and she had to fight for breath against his alien beat, but there was an extraordinary gentle power in this that made Elgith's heart thump. She ran her tongue down the gaping slit of his glans and shivered inwardly in wonder as he reacted, quivering at her touch.

When Tarkelion Dirskis was assured that she had found her proper rhythm he relinquished his hold of the other man and pulled back behind her again, kicking his hose off and sliding his own hot cock up between her rocking thighs. Elgith found herself hung on the hooks of two men, the one at her rear working carefully, the one in her mouth thrusting more and more quickly. It was the strangest sensation she had ever yielded to, frightening and comforting all at once. Hot shivers of pleasure chased up her stomach. She lost her rhythm for a moment, forgetting Soron Shal's demands in a wave of her own desire. The soldier seemed to realise that she was losing control; he tightened his grip on her and let her go passive, moving his hips to compensate for her and pushing her head from side to side. Tarkelion Dirskis slipped one hand around the front of her thighs and plunged his fingers into the swamp of her groin, finding the agonised focus of her pleasure, whipping her excitement to an unbearable pitch until she started to shake all over, muscles screaming in spasm, unable to rock or lick or breathe. She felt Soron Shal tighten up. Tarkelion Dirskis was slapping into her wet pussy like a man hammering a stake into the ground, his hand was making her boil – and she came in a wrench of ecstasy, felt Soron Shal arrive at the same moment, her throat opening slackly to him, his hot distillation foaming into her, filling her mouth as she convulsed on him, on them, both men holding her up, filling her, tearing her apart with their caresses.

At the moment she felt she could finally open her eyes again, Tarkelion Dirskis pulled her from his companion, rolled her over on to her back and parted her thighs anew. He was not rough but he was quite urgent, his own neglected weapon a small fist punching into her gaping crotch. She spread her legs wide for him, soft with gratitude and joy, wrapping her legs around the small of his back so that he might impale her deeper and deeper. His mouth closed over hers and his tongue slipped into her; he tasted Soron Shal's semen in her and groaned.

Then he froze. Elgith opened her eyes and saw Soron Shal hovering over them both, falling like a shadow, like a winged bull. He held himself up, pushing no extra weight on to the woman at the bottom, but Elgith felt his descent through Tarkelion Dirskis' flesh, felt her rider yield and flatten and open to the warrior, saw his eyes roll back and sweat spring from his brow, his throat a taut line of unutterable sensation. In that tiny still moment, she licked the sweat from the bronze amulet that hung there. Then Tarkelion Dirskis, impaled between heaven above and below, fell – and cried out as he plummeted.

Elgith woke to the sound of the cockerel, as she did every day, and saw the pale predawn light ghosting the bare floorboards. It took her a few moments to recognise the transformed room from such a strange angle. She raised her head. The shutters had been left open all night; she could see a slight haze of mist creeping in from over the rooftops. Soron Shal had retired at some point to the big bed, where he lay shrouded in white sheets and black hair. She was still on the pallet with Tarkelion Dirskis, wrapped in a tangle of warm limbs, her back to his chest, his breath slow and even in her ear. She stretched cautiously and then began to ease out from the mattress on to the floorboards.

The circle of his arms tightened around her at once.

'I have to get up,' she whispered.

'No,' he grunted, half or fully asleep.

She smiled tentatively to herself. 'It's nearly dawn. I have to make breakfast for everyone. You too.'

'Mmm.' He stirred groggily. 'All right. Come back here afterwards.' His arm sagged rather than loosened and she slipped out from beneath it.

She pulled her clothes on, not bothering to lace up the bodice, and approached the door. For a moment, she entertained the horrible fear that Marlam would be standing on the other side as she opened it, waiting for her as he had waited all night. But when she lifted the latch and pulled it open, there was no one in the darkened corridor.

'Tell your husband,' came Tarkelion Dirskis' voice thickly from behind her, 'that he's not to touch you again. If he does, I'll see him dead. You tell him that. I will, too.'

'Thank you,' Elgith whispered.

She went out into the silent house and felt her way down into the kitchen. Flinging open a shutter to let in the light, she leaned out into the courtyard. The world seemed very still; even the cockerel had ceased crowing for the moment. She breathed in the cool misty air and smiled to herself. She stank of sex. Her legs felt wobbly, her throat was raw. She had hardly had more than a couple hours of proper sleep. Her position was scandalous, dangerously insecure, entirely foolish. But for the moment – just at this moment and for the first time she could recall in years – it tasted like freedom.

Captive Audience

*J*ade woke knowing that there was a man in her room. Through the soft, embracing darkness, the chime of the wind-bells in the night breeze and the gentle scent of musk and jasmine that perfumed her chamber, something alien had come to her and roused her from sleep. Some scuffling foot upon the ebony boards, perhaps, or a stifled masculine cough, or the warmth of a stranger's body.

The moment she awoke, the caryatids at her bedhead sprang into motion. There was the sound of pounding feet, a gasp and a thump, the squeal of a knife-blade skidding across metal.

Jade sat up in bed, the silk sheets sliding from her, and clapped her hands. Flames leaped up in the lamps and disclosed the scene before her. A man was pinned, twisting, in the grasp of two life-sized bronze statues. The metallic figures gleamed in the lamp-flame: one masculine, one feminine, both muscular, faceless and inhuman. The man was unshaven, dressed in soft shoes, close-fitting trousers and a leather jerkin that left his arms bare and now cruelly pinched in the unyielding hands of his captors. He stared wildly at them and gaped at her. She could see the whites of his wide eyes. A fallen knife gleamed on the sheets at the foot of the bed.

Jade pulled a fold of silk up to hide her breasts, her sapphire gaze as startled as his. She had never been seen naked by any man since babyhood and she was not sure she wanted this intruder to be the first. She could feel her pulse dancing in her throat. This was a man of the city – she could tell that from his plain attire and his rough demeanour. Not a slave, not a eunuch, not a court official or a nobleman. One of the common people. She had never imagined that she could be so close to one. It was repulsive and yet exciting. She kneeled up in the bed.

'Lady,' said the man hoarsely. 'Princess. Forgive me. I never meant to spy on you. I am not going to hurt you.' He was recovering quickly from his first shock and now held his head up high. Jade saw his gaze flick around the room, looking for some means of escape, but it kept returning to her face.

A little smile moved across her lips. The man took it as a good sign.

'Are these yours?' he asked, daring to grin crookedly at the bronze figures holding him. 'You are well guarded, Princess. If I had known, I wouldn't have chosen this way in to the palace. Forgive me, please. I never intended to frighten you.'

His voice, though hoarse, was low and gentle. Jade climbed down from the bed and walked around to where he was held. The caryatids turned him to face her. She dragged the sheet with her as a sheath to cloak her slender nakedness but, under the silken-black gleam of her unbound hair, her amber shoulders and arms were bare. She stood within a pace of him, so close that he might have leaned forwards to touch her if he had not been gripped so tightly.

Jade gazed up at the man's face. He was somewhat

taller than her and, she guessed, twice as old. His hair was sandy-brown and the stubble on his cheeks caught the lamplight and looked blond against his tanned face. She open her nostrils to breathe in the scent of him. She had never in her life before encountered a man who did not reek of perfume – but this one smelled like a man. It was a heady, dark, salty scent like clean leather, strange and yet pleasant. Jade allowed another smile to creep on to her lips. She decided she liked the look of this stranger. He was compactly built out of hard muscle and his brown eyes were keen.

'Are you a thief?' she asked, inclining her head.

He held her gaze and attempted a wry shrug. It was almost possible to hear his mind working furiously as he replied, 'They say in the city of Ilaun that no man can steal the Emerald Pendant of Yoharneth-Lahai. It was my ambition to prove them wrong, Princess. For three years I have been uncovering the safest route into the Palace and from there to the Imperial Treasure House. My path, sadly, led through your chamber.'

Jade spared a glance at the litter of tools and rope that lay discarded near the window. She wondered what the man thought of her, so close to him and so flimsily clothed. Did he see a pretty girl, still a child, or a lovely young woman? Did her slight, small-breasted figure in its pale veil and its long cloak of hair speak to him of untouched pleasures? Or would he dismiss such inexperience as not worthy of his interest?

Whatever he was thinking, he hid it beneath a studied mask of respect and self-deprecating trust. Even his diction was carefully honed.

'What is your name?' she asked.

'Petrus,' he said. 'I am at your mercy, my Princess. If you should choose to give me up to the officials, I would be subjected to a terrible death. You cannot imagine the tortures that would be laid upon a thief caught in the Imperial Palace.'

203

'You are mistaken,' Jade told him coolly. 'I know what they would do. I have seen it done before. You would be flayed across your back, chest, lower legs and palms, and then you would be taken out to the salt-pits beyond the city gates and thrown in.'

It was like watching a light die in his eyes.

'Princess . . .'

'Do you know who I am?' she enquired gently.

He swallowed. 'Princess Flower of Jade,' he murmured. 'Daughter of the Emperor.'

'I am the eldest child of the Emperor,' she corrected. 'I am the Celestial Light of the People. The Diamond of Ilaun. The Golden Dove of the Twenty Kingdoms. And when my father is dead I shall be Empress.'

Petrus bit his lip. 'There has never been a ruling empress,' he said. 'And you have brothers.'

Jade smiled benevolently, a smile she had practised in front of her mirrors until she knew it was devastating in its charm.

'For now,' she said. 'But I will be Empress. And you are to be my first subject, Petrus.'

She had him confined to her bathchamber. As she indulgently explained to him, there were seven rooms assigned to her in the palace, and of these only three were never visited by human servants. 'If you were to be seen by anyone else, that would be the end for you. You cannot trust slaves. That is why I have Anima and Animus to serve my needs,' she said, indicating the two caryatids as they dragged him into place at the back of the chamber. 'They are quite sufficient for my present requirements – they are without speech, unswervingly loyal, and they make excellent guards. Do not bother to struggle, Petrus. I have kept the palace servants out of my bath and bedchambers for years. They know I require privacy. But I would not shout, if I were you.'

The echoing, marble-walled chamber with its central circle of columns around the sunken bath was lit only feebly at this hour by the open skylight above the pool, through which the fat yellow moon was shining. But there were also five great metal chandeliers hanging from the ceiling, each bearing a crown of candles. Anima released the long chain supporting one of these and lowered the ornate structure to within reach. The living statue broke and twisted the bronze fittings of the chandelier, wrapping them around Petrus' wrists and securing the metal back upon itself. When the caryatid had finished, Petrus was held firmly in a standing position, his arms spread apart at head-height, his feet free but taking his weight. He was capable of moving no more than two steps in any direction before losing purchase on the smooth marble floor and swinging back on the length of the chain like a living pendulum.

Anima crouched behind him at his feet, ready for action. Animus stood to the side holding the single lamp. Their terrible unbreathing stillness only accentuated the isolation of the room.

'Comfortable?' asked Jade sweetly. She was still holding the silk sheet around her with one hand. She had noticed that the raised position accentuated the muscles on Petrus' arms and revealed the soft skin of the armpits beneath, fluffed with sandy hair.

'What are you doing with me?' Petrus asked. 'Is this some game little rich girls play?' He had gone quite pale and she could see sweat standing out under the untidy line of his ragged hair.

'Ssh,' she admonished, laying one finger on his lips. His stubble felt rough against her hand. Fascinated, she explored with her fingertips the hard line of his jaw and the softer skin beneath, the warmth of his neck and then the ridge of his larynx, hard as a peach-stone wedged in his throat. His hair was coarse to the touch as she wrapped it round her fingers, but the tuft under his right arm was soft as carded flax and he quivered under her cool hand.

Petrus made a little noise in the back of his throat.

She liked him. She liked the little lines under his eyes got from smiling in the sunlight, liked the pads of muscle over his cheekbones, the softness of his dry lips, the smell of him, the size of him. She liked the neat lie of the hairs on the back of his forearms, and the muscle beneath that felt hard as wood. He was twice her bulk, all meat and bone, but he was there at her whim for her to touch and explore. She laid one hand on his breastbone but her quest was blocked by the tough leather jacket he wore.

'Anima,' she said, stepping back. It was not actually necessary for her to vocalise but she sometimes did so out of natural habit.

The feminine caryatid stepped over and tore the leather from Petrus' torso as if it had been wet paper. The man flinched and the breath hissed over his teeth.

Jade looked at his bared chest with pleasure and ran her hand over his ribs as if he were a beloved dog. The muscle definition on him even stretched to his belly; not soft and rounded like a woman's but sculpted into ripples like the sand on a flat beach.

'Princess,' said Petrus. His voice sounded strained.

She ignored him. She stroked the kite-shape of hairs that grew across his upper chest, tugging them softly. They were darker than the hairs on his head. His nipples were flat and pale brown. She wondered if they were as sensitive as her own and toyed playfully with one; when it responded within seconds to become a hard little pea of flesh she could not help giggling to herself.

Petrus bared his teeth and grunted. Jade took both nipples in turn in her fingers and pinched them, softly at first and then harder. When her nails bit in he shuddered under her touch as if an earthquake was shaking his body.

'You are strong,' she breathed. 'And big.'

She laid her head on his chest and listened to his heart pounding. She pressed her face against him, exploring the extraordinary textures of his body with the sensitive skin of lips and cheeks. Softness of warm flesh, tickling little hairs, nipples hard and slippery under her tongue. He smelled of warm bread. She crouched to brush her lips across the skin of his belly and sides, found more hair leading from his navel down under the unkind edge of his trousers. Her shoulder rested against his crotch and she felt the hardness of the unseen member beneath it move suddenly and savagely.

'Princess,' said Petrus urgently, 'if this is what you want, let me go. Oh, I can help you. Let me free. I can give you what you want. Just . . .'

'Ssh,' said Jade, distracted. She straightened to face him again, reached up to lay her cheek against his and let her body rest lingeringly against him. He tried to press into her but she would not push back. She rubbed her soft, golden cheek against his prickling stubble, eyes half-shut in an ecstasy of exploration and sensation. Her lips closed around the lobe of his right ear and she tugged the helpless morsel of flesh with her teeth.

'Gods, you really need it, don't you?' he groaned. 'You're dying for it. Go on, let me give it to you. Let me give you what you want. I'll show you. I'll give it to you hard and long, Princess. Everything you want. Everything.'

Her sharp little canine teeth sheared through flesh and met in his earlobe.

He did not cry out, or pull away. He convulsed silently under her and she felt the damp heat of his sweat hit her like a wave. When she stepped back she found him pasty white and starting to shake.

'Brave, too,' she whispered.

She kissed him gently and left his own blood on his lips.

Then she walked away and went back to bed.

Jade did not return to her prisoner until the following night, except for a brief visit at dawn just to instruct Anima to lower the chain so that he could rest on his knees. She had a full day planned. After dressing she breakfasted with her mother, the Emperor's fourth wife, and, with her younger sisters and the female children of the concubines, she inspected the wares of a merchant who had brought in for their perusal goods newly arrived from up the river Yann. Slaves, silks, jewels and perfumes were the bulk of the merchandise on offer. The merchant, being a commoner and a man, was forced to kneel behind a screen in the Court of Women to call out his descriptions and explain the delights of his wares, while eunuchs carried or led the objects of trade before the assembled women.

Jade bought nothing from the merchant in public except a small monkey in a red silk shirt. Two of her sisters commented audibly upon the great number of pets she had purchased in the last few years, and upon how few of them had ever been seen again. Jade made a mental note to herself, to be reviewed at an appropriate point in the future, but was not distracted from the next event of the day – the public beating of a slave-girl – and watched the proceedings with dutiful concentration.

The objects she bought from the merchant once out of the public gaze were a heavily wrapped book and a very old, tarnished, silver ring, both of which she had instructed him to acquire for her. She was greatly pleased with both objects, and for several hours she sat upon the balcony beyond her bedchamber and read the book.

She ate alone during the hottest part of the day, then spent the afternoon with one of the tutors she employed, a wizened old man who taught her the astrological lore of the ancient people of Runazar. And when the day had cooled she went down through the gardens to the river Yann with the oldest of the concubines, a woman who had always shown a special care for the young Princess, and they embarked on one of the royal boats. For three hours they watched the oarsmen row them up and down the river, while fanning themselves to encourage the sultry evening breeze and listening to one of the city's poets who crouched blindfolded in the prow, earning his hire with words that few would have understood but many decent people had reviled.

The blue night was settling on the palace by the time she finished dining with the concubine and returned to her rooms, humming to herself and absently stroking the monkey on her shoulder. Animus stood before the door to her bedchamber, arms akimbo, guarding it and the rooms beyond from any intruders. It slid aside as she entered, metallic limbs moving noiselessly, eyeless head turning to watch her.

Jade deposited the monkey in its golden cage and stretched her arms. She felt sticky and unclean from the long day and ached for a bath. Slaves had already been sent to fetch water to her chambers. At the flick of a glance in its direction Animus picked up a lamp from the room and preceded her into the bathchamber to prepare the candles.

By the time she entered that room, all the chandeliers but one were blazing and scented tapers were lit on every surface, filling the room with attar of roses. Reflected light gleamed from the white marble and green malachite surfaces. The water in the bath looked gold under the candle-flames as Animus poured bucket after bucket into its creamy depths.

Petrus kneeled under the unlit chandelier, his head sunken on his breast. He raised it up when she entered, then pointedly looked away.

Jade was wearing a gown of silk strands so loosely woven that although it draped her from neck to ankle her small nipples poked through between the weave and snagged upon the weft as she walked, a nagging friction that she found gently pleasurable. She walked without haste up to Petrus and looked at him solemnly. His head was at her breast height but he stared into the distance past her arm, his jaw set and his eyes hot with loathing. Dried blood was still tracked across his neck and shoulder.

'Petrus,' she greeted him, laying one hand along the line of his jaw. She could feel the muscles clench at her touch. 'Would you prefer to stand up again?' she asked.

The eyes he turned to meet her gaze were bloodshot. 'I need to piss,' he said harshly. 'And I need to drink.' She could see that his lips were dry and cracked. Despite the marble vault in which he had been incarcerated, the day must have been hot for him, and very long.

Jade turned to look for Anima. The caryatid was sprinkling flowers on to the warm waters in the bath; the white, waxy flowers of the Tree of Stars whose four stiff petals gave out such a perfume that it was said that bees would not forsake them to return to their hives, but hover lovesick around the tree until they died in the night. At her glance Anima ceased its task and brought over from the side of the bath a small bowl of fruit.

Jade selected a pink, fleshy persimmon and held it to Petrus' parched lips. 'Drink,' she said, squeezing it. The thick, sweet juice ran out between her fingers over his chin but he grimaced and made no attempt to suck the liquid. Jade shrugged and dropped the empty rind on the floor.

'Stand up,' she said. Anima instantly went round behind Petrus. While Animus shortened the chain to take the weight of the bronze chandelier, Anima hoisted the man from his knees to his feet. Petrus groaned in pain, his calves unable to brace themselves under him. The two caryatids freed him from his shackles and Anima simply propped him up in its cold bronze arms, supporting him as he slumped against its obdurate length.

'You have made a mess,' Jade observed and, gripped by impulse, she leaned into him and licked the pulp from his chin and chest with soft lapping motions. On her tongue she tasted both the sweet fruit and the salt of his sweat. Petrus groaned again.

She pulled away with a smile, licking her lips, but when she saw his tightly shut eyes she turned towards her bath.

'I have had quite a tiring day,' she said conversationally, sliding the robe from her shoulders and stepping into the scented water below her. 'It is nice to bathe and relax, don't you think, Petrus?'

She turned in the water to smile up at him, and was gratified to see the man staring at her. But as soon as she glanced in his direction, he looked determinedly away, fixing his gaze upon Animus, who waited against the wall. Jade stretched out in the warm water, opening her legs to its caress and resting her head back on the rim of the bath.

'Do you like them?' she asked mischievously

'What in the Seven Hells are they?' he muttered.

'They were sculptural bronzes. They used to support a fountain in the Court of Women. Then I summoned *efrit* to animate them.'

He looked over at her blankly and she wriggled in the water beneath his gaze.

211

'They make perfect slaves,' she concluded.

She could not hear his voice, but his lips painfully shaped the words 'Oh, shit.'

She ran her hands up and down her body lingeringly. It was not a lavish, fleshy body but she was proud of it and knew she was beautiful. She pushed her hand between her legs and rubbed the perfumed water into the petals of her sex, but somehow the aches of the day just seemed to grow worse.

'Do you like me, Petrus?' Jade asked, lifting her breasts so that they bobbed upon the surface of the water, stiff nipples pointing like fingertips. Flowers clung to her body. Her black hair spread through the water like mist or darkness.

'Like you?' He coughed; it might have been meant to be a bitter laugh. 'I did think you were a poisonous little bitch-puppy. I must apologise. It turns out you are a black sorceress as well.'

Jade laughed and wriggled over on to her stomach, her buttocks arching. Every part of her that broke the surface gleamed. Petrus was not even trying to look away from her now. She could feel the warm water pressing into her sex and see the rise and fall of his chest sharpening. Both facts delighted her.

'I'm going to be the Empress, Petrus,' she explained kindly, squirming softly from side to side. 'I am going to rule the Twenty Kingdoms, and then I am going to conquer the world. That's why I need to be a sorceress. You understand, don't you, Petrus? Nobody ever became great by being weak and gentle. I will have to fight for my throne. I know that. People will have to be killed. It does not matter. I am going to be the greatest queen that ever lived. And I will rule forever. I can do that, you know, with the right magic. And everyone will be happy, because everyone will love me.'

She kneeled up slowly, water pouring from her high breasts and from the thigh-length black hair that cascaded down her narrow back. Where her hair ended and the water began, no one could have said.

'You love me already, Petrus, do you not?'

He did not reply or move, but his eyes were starving – so hungry that they would have devoured her down to the bones if they could. Ravenous and appalled. She stood and shook out her hair. He tried to lick his dry lips with even drier tongue.

'You needed a drink, you said, Petrus,' she reminded him. She raised one leg and placed her foot upon the side of the bath, then ran slender fingers through the wet black ringlets at her groin. 'If you love me, I will let you drink.'

She pissed into the bathwater, long and hard. Petrus' eyes never left her – he hardly even blinked. When she had emptied herself, she took up the blue glass bowl which had held the flowers and stooped to fill it from the bath. She brought it to him. Part water, part flowers, part piss, she offered it up to his cracked and blackened lips like the Water of Life itself.

He only hesitated for a moment before he drank. She watched his throat work with a sense of pure satisfaction.

When he had emptied the bowl, she brought him more and he took that in great gulps too, slopping it down his throat and chest in his eagerness, washing away the last sticky traces of fruit. Only when he had drained the bowl a second time did he lean back against Anima's metal breasts and stare at the roof, trying to regain control of his breathing. Jade put the bowl aside.

'You have wet your clothes,' she said, reaching for the waistband of his trousers.

He had enough freedom of movement to get his hands down and grab hers, but the moment they touched her Anima's grip transferred to his wrists, twisting them open then wrenching his arms up and apart.

'Bitch!' Petrus gasped. But he did not struggle as Jade unpicked the knot at his belt and slid the cloth past his hips down to his ankles. She kneeled slowly before him, her face on a level with his crotch and rapt with wonder.

She had seen pictures of naked men in books that depicted every sexual position imaginable, and even heard the parts described in lurid detail by concubines and slaves, but she had never seen the phallus in the living flesh, nor smelled the sour musk of it. To her delight, his whole groin radiated a heat that she could feel on her face. From a wild thatch of hair, the cock arced up like a rainbow rising into the sky, the eye in the hooded head wet and weeping. It swayed like a palm-tree in a high wind and when she laid her hand upon it it bobbed and twitched in an ungainly manner. It felt surprisingly hot in her hand. Petrus moaned beneath her touch. She tightened her grip and felt the cock thicken and harden in response, spreading her clenched fingers.

'No, Princess, I need to piss!' Petrus begged through gritted teeth.

Jade ignored him and pulled the thick member upright as if it were some dagger she were raising to strike. The hairless balls pendent beneath were fatter than she had imagined, the scrotum wrinkled as a walnut with a seam like a scar bisecting the two sacs. As she looked she saw the scrotal skin was crawling almost imperceptibly, the different parts puckering and relaxing in a secret dance. She drew back the foreskin and saw the glans glistening beneath, fat, angry-looking, almost purple in colour, the inverted 'Y' of the slit cupping a wedge of tightly-packed ridges.

Petrus was writhing with frustration or discomfort, she could not tell which. She released his straining cock and stood to one side. 'Piss, then,' she said curiously.

'Ah!' Petrus gasped. 'Gods, no, I can't – I'm too hard, you lamia!'

Jade smiled to herself. At once the two caryatids moved and in moments they had Petrus bound to the chandelier again. This time the chain was pulled tighter so that his arms were stretched right above his head. His erection stuck out from his body like the handle of a knife that had been driven into his guts.

She walked behind him to examine the view from that angle. The broad expanse of his back tapered down to hard buttocks totally unlike anything she had seen; not the rounded globular softness of a woman's arse but two sharply defined muscles like great clenched fists. She laid a hand on one of the cheeks and almost flinched to feel it so rock-hard. The skin of his rump and legs were rough with nearly-invisible hairs, but a small swirl of them like a fingerprint could be seen at the top of his arse-crack. Jade raked her gilded nails across one buttock, admiring the little pink lines evoked.

A shiver crawled visibly up his spine.

She crouched again in a drift of her own wet hair to examine the contours of his legs, the rigid planes of his thighs like planks of wood. She laid her face against his hard thigh and stared at his rampant erection.

'Piss,' she commanded.

'I can't,' he groaned.

Standing, she pressed herself against him from behind and wrapped her arms around his waist. 'Piss,' she said, pushing the heels of both hands in at the base of his belly.

Petrus cried out. Then he let go and pissed like a horse on to the costly floor.

By the time he had finished, two long tears of humiliation were running down his face and there was little left of his tumescent erection. Jade picked up her robe and walked to the door. Just before she left the room she turned and said – for his benefit, not that of the caryatids, 'Clean up. Clean him. Let him lie down to sleep. When he wakes, chain him up again.' Then she departed.

On the second day, Jade trained her monkey to bring her peaches from the top branches of the palace orchard. She learned from a different tutor of the wisdom of the High Prophet Imbaun, both his public sayings and his secret writings, and it made her laugh. She watched the execution of a minor court official who had been caught reselling the imperial supplies of grain. She copied the faint lettering inscribed on the interior of the silver ring and spent a little time trying to decipher them, although she was careful not to pronounce any word. She did not think about Petrus.

She came back to him in the cool of the evening, dressed in a belted robe of scarlet silk embroidered with azaleas. Anima followed her in bearing a tray of food and drink. He was chained in the kneeling position once more, and lifted his head to glare at her sullenly.

'Drink this,' she said, pouring him a glass of wine thinned with iced pomegranate juice. He drained the cup twice, though with some show of reluctance.

'Are you hungry?' she said. 'You must be. It is at least two days since you have had anything to eat.'

'Don't bother,' Petrus growled.

'Now now, I want you to keep your strength up,' she chided him as she broke white bread in her hands and dipped a piece in a bowl of golden olive oil. 'I am trying to look after you.'

He tried to laugh but it came out as a resigned croak. 'Listen, bitch, I know you're going to kill me. Do it quickly. Get it over with.'

'I am not going to kill you,' she smiled.

'I don't want to play your games, little girl. I am not

here to be the toy of some *couzie* with a scorpion for a heart. Fuck you.'

'Oh, no, Petrus,' she murmured. 'You do not understand. I have no intention of killing you. I have plans for you. I need you to be big and strong. Go on, eat up. You must be starving.'

She stroked the hair back from his forehead and he groaned. She loved that. The mixture of frustrated anger and despair made her blood race. He was so strong, yet so helpless. She held the morsel of bread to his lips and he took it from her, his face a mask of pain. She fed him gently by hand, stroking all the time his temples and jaw and neck. When he had finished the small loaf of bread she offered him grapes, green as poison, feeding them fastidiously one at a time between his scarred lips. He submitted to her touch for the sake of the food.

Then Jade broke open the piece of honeycomb on the tray and ran her fingers through it until they dripped with the sweet sticky stuff. She held out her honeyed hand to Petrus and he opened his lips to her, sucking her slender fingers into his hot, wet mouth, probing up hard between the digits with his tongue to chase the last fugitive dribbles of sweetness. When she withdrew her fingers, he stifled a whimper and tried to reach for them, straining against his fetters.

His cock was thickening already.

Jade loosed the belt of her robe and let it swing open to reveal her delicate frame, her small breasts. Her copper-coloured nipples were soft but, when she broke more honeycomb and smeared it lasciviously over her breasts, they hardened at once to little peaks. Sticky droplets of honey dripped slowly from her bubs on to the golden skin of her thighs. She took more honey in both hands and worked it across her belly and flanks, rubbing it into the curls of hair at her groin until they glistened. Petrus' eyes were shining like those of the damned; he could not restrain his reaching lips or his rising cock.

She took that one step that brought her within his reach and his mouth closed hungrily on her right breast. Jade gasped as warmth rushed through her from spine to scalp, and she grasped his head between her hands. He began to suckle desperately, licking and mouthing her virginal breasts as if he were clinging that way to life. His tongue was everywhere on her little tits, under and over and between them, whipping her nipples, lapping across her breastbone, scouring her stomach with hungry kisses. He worked his way down her body, stooping awkwardly to her crotch, mumbling at her honeyed bush. Jade tilted her pelvis up towards his mouth and he thrust at her soft pubic mound, reaching for the sweet slit that was just beyond his reach with a tongue that must have been almost tearing itself out at the root. The rough stubble of his chin raised welts across her untouched thighs. He groaned and gobbled and strained against the fetters until the bronze bit into his wrists and the muscles stood out on his shoulders, but he could not quite reach his goal. Jade staggered, weak at the legs. She was wet now, her sex hot and swollen, the slipperiness between her thighs nothing to do with honey.

She grabbed his head and tilted his face up to look at her, stilling him. His chin was pressed against her belly.

'Petrus,' she hissed. 'Do you love me, my slave?'

And still, eyes hooding, he pulled away from her, though his cock stood like an obelisk, a monument to the bone-breaking, entrail-tearing tyranny of his lust.

She sloughed the silken robe and stood naked in front of him. 'You are the first man to see me, Petrus,' she told him. 'Can you believe that? The first man I have ever touched. The first ever allowed to touch me.'

He laughed in disbelief. She stooped to bite his lips

softly. They tasted of honey. He writhed under her, hot and afraid.

'I am telling the truth.' She posed for him, running her hands up her filthied body and lifting her breasts in crushing, clawing fingers. 'I am an imperial princess. I have never seen a man. I am not allowed near them. Never had a hard, salty prick pushing between my legs. Protected. Cosseted. Indulged. Nothing to relieve my curiosity. I have made do for years with tickling and dreams and frigging. Even Animus –' she jerked her head derisively at the caryatid '– cannot do for me what the filthiest street-sweeper can do for the lowest slut in the bakery. He was carved to look like he had a member, but it is a fake, a blob of metal; it cannot rise to the occasion. Do you know how I feel, Petrus? I am burning with curiosity. I want to know what it is like. I want to find out what a man can do. I am sick of ignorance. If I am to be Empress, then I have to know everything. You are my instrument, Petrus.' She giggled, her body quivering all over.

'I will fuck you till you scream, you bitch,' he promised.

'No.' Jade froze, her hands in her midnight hair, her flushed breasts tilted high, her sapphire eyes aglow. 'You will not fuck me, you filthy gutter-crawling thief. You common little piece of shit. You will not fuck me. You will beg me to fuck you.'

And Petrus could not reply. Into the silence of the room, from across the city rooftops, there drifted the faint sound of the priests calling the people to prayer at the Temple of All Gods But One.

Jade grew straight and proud and cool once more. 'Let me show you,' she said. 'Let me show you, Petrus, how I pleasure myself. Would you like to see that? Because I can keep you chained forever, unable to touch yourself. I can make you watch me grind myself into exhaustion, if I like. Would you like to see me play with myself, Petrus?'

He said nothing, but his eyes burned and his cock surged like a chained dog.

'I like to use a candle,' she said, surveying the ranks of fragrant incandescent columns that filled every ledge and holder in the room. 'At first it had to be a narrow, smooth taper. But now I like something a little more substantial. Like this.'

She chose a waxen column and carried it over, still burning, to Petrus. The candle was nearly as thick as his turgid cock and had been moulded with a pattern of flowers, as would enhance a lady's bedchamber. Since it had been only recently lit for the first time, the head was still domed and convex, the wick rising from a tiny pool of molten wax.

'Would you like to watch me use this?' Jade breathed. 'You must be brave.' And she tilted the candle over his chest. Hot wax dribbled down on to his nipples, causing him to flinch and shudder – but he refused to cry out. Jade purred with pleasure and brushed the congealed dribbles from his reddened skin. Then she snuffed out the flame by pressing the wick to the sweat-sheened skin over his solar plexus.

Still he barely flinched.

'Now,' she whispered, smoothing the wick down into the soft wax of the candle tip. She rubbed the lumpy shaft against Petrus' own teasingly, but not for long. Just enough for him to feel its rigidity.

There was a single piece of furniture in the bath-chamber, a carved rosewood bench close by where Jade would sometimes sit while Anima dried her feet. She went over to it now and perched on the edge, her legs spread so that Petrus could get a clear view. Gazing directly at him, she rubbed the still-warm tip of the candle against her plump pink sex lips, using the unyielding object to probe between them and open

220

herself up. The candle sank rapidly into the hot depths that awaited it. She began to draw it in and out, rubbing the thick ridges of the decorative moulding against her inner folds. The pleasure of the physical sensation was indescribably enhanced by the sight of Petrus with his whole agonised attention glued to the inches of thick wax disappearing into, and reappearing from, her stretched pussy. She let herself whimper with pleasure. She could see the sweat gleaming all over him, his cock jerking with frustration. With her free hand, she groped at her own right breast, but she could not divide her attention for long. As the stabs of pleasure grew ever more demanding within her, she raised one foot on to the bench and lay back, both hands reaching down between her legs to grip the candle base and pump it harder and deeper into her wet hole. Petrus gave a strangled, inarticulate cry.

Then she came, her voice drowning his.

When she sat up she was flushed and smiling, but as poised as ever. She pulled out the tool of her self-gratification and brought it over for Petrus to inspect. The tip was filmed with milky fluid. His nostrils flared at the scent of her juices.

'Hungry still?' she invited.

His throat worked. He licked the candle dry as if it were some great white phallus he was trying to pleasure. His cock was the colour of rosewood, so flushed with blood it was. She laughed softly under her breath, then dipped the candle tip into the little bowl of olive oil. Stepping behind him, she reached between his hard arse-cheeks and located the tight and wrinkled hole of his anus.

'No!' Petrus whimpered.

'If I can take it, surely you can?' Jade said reasonably, but she did not wait for any consent before pushing the slippery tip into the muscular orifice. 'Relax, Petrus. The more you fight it, the more it will hurt.' And inch by quivering inch, twisting it, turning it, working it in and out against the flexing, clenching grip of his arse-hole, she pushed the thick wax dildo a hand's depth into the shuddering body of her victim.

'There there,' she soothed as she worked. 'Gently now. Open up. Take it further, my lovely Petrus.'

He thrust out his head, mouth open. He panted, shrieked and moaned, all pretence of dignity and restraint lost, but his hard-on did not die. Jade reached round to spank it with her free hand.

'Ah!' cried Petrus. 'Please – you bitch, you cunt, you monster – touch me. Stop it. Touch me. Stop. Oh, shit. Please, Princess. I can't. You're killing me. You bitch. Please!'

'You want me to fuck you?' she murmured into his shoulder, stirring the rod in his arse like a pestle in a mortar.

'Yes, yes, yes, anything, please –' was the gobbled reply. 'Fuck me. Fuck me!'

In a blink of an eye, the caryatids sprang to his side, breaking the chains that held his wrists. They dragged him over to the wooden bench and spread him out upon it face-up, his arse jutting out over one end with the candle still projecting from between the cheeks. Anima crouched beneath him and gripped his feet against its hips, gazing up sightlessly between his spread thighs, his balls hanging nearly in its face. Animus stretched his arms out over his head and held him. Nothing was left but for Jade to straddle him in the centre, bracing herself upon his chest as she lowered her pelvis to meet his. He felt hot and clammy under her hands, and his face was twisted in an agony of fear that she would not fulfil her promise. As she leaned over him her hair fell about their shoulders like night.

'Please,' he said.

'Yes,' she whispered, sheathing him in her tight flesh. A sigh escaped her as she realised that nothing she had tried had ever been quite like this. The member penetrating her was for the first time neither cold nor unyielding, and it rose up to meet her through an aura like the clashing of brass cymbals in her head. She smelled the sweat of his lust, felt the slight yielding of his ribs, heard the quick hard breaths he was taking beneath her. His hips thrust and she rolled against them. His belly was hard and ridged with effort. His pubic hair ground against her mound. She pushed her toes against the floor – her legs barely long enough to meet the ground – so that she could rise from him in order to sink again further. He groaned and met her in rhythm, his face twisting with effort. Already burning from her first orgasm and from the titillation of his agony, she began to quicken almost straight away. She dug her fingers into his sides and he breathed a short gasp of pain that aroused her further. Flames seemed to be climbing up the wall of her belly. The wet slapping sounds of their synchronised movements filled her ears. Her stuffed flesh was churning; though he filled her completely she wanted him bigger and bigger inside her. Then quite suddenly she felt her climax within her grasp and she seized it, her whole body opening up into a burning maelstrom of pleasure. She threw back her head and thrust down on to him, drawing his thick cock as deep into her as she could, and she howled with triumph.

As she came down from her peak, she locked her thighs and raised herself slightly from him. Petrus flailed under her, his hips thrusting wildly. She was surprised by the violence of his need; he seemed ready to tear himself bloodily from the grasp of the two caryatids. His balls slapped against her as he thrust and his jaws were locked into a rictus. Jade placed one sharp fingernail against the skin above his right nipple and began to carve.

'Yes, Petrus,' she said. 'Now.'

That was enough. He spasmed as orgasm punched through his vitals but he kept thrusting. Jade had to hold on tightly as she cut stroke after delicate stroke; instead of trying to separate from him, she had to cling closer as thrust after thrust to her pelvis threatened to knock her off altogether. Then she dropped her entire slight weight on him and rode him in as the last waves ebbed from his racked frame.

The caryatids let go but Petrus was incapable of movement, gasping like a beached fish. Jade wiped the blood from his chest and surveyed the sigil marked in his flesh with satisfaction. Her sigil, delicate as the footprint of a bird, imprinted in scar-tissue on his skin forever.

'Time to go now, Petrus,' she told him as she leaned over to kiss his swollen lips. 'I have finished with you for now. Animus will take you down to the river gate in the gardens. I am sure you can find a boat, and then you are free.'

'Princess,' he groaned thickly.

'Ssh. It will not be for long,' she soothed him. 'When I need you again, you will come back to me. You are mine, Petrus. The first and most loyal subject of the new Empress.'

White As Any Milk:
Black As Any Silk

*A*s if it had emerged from some child's tale, the witch's castle was smothered in the thick, spiny briars of wild rose and black rooks fled cawing from the roof as I approached. Except that it was not a castle; rather a fortified farmhouse with a round tower at one end, stone-built sure enough, but the defences neglected. The tower showed the old scorchmarks of fire on the highest storey, which was jaggedly open to the sky, and the wooden palisade around the building was sagging and rotten. No guard stood at the open gate and no steward came to meet me as I rode in. I slipped from the saddle and looked around me at the deserted yard.

The farmland around the house had not been empty; I had just ridden through the village of Pedwell at the foot of the slope and there children had been playing and women spinning in the sun. There had been serfs in the fields hoeing the vegetable strips. Every one of them had stopped to watch me pass – I suppose travellers must be few here, where the road ends. There is nowhere for the track to go, for here the long humped spine of the Polden Hills concludes with a drop into the great Sedgemoor Marsh and only the witch's farm marks the termination of the dry lands. But none of the serfs had spoken to me or challenged my passage; my robes and my horse marked me out as too far above their station. And there was no one up here on the wooded hilltop to receive me, only a few brown hens scratching in the mud.

I tethered the mare to the slumped remains of a handcart and walked around the perimeter of the building. The tower, partially ruined as it was, had clearly been built to keep watch over the marshlands to the east, and a gap had been cleared through the trees on that side which was not yet entirely overgrown. Light glinted off distant pools on the Levels beneath me. The rose-bushes that scrambled up the stones were in full bloom, a mass of open white blossoms with pink and gold hearts. Bees questing among the flowers made the whole area a thrumming stir of sound. I pulled a flower from the thicket, careful not to prick my fingers on the thorns, and tucked it into the pouch at my belt.

There was no door at the foot of the tower and only one in the length of the house-face, a heavy oak barrier that was firmly closed and secured with a bronze barrel-lock. Clearly the witch was not within. I made my way around the outbuildings and then into the orchard – the walls had slumped almost to the foundations in places – at the back.

She was there. She lay on a blanket in the dappled shade of an apple tree with one arm curled under her head, fast asleep. Her small feet were bare, the soles stained green by grass. A layman might have wondered that the Baron saw such menace in that slight figure, but I knew differently. She was asleep in the middle of the day, which meant that she had been up last night at her work. Scratchy tiredness prickled at the back of my own eyes, but I had ridden out ten miles to confront her today, under the sun where we would both be unarmed.

That deep curve of a woman's waist and hip when she reclines on her side has always seemed to me to be one of the most beautiful things under the heavens.

I squatted down carefully with my back to another trunk and then coughed. She stirred, flexed her legs and then sat up, brushing the hair back from her face. As soon as she saw me, she froze, and we faced each other across the long orchard grass. What I saw was a young woman with a wide face, pointy little chin and dark eyes narrowed now with apprehension. Her waist-length hair was the flecked grey of moth-wings, despite the youth of her features. She wore no jewellery, which I had anticipated but yet made my heart sink.

'Galiena Pedwell?' said I. 'Peace to you, Sister.'

What she saw when she looked at me was unambiguous, I suppose. A man in white robes with a black over-mantle; no peasant. Rather pale skin, slender build; no warrior. Very black hair worn to the shoulder and a small black beard that framed the mouth in the latest fashion; a courtier of some kind, priest or scholar. Silver ring on my finger, silver collar about my neck, silver clasp about my left wrist. A mage. A Moon-mage.

'Who are you?' she demanded.

'Julian of Oxford,' I said. 'Magus to Baron Chedzoy.'

She stood up. She was, I judged, a little shorter than average and her slenderness – visible through the simplest of homespun linen dresses – made her look weaker. I didn't fear her in daylight; she wasn't even carrying a knife, the only thing at her belt being a bronze key.

'What does he want now?' she said, her gaze sliding sideways from me. She was seriously considering flight.

She had allowed herself to be caught unawares and now she was in a very vulnerable position.

I spread my hands and tried to look as unthreatening as a strange man can look to a woman. 'He wants me to talk to you,' I said, not entirely accurately. 'He wants me to uncover the truth. There have been accusations, and he is bound by law to protect his dependants.'

'Accusations?' She fixed me with a hard, appraising stare.

'There are those who say you have been dealing with Darkness magics.'

Her lips moved in a little humourless smile. 'Really? How so?'

I had no written list, but I could remember the litany of blame well enough: 'That you cursed Chedzoy's bailiff with a madness that caused him to drown himself. That you have caused good wives to fall in love with men other than their husbands. The Sheriff's wife in Chedzoy has had fits and miscarried. The Baron himself says that you walk in his dreams.'

She folded her hands over her waist and grimaced. 'People kill themselves, and they lose their children, and they fall in love. Every day. It does not need witchcraft to cause that. And many women walk in the Baron's dreams,' she added offhandedly. 'He must see witches in half the kingdom.'

I could believe that. I could also believe that Galiena, once met, would be easy to dream of. 'There are stories of you summoning creatures from Hell,' I said softly.

'Have you witnesses?' she demanded.

'So I'm assured. I haven't yet questioned them all.'

Her eyes gazed steadily into mine and she seemed to consider her answer carefully. 'Julian of Oxford,' she said at length, 'have you been in the Baron's employ for long?'

'A month.'

'Did you know he is a cousin of mine?'

228

I didn't, but I nodded.

'Oh, it is only a weak relation. My forefathers were the bastard branch of the family and not favoured by Fortune. I hold only a few fields, and a towered house, and Pedwell village. It's not much to be envied, and I'm the last of my family. That's the only reason I came back here. But –' she raised one hand '– those few acres are the only ones on the Poldens that don't belong to Chedzoy. And he wants my lands. Can you not see that he has a motive to lie about me?'

I shook my head then. 'I'm not stupid,' I said, 'nor any man's lapdog. Why do you think I came to talk to you? There's more than one reason for accusing a mage of witchcraft. And believe me, Sister, it's not something I want to hear or want to be true of any one of us.'

'Then what do you want to hear?' She took a couple of paces towards me and lifted her chin. 'I am not a witch. Does that satisfy you? My art is of the Moon; I am not aligned to Darkness.'

'I might believe you –' oh, no, her word alone was far from sufficient '– but the Baron I think will not. Particularly if it is your land he wants.'

She rolled her shoulders in an angry shrug. I had hardly ever met such an intense gaze as hers; it pinned me where I sat. 'He knows nothing about these things.'

'He is my liege-lord,' I warned her. 'He might send me against you, whatever my convictions. He might hire in a Sun-mage. Or call for the Witch-hunters.'

She flinched then, though she tried to hide it. 'They will not find me,' she muttered.

'No? I think they would, eventually. They might prove you innocent, in the end. But . . . you know what it would be like for you.'

She turned her face away.

'Listen,' said I, getting slowly to my feet. 'He wants rid of you. I think you would be wise to leave. Let him have your lands.'

'I don't cave in to threats.'

'This,' I said, suddenly weary, 'is a warning, not a threat. Do you think I want to fight you?'

'You had better not, Brother. I would break you.' Her voice was colder than midwinter.

I could only sigh and turn away. She was not going to listen to me. 'The moon shine on you,' I said, but the words stuck in my throat. I strode back through the lush grass to the wall, and rode off without glancing at her or her holdings again.

But she would not get out of my head. The mare skittered under me, feeling my agitation. Galiena's dark gaze, the defiant tilt of her head, the little pale hands clenched at her small waist – these things stayed with me even as I left her demesne and rode the long way along the hill's flank into Chedzoy's fields. The thought of her kept dragging my concentration down to my groin. She made the blood beat hard under my skin – and she made the hair prickle at my nape. I have never been one to relish confrontation, neither in victory nor defeat, and this business seemed a bad one to me.

Even her belt-buckle had been of bronze. No steel. No silver. I did not like this one bit.

Chedzoy's serfs stood respectfully by the side of the road as I passed, doffing their caps. Even after only a brief time in his service, I was known to them, more so because my first task had been to walk all the boundaries under a waxing moon, sealing the fertility of the land. I will have to visit each village in turn over the rest of the summer and bless them for a safe winter free of sickness, and in the spring work the weather for the benefit of their crops. Most of my duties will be of that nature, domestic and unobtrusive. Had the Baron planned to go to war soon, he would have sent to Oxford for a Sun-mage instead.

She might have been an ally to him, had he chosen

so. I thought about her pride and her feral watchfulness, but I could not imagine her small figure dressed demurely in robes of office, or patiently acceding to Chedzoy's commands.

There was a new occupant swinging from the crossbar of the gallows at Chedzoy bridge, but any crowd had dispersed. The mare shied from the sight and I had to rein her in hard.

When I asked at the gate as I entered the castle, I was pleased to find that the Baron was out hunting. I passed the mare into the hands of a stable-boy and ascended to my own chambers, where I flung myself fully clothed upon the bed and tried to snatch a few hours sleep for what was left of the day. Sleep did not come easily; I found myself picturing Galiena's contemptuous eyes and strange, dappled hair. I was forced to turn my mind to listing each of the summer stars in turn before I could sink down the spiral well into unconsciousness.

Sunset woke me with a start. If I am asleep I am rarely disturbed by sunrise, but the end of the day always shocks me to wakefulness. I felt the tide of empowerment filling me like a cold wave, my fingers tingling as strongly as if I had slept upon them. I rose from my bed and kneeled before the small shrine to Gwydion in the centre of the room, offering the nocturnal prayer of dedication and thanks. When my mind was stilled and focused I began my preparations for the ritual I planned.

My chambers consist of two large rooms, one for my everyday use and the other, the inner, for thaumaturgical purposes only. The Baron has been generous, or at least fully aware of the value of his investment in me.

I needed to check on Galiena.

Still in my sleeping quarters I stripped my travelling-clothes from me and washed thoroughly in the bowl of chill water collected from the rooftops, pouring out the waste down the garderobe where it would mix harmlessly with the collective effluent of the castle. I stood naked in the dusk air, meditating on my own breath until the water had dried from my skin, then I donned the clean linen vestment of the Church and my silver.

Within the inner chamber all was as I had left it. The single open window looked out over a darkening landscape. Clouds covered the stars; I could not see the moon, if it had risen yet, but I could feel the tides of power at the flood within me. There were two bare tables against one wall; I laid out the tools with which I would be working. All this was very familiar to me. Years of training and practice smoothed the path of my art and I hardly had to think about the detail of the rite, my concentration instead on my goal. Fluently I spoke the words of consecration that made the room a holy place; smoothly blessed the salt, the flame, the incense and the chalice; confidently constructed my ritual circle upon the lines I had inscribed on the bare slate floor. I asked the blessing of Gwydion using the longer form of supplication – it might be difficult work ahead of me – and invoked the power of the moon, drawing it down into the circle. Only then, when all the preparations were made and the power buzzed in my ears like racing blood, could I embark upon the core of my rite.

I used the flower I had plucked that noon from Galiena's tower. It had wilted a little but I laid it within the silver chalice of moon-water and, when it had sunk, focused my gaze upon the surface of the liquid. The work would have been far easier had I been able to use something closer to Galiena's person – her hair, her blood, her tears – but there would have been no way to steal such precious items from her on our brief acquaintance. I had to make do, and compensate for my poor tools with my own skill and the power of my will. The words of the rite slipped, almost unheard, from my lips. The surface of the water took on a silvery sheen. I felt the metal at my throat and hand and wrist grow cold.

Though there was no moon visible through my window, and only the light of a little white candle at my right side, the image of a waxing moon appeared slowly in the mirror of the water. I focused my search upon her tower, the rose-clad stones at the base, the crumbling walls open at the top to the sky. That would be where she worked, if she was active now – and that I did not doubt for a moment. I sought her own chalice, the reflecting pool of water that she must surely have among her tools.

I saw her. The image in the pool suddenly became one of movement. I was gazing into my own basin, but up out of another miles away. There was no sound, and my view was restricted. I could see the edge of a wall, and the clouds beyond, and Galiena when she moved into my field of vision. She was walking around her own circle, her lips moving inaudibly, and she wore only a silver girdle.

For a moment I allowed myself a very small taste of relief. It is actually easier to slay with Moon-magics than with Darkness, but at least I had the resources to counter that mode of attack, should she be trying it. Then the distraction of her form swept over my every other emotion. She was a small woman; I could easily imagine circling her waist with my hands, or enfolding her in my arms – but there was nothing childlike about her body. My flesh responded instantly and insistently to the sight; the image in the chalice quivered for a moment. I felt the skin tighten not just across my scrotum but all over my groin and up over my rear to the base of my spine. Blood ran thick into my member and my stones felt as heavy as lead slingshot.

There were glowing lines of silver all across her skin;

spirals and twisted loops like the fragile tendrils of climbing plants. They outlined her spine and encircled her limbs delicately, and they seemed to be rooted in the cobweb-coloured down at the meeting of her thighs. Tattoos, I suspected. I had heard of the practice though it was not common, even among clergy of the Church.

My mouth was dry. The moon-lines encircled her breasts, emphasising their roundness, and radiated from her small nipples like star-bursts. She moved in a graceful dance about the circle, her hands describing elaborate passes, her naked breasts and buttocks wobbling gently with her motions. You might easily cover each of those small breasts with a hand. They would be as warm and soft as doves. The head of my member was swollen like a plum now and its shaft stood up erect as a tent-pole under the coarse cloth of my vestments.

She finished another rotation and without warning loomed close to the field of my view, her moon-washed torso and then her face filling my chalice. Her eyes were wide and filled with light, the pupils dilated, and her lips were softly parted, shaping unheard syllables with a caressing action that made my stones burn. She gazed into the silver basin of her own ritual circle and I gazed back, so close to her despite all the miles that I might have leaned forwards and kissed her. I could see the pulse beating in her throat. My loins tightened as if they were ready to burst.

A thunderous knocking sounded on the outer door of my chambers and shattered my concentration. I jumped like a guilty boy caught spying on his sisters and wrenched my gaze from the chalice.

'Lord Magus!' the voice of a guard roared from beyond the door.

The image in the chalice had gone. There was nothing in the silver cup but water and a drowned flower.

'Wait,' I croaked. I was unable to risk further speech.

I rose to my feet, ignoring the furious remains of my erection, and gathered my concentration. Raising a ritual circle is like dragging a heavy net full of weeds and fish into a very small boat; it is done slowly and with a great deal of effort, and releasing the net once more must be done with equal care, or else you will find yourself pulled down into the depths with it. I dismissed the circle as quickly as I safely could, then threw a heavy cloak about me. Only then did I go to the door, forced to leave the accoutrements of my rite scattered about the inner room.

The guard shrank back a little from me as I flung the door open, which was mildly gratifying since he was somewhat taller than I and wider at the shoulder – I never quite lose the satisfaction of moments like that, however childish it might be. His meaty hand tightened around the halberd he carried.

'Interrupt another ritual like that and you'll spend the rest of your days as a frog,' I told him.

'Lord Magus,' he muttered: 'Forgive me. The Baron of Chedzoy requires your presence in his chamber straightaway.'

I pulled on some clothes and reluctantly followed him through the castle to the Baron's private rooms, which filled the southern face of the keep and were thus the warmest in the building. I was shown in past two more guards and bowed low before my employer.

Chedzoy was wrapped in a fur-trimmed robe and stood before a perch on which a hooded gyrfalcon stirred uneasily. White bird-droppings spattered the floorboards beneath it. The room was warm – the fireplace was ablaze, despite the season – and smelled of male sweat. The curtains of the great bed were drawn closed, presumably to shield his wife from my ignoble gaze.

'Fine creature,' said he, stroking the falcon's breast-feathers. I was not expected to answer and I waited patiently for his attention to drift in my direction.

'Julian,' he said at last.

'My lord?'

'A good day's hunting, but I lamed a horse. The bay gelding. You'll go down to the stables and cure it.'

'Of course, my lord,' I agreed.

He turned his pale eyes upon me. I wondered how such a bland face could be so disagreeable. 'Have you seen to the Pedwell witch yet?'

'I have made enquiries, my lord.'

'She is a witch, is she not?' he said pointedly.

'She may well be.' My reply was guarded. I had seen no evidence that she was not – but then I could not imagine what such evidence might be. 'I think she may also be an Immaculate, my lord.'

'What in the Hell's that?' he asked.

'A Religious, my lord.' Like the Archbishop, I added mentally. His ignorance appalled me. 'She may have vowed herself to Gwydion; sworn abstinence from certain things. Iron, for example.'

'So?' His sandy eyebrows rose.

'They are very powerful, my lord. It may be difficult for me to confront her – and impious, at that.'

Chedzoy tugged irritatedly at the falcon's jesses and the bird took offence, flapping its wings. 'I didn't employ you, Julian, to tell me that *maybe* you can't deal with problems. I want you to get rid of the witch. If you can't, I'll send for someone else.' His half-snarl showed a row of rotten teeth.

I bowed very carefully. 'I will see to it at once, my lord,' I promised.

'Good. You may leave. Don't forget the horse.'

I went down to the stable bristling like a cat that had landed in mud. I was already beginning to rethink my prospects with this liege-lord, though I had in law no right to refuse his commands or shrug off his authority.

My attitude infected the gelding, which despite its swollen fetlock danced nervously around its stall in my presence and would not let me examine the injury. Horses generally do not like the feel of magic and this one could smell my ill-will. I had to raise up a circle in the corner of the yard and cause a groom to lead the beast within – I did not bother with the proper tools of my art for such a simple rite, making do with the silver knife I carried at my belt to inscribe the pattern in a layer of mud, and a wooden bowl of well-water, and letting the outdoor setting compensate for lack of fine detail – the man holding its head tight while I worked my way along its flank to within touching range of the injured leg. The beast tried to kick me even then, but I forced healing into the ungrateful animal and backed out of range without too much loss of dignity. My pride was already smarting badly.

Of course, if I had been aligned to Darkness too I could have charmed it to absolute obedience.

I retreated from the awed but nevertheless untrusting admiration of the grooms to the Great Hall in search of food. The household had eaten their evening meal just after sunset and the tables had long been cleared. I found a servant scraping the wax from the sconces for remelting and sent her down to the kitchens to find me dinner, which I ate alone sitting next to the embers of a fireplace larger than my own bed. The repast – what remained after the servants had made their own meal from the leftovers – consisted largely of bread and congealed cider gravy, with the pickings from a fowl carcase, but I had hardly eaten anything all day and I finished it with a will. Nobody waited on me, but nor would I have been welcome in the kitchen. I fell between the two poles of the household, neither servant nor nobility, and in consequence I was forced to become familiar with my own company.

I was tired too, I realised as I recognised the melancholy stealing upon me in the echoing gloom of the hall. My sleep had been patchy recently; it is one of the obvious yet curiously disorienting results of being a nocturnal mage. I climbed at last to my bedchamber, praying that I would not be needed further that night.

But my rooms had been invaded. I noticed the smell before I could make out anything by the light of my small cresset-lamp; a sweet hedgerow scent partly rank but mostly floral. My rooms were full of roses. I sagged in the doorway and began to laugh weakly. A vast tangled wave of briars, rootless yet in glorious health and full bloom, sprawled through the doorway from my ritual room, heaped right up to the lintel, swamping most of the furniture except the shrine. The inner room was totally inaccessible, the outer room held by the vanguard of thorns. Serrated leaves glinted glossily in the lamplight. The air was full of moths feeding on the open flowers.

It was the rose I had left in the chalice.

I shook my head, not wanting to believe what I saw. Galiena's message was very clear: *I know you have been watching me; now see how I turn your tools against you; see the strength of my art that I can grow briars from air and stone without even being present.* Flowers and thorns. It was an open threat, yet it was also extravagantly beautiful.

And it cut me off from my circle and my tools. If I wanted to dismiss the enchantment, I would have to stretch myself to the limit.

I paced the room as best I could, considering my options, and in the end elected to do nothing that night. Though there were hours of darkness left, exhaustion already had a claim on me. I made my way carefully to my bed which was only partially covered, crushing a few outlying tendrils underfoot, and then cut away enough of the stems to allow me to sit down upon it, and even to lie at a pinch. My head was thumping. Galiena had me worried and impressed, but I did not anticipate her launching a direct attack so soon after her symbolic challenge. Or at least, that was my hope. Kicking off my boots, I stripped and crawled under the blanket and was asleep even before I had pulled in my feet.

I woke with the early morning light streaming through the window over my bed. The sun was rising behind a wall of summer mist, filling the world and my chamber with a brilliant white luminosity. Little tendrils of fog drifted across the flagstones. Dew had dampened my blanket and my pillow and left tiny droplets in my hair. There was no sign of the roses of the night; they had faded to nothing with the dawn.

I hardly had time to notice this and to stretch out flat across the reclaimed expanse of the bed when the inner door to my chamber opened and Galiena walked in. She was naked but for the ash-drift of her unbound hair and the blue filigree of tattooing on a skin white as moonlight itself. Her eyes were hard, but her mouth twisted in a smile when she saw me.

I was struck dumb and frozen motionless with shock. I could not react even when she reached the side of my bed and looked down on me.

'Chedzoy's dog,' she sneered. Her voice was soft, nonetheless. She reached for the blanket and drew it from the bed in one motion, dropping it at her feet. I think I raised my hands in silent protest. And my prick moved too, stirring to life under her gaze with a wrench so sharp it was almost painful. Her glance was not modest; it was cool and appraising, conducting as harsh an examination of my supine form as it had of my character. She raked her glance down my body from head to foot, taking in all from my startled face to my chest with its delta of black hair, down the flat stomach bisected by a line of hair that flared into the thicket of my groin – lingered there while my prick quivered and thickened visibly – and then travelled on down the long stretch of my legs right to my toes. I felt self-conscious about every inch, even my entirely neat and inoffensive feet – but she did not seem displeased. Her smile relaxed a little. She laid one hand upon my burgeoning member and it leaped under her touch like a hound greeting its mistress. If it had been a dog it would have fallen fawning at her feet – if I had been a dog, so would I.

I groaned like a stunned ox, and stared helplessly as she slipped her hand around my shaft and caressed it from root to tip.

The smile, still not entirely gentle, suffused her face further. Still stroking me, she sank down on the edge of the bed, laid one finger on my lips and then explored my face with her free hand; my short beard, the stubble on my cheeks, the soft skin of my throat. I could not have resisted even if she had produced a knife and cut my jugular. Her left hand cupped and weighed my quivering ballocks, pulled tenderly at my hairs, then slid up and down the rampant length of a prick that was now harder than rock and hotter than fever. I felt like the giant of Cerne Abbas. I spread my thighs further and pushed up into her kneading grasp.

She bent over my face. Her lips brushed mine, very softly. Her hand, relentless, worked my long staff. I felt her breath mingling with my own, tasted her warm mouth. I could move now; enough to pass one hand up to the back of her head and pull her against me, our tongues melting together in a warm, hungry, terrifying dance. Her hair was thick and soft under my palm. Joy stabbed through me so sharply that it hurt.

Then she pulled away, ignoring the pressure of my hand, leaving my lips bereft. Her expression was heavy-lidded and grave. She kissed my face and my chin and my throat, began to work her way down my body with her mouth. My skin was cool; her mouth felt like fire, her tongue like a salamander though it left a cold trail across my flesh. She tongued my flat, sensitive nipples until they hardened to hailstones and I writhed under her touch; she tugged my chest-hair with her teeth; she blazed a trail down my breastbone and belly and licked a tickling, tormenting path around my navel. My right hand was entwined gently in the abundance of her hair. It fell like a living fountain washing across my skin, cold and warm all at the same time, soft as nightfall, puissant as moonrise.

The bell in the castle tower began to toll the hour.

Her lips joined her hand at my prick. I nearly wept with pleasure; I know I did cry out. Her hot mouth slid over the turgid bulb of my member, pushing back the velvety foreskin, her tongue stroking the ridges and the furrows. She took me all the way down into her throat, sliding me into the moist velvet tunnel, then eased me out again that she might whip the most sensitive tissues of my prick to a frenzy with her tongue. She sucked and she licked, her head rising and falling at my groin, her every breath dragging in my scent, her hands stroking my thighs and balls. She was unstinting and ravenous. My shaft glistened with her saliva as it emerged into and receded from the light. My right hand raked across her scalp, stroking her hair but also pushing it back so that I might better see her full lips distended on my gleaming rod. Blood was racing through my veins; fire building in my loins. The bell rang for the fourth and last time in my head.

She was more beautiful than any woman I had ever seen. Her right breast was just within my grasp as she kneeled over me. I slid my left hand down and that warm, perfect globe nestled into my palm. My other hand tightened on her scalp. My muscles locked, only

241

my pelvis thrusting as she forced me unrelentingly to my crisis.

The air was filled with the scent of roses. An owl cried.

A single moment from my climax, in a white-hot blur of desire and panic, I wrenched Galiena's head from my groin and threw myself across the bed.

I regained my reason to find myself lying face down, the blanket wrapped around me in a strangling grip, my feet thrust into the briars that framed my bed and my calves on fire with a thousand bloody scratches. It was dark, with that steely luminescence that comes an hour before sunrise, and I was alone. I had always been alone. She had never been there. My own hand was on my straining erection. My body was a lather of sweat.

I thrust my face into the mattress and groaned in torment. Then I rolled over on to my back again, stripping the knotted blanket from my hot limbs. My prick stood like a megalith, in an agony of denial, but though I kept it in a firm grip I did not dare give it the relief it demanded.

Galiena! The bitch had walked in my dreams . . .

Had she not?

I pushed the sweaty hair back from my eyes and tried to think straight. No man thinks best with his prick and mine was staging an open bid for control. I struggled to reassert mental dominance over my mutinous flesh.

It would have taken the utmost arrogance for her to dreamwalk with me; it would be an admission of guilt so blatant that it could only be interpreted as a challenge to the death. I tried to focus on any lingering trace of Darkness in the room, but my nerves were so much on edge, my thoughts so deranged, that I did not have a hope of detecting such a delicate spoor. Moonlight was chasing across my skin and singing in my pulse; it compounded my lust and made self-denial almost impossible.

But not quite. Despite the throbbing in my balls I kept my hand still and my mind active. If she had come dreamwalking, then why like this? To torment me? To humiliate me? To cripple me in the last hour of night so that she could launch some more deadly attack? That thought was not pleasant. Nor could I wholly believe it; I did not think our meeting had been so hostile as to warrant all-out war. If it had, she would not have wasted her energy on sending me roses.

Probably she meant it as a warning: *See how powerful I am; even without your tokens, I could find you.* And to mock me. To point out how easily I could be fooled and trapped.

Oh shit, thought I. My prick struggled in my hand like a wild creature. I had experienced orgasm during my time of empowerment only once, when I was at college and young enough still to be testing the boundaries. I suppose most novices try it out at some point – all except the truly holy and the truly ambitious, of course, among whom I did and do not number. The experience had been terrifying; physical ecstasy beyond description, a period of unconsciousness, and then waking shaken under the moonlight bereft for the first time of even the residue of power. And blood everywhere. And it had felt like I was pissing fire for a week. I had heard of some mages who found the experience addictive, but after that I had always shrunk from temptation during the night.

Galiena's tactics were below the belt, to say the least.

Unless of course, it had not been her doing after all. Perhaps I was blaming her for my own lechery. Perhaps she currently slept the sleep of the innocent, and it was my own arrogance that flattered me with the illusion of her presence.

I gritted my teeth and stared at the ceiling.

I could do nothing until dawn – and I did precisely that, though it seemed like the night was crawling away at a snail's pace. But there was no chance of me dozing off again and I had to wait it out, moment by agonising moment, my hand clenched so firmly around my erection that I started to suffer cramps in my forearm. I have never been so glad to feel the sun rise, to feel the power ebb from my bones, to know that I was only a mundane man and thus free again. With a groan of relief, I let my hand sink to my shaft-root and slid it up to the tip again, squeezing the foreskin closed over the swollen dome, pulling it back so that the tight cowl rubbed life into its neglected head. My own moisture quickly seeped out from its leering slit to lubricate my knob-end and my hand found a glorious rhythm, seeming to fly over the crest of my prick. My other palm hefted and caressed my balls. The image of Galiena's pouting mouth stuffed with my hot meat filled my inner vision, and my hand became a blur, and in a very few instants I thrashed and stiffened under the blows of the most savage, satisfying, mortal climax. My come splattered my belly and chest with wet bombardment; four jerking spouts of moon-pale seed falling upon my skin.

The roses were withering with an audible sussuration, like the sigh of old ghosts.

Lying in my bed surrounded by yellowing briars, cock in hand, staring at the roof beams, I conceived my plan and came to my decision.

I did little that day except tidy up and prepare. I washed, and disposed carefully of the water, and I shaved my cheeks and trimmed my beard – seeing in the polished steel of my mirror a face that, although still young, was already settling in sombre, pessimistic lines. After that it took some hours to gather up the heaps of brittle stalks that were all that remained of the briars and to clear my rooms. Once the way to the fireplace was open, I stripped the sheet and blanket from my bed and burned them; this was no time to take risks.

An hour after sunset, wearing the shape of a crow, I was circling Galiena's tower. She was not on the roof and the only light from the farm came from the window in the storey below the deserted ritual circle. There were no wardings about her home; the flowering woodbine I carried in my beak gave off only a faint, natural scent. I flew to the window and settled on the sill with a flick of coal-black wings.

Galiena raised her face to me. She was sitting by the fire, a basket of carded fleece at her feet, a drop-spindle hanging from her left hand. Absently she drew another few inches of fluffy wool into thread without looking at it, then lowered the spindle to the floor and stopped its turning.

I dropped the wild honeysuckle stem from my beak. The sweet scent of the night-blooming flowers suddenly redoubled.

'Julian,' she said.

There was a taint of power in the room; she had some spell already prepared. Hurriedly I slid out of crow form and into my own shape which, even cross-legged, barely fitted into the window-recess. The stone was intensely cold beneath my butt – I was naked, of course, there being no choice when it comes to shape-shifting. I raised my hands apologetically and just managed to forestall the complex gesture she was making with her own.

'Wait, Sister – I haven't come to fight.'

'What for, then?' she asked, then suddenly laughed. 'To bring me flowers?' She nonetheless stilled her hands in her lap.

'It seemed appropriate. I wanted to thank you for your gift last night. I appreciated it.'

245

She flashed her eyebrows but did not reply. Her colour was high in her cheeks and she was failing to look at me directly, watching me from the corner of her eyes instead. I did not quite know what to make of this; I doubted she was merely being polite. My shins were crossed before my crotch anyway, so I was not forcing her to look at anything she might find too offensive.

'I want to talk, Sister. If you will permit it.'

'Yes?' She was wary.

'I'd like to propose a bargain.'

She retrieved her spindle and began to wind the wool on slowly. 'Why should I be interested in that?'

'We are both trapped,' I said. 'We are cornered like dogs in a pit and will be forced to fight. Even if you kill me, they will only bring in other hounds against you. So I propose a deal. A duel, if you like; *certamen singulare inter magos*. Would that suit you? Then neither of us will have to end up dead. And if I win you'll leave this place and let Chedzoy have the lands.'

'But if I win?' she asked.

'I'll bring you a lock of the Baron's hair, and you can deal with him any way you see fit.' My throat was dry.

She stared at me, unbelieving. 'He's your liege-lord,' she objected.

I felt cold. 'I'll do it,' I said. 'I have no love for him. And after fighting you ... I'm sure I will not fear the Witch-hunters.'

She bit her lip; it was an oddly childish expression. 'No. I don't trust you,' she said at last, very softly.

'You should. You could trust me with your life, Galiena,' I said. 'I would ...' Then I shut up, because I was all but offering my throat to the knife.

'I would require a lock of your hair as well as his,' she whispered.

I shrugged. 'If you wish. You won't need it.'

She pondered in silence, holding my eyes in her dark gaze.

'What form of contest?' she asked at last.

'Shape-shifting.' It was the traditional form between Moon-mages.

'Tomorrow is a full moon,' she said. 'Meet me in the woods after sunset. Whenever you are ready.'

I nodded. 'The moon shine on you, Sister.' I folded my form back into the small feathered shape of a bird – an owl, this time, for it was getting too dark now for a crow to fly. I was perhaps too conscious of her gaze and neglected to alter my colouring, so that it was a glossy black barn-owl that dropped from her window and sped off into the blue night.

I had told her the truth. She did not need any tokens or rites to hold me, for I was already caught fast in an enchantment stronger and crueller than any spell.

Which is how I come to be standing naked under tall trees by night. I can just make out the dark shape of Galiena's house against a sky flushed with stars. My ritual circle is unmade once more, my accoutrements – even the silver I normally wear always – hidden under a rotted log. There is a night breeze, but I hardly feel it; every inch of my skin prickles with power. Into this rite I have woven every strand of my knowledge, invoked the dominions by every name, prayed for Gwydion's aid in the longest forms and bound in any and every token that might strengthen my hand. I have bathed in water steeped from mugwort, whipped myself dry with willow twigs and forsworn the use of steel since sunrise; even my horse's bit was made from bronze.

If she is an Immaculate, then all this will count for nothing.

It is two hours after sunset. A late blackbird is still singing in the undergrowth to my left, no doubt disturbed by the strangeness in the air.

This contest cannot be fought with magic, but with cunning and will – or else I have no hope.

She is here. I see her slight figure, ghost-pale in the darkness, coming towards me through the trees. Her hair is loose and drifts like a cloud about her. Silver glints from her naked skin; the spiralling lines on her flesh are aglow. I can hardly breathe. She is a storm-cloud ready to unleash its fury upon me.

We face each other, knee-deep in the lush woodland undergrowth. The gloom shields us from mutual exam-ination, but I can make out that the expression on her face is one of calm, almost joyous, and I understand it; the power beating in our blood, the moon rising full beyond the branches – it is difficult to feel anything but pleasure. Our mutual nakedness, so close. I want her, very much. My prick rests heavily between my thighs, thick and filled with moonlight as the rest of my flesh is, but not yet rampant. In another few moments it will betray me.

'Begin,' I suggest.

She, the challenged, has the right to make the first move and the right to take the defensive. I must prove my mastery over her to win. The rules are ancient, worn thin with time; defeat the other, cause them to yield from exhaustion, or spend their last dregs of power before dawn. My only advantage is that it is in Galiena's interest to refrain from killing me.

She smiles and is gone. So quickly, so smoothly does she pull herself down that it looks as if she has simply vanished. My heart jumps and I cast around for a moment in fruitless search. There is no movement under the trees except for the breeze stirring a few leaves on the ground-flora. I am wading through dog's-mercury and ground-elder and ramsons, my feet crush-ing a pungent odour from their bruised stems. From the banks of green foliage tall spikes of fox-glove lift their heads. She hasn't fled, I realise; she has hidden herself here.

I change, becoming less. I fold myself down no larger

than the joint of my own thumb, becoming a honey-bee, fat and furry with shiny black legs. It is dark and a little too chill, but now I can smell all the scents of the woodland, the flowers and the leaves and the earth. I can smell her. I quest from plant to plant, wings droning softly, tracking down the one that tastes wrong or feels strange under my feet.

Here she is; the leaves a shade too warm, the scent a note too musky. She is a spire of fox-glove, pink flowers in ascending tiers. I crawl into one of the blooms, satin petals beneath my feet and over my head. It covers me entirely and her perfume surrounds me. I uncurl my long bee's tongue to stroke the nectaries. She tastes sweet. I lick and dabble, my furry body vibrating and heaving inside her velvet flower. My feet tickle her. Strength flows through me, I feel a quiver from the plant – it is moving.

She changes. I am thrust back out into the night as the flower convulses shut and she stretches for the canopy overhead. I catch a rushing glimpse of motion too vast for my smallness to comprehend, and then the foxglove is gone and where it was standing is a wall of bark. I resume my own shape briefly, just long enough to study what I am facing. She is a great ash tree, grey-skinned, in the prime of maturity. Her branches reach to the sky, her feet are buried in the forest soil. I lay one hand on her trunk.

I am the ivy that grows from the soil at her feet. I coil up the column of her trunk, close as her own skin, feeling her stretched taut and quivering beneath my embrace. My tendrils explore their way into every crack and crevice. I wrap my thick green arms around her branches and pull her close. I feel the wind swaying her and I sway too, we are like lovers dancing, leaf brushing leaf, my rootlets are in the crotches of her limbs questing for moisture, my fingers are everywhere on the rippled texture of her skin. I find purchase, pull and push myself higher up her. My crown is entangled with hers. Her breath and mine are one. I feel her creak and groan beneath my weight and I embrace her tighter; prising, stroking, caressing.

She withdraws. Suddenly she is not there and there is nothing to support me and I crumple to the forest floor – but there is no time to consider my next move because something is on top of me tearing and trampling, snapping brittle old wood and pounding new shoots into the mud. Ivy leaves fly everywhere. It hurts.

She is a deer, raging among my greenery.

Shit – she is trying to kill me. In a convulsive motion, I drag my sundered self back together, coalescing in a knot of hot blood and coarse hide, wood becoming horn and bone. I rise from the earth as a stag, snorting and belling. My head is crowned in nine-pointed splendour, my legs are like iron, my neck thick, muscles rippling beneath the bristling hair of my shoulders. She shies from me, outmassed, and attempts to dodge off into the woods, but I am there before her, barring her way with heavy limbs and a savage thicket of horn. Her nostrils are distended and I can see her flanks heaving. Twice and then three times I parry her escape, pushing her back. She is only a hind, built for speed not battle. The stink of my rut is rank on the night air. I fence her round with my own presence, letting her flee no more than a few paces in any direction, until she at last stands still in confusion and I can approach. I lay my heavy neck across hers and although she shudders she does not shrink from me. The scent of her is rich and inviting; borrowed flesh is betraying her as it will every mage, for shape-shifting is not simply a matter of appearance. Animal instinct clouds her human wit. I lay my head across her withers and then her haunches, feel her brace her legs, smell her submission.

She is a wolf.

She goes for my throat, swift as a shadow, and her teeth meet in my hide. She wrenches, slashing a gash open across my shoulder, then springs back out of reach as swiftly as she had closed. I founder, numb with shock, swing round to face her. She feints again but is repulsed by the points of my horns. She crouches, snarls then springs away and begins to circle me, pushing in low and mean at every opportunity. She is furious. Blood gleams on her muzzle and darkens the long points of her fangs. My own right foreleg is cold and weak, though drenched in the hot blood that is sopping from the wound at the base of my neck.

I have to change.

She is taking no chances, never quite closing enough that I can strike her. The advantage is with her, the unwounded hunter. I will weaken rapidly. I have to counter her in this new form before I am forced to yield.

She is now male; I can see that as she circles me. She has chosen the shape of a huge dog-wolf, big as a calf. She does not mean to repeat the mistake she made with the deer.

I am a wolf too.

She leaps in at me, snarling, then stumbles and halts in confusion. Instinct claws at her guts. She has anticipated a fight, but I am much smaller than her, crouched flat on the ground. And I'm a bitch. She snarls at me, froth dripping from her jaws, but though she closes in she does not bite. I whimper and roll over on my back, exposing belly and throat – it is the most terrifying thing I've ever done. I am staking everything on her wolf-instinct. She sniffs me, hackles up, and I wriggle flirtatiously and beat the earth with my tail. There is nowhere for her anger to go except to die, and at last I smell her aggression fading into curiosity. I flop over on to my stomach and lick her jaws gently, tasting stag-blood. She closes her great teeth over my muzzle and

251

holds me motionless. There is a long pause before she releases me.

She is wondering if she has won, that I am no longer challenging her, what it is she should do next. I do not assume my own form to declare her victor, which warns her it is not over so easily as it might appear. She is quite aware of the scent of me, of my willingness which is more than conciliation. Despite herself and her human suspicions she is aroused. The big dog-wolf noses me gently, looms over me, shifts behind me. I dance with pleasure and present myself for her. She nips me teasingly and I writhe beneath her teeth. She makes to mount.

She knows.

I feel her freeze. She has recognised my strategy. She hits the ground with a thud, changes so fast I can hardly see, and I find myself alone with – a rock.

I slide back into human shape again and crouch over her. She is a boulder as big as my torso, green with moss, half-sunken into the soft soil of the hillside. I clasp her in my hands, feeling the unyielding cold hardness of her curves. She has withdrawn from me as far as she can, become entirely obdurate. A rock cannot be betrayed by its appetites as an animal can. She has been forced thoroughly on the defensive. I smile to myself in the dark. She has realised the nature of my ignoble purpose, but her awareness is also a weapon in my hands.

I become water.

I am a spring welling from the ground beneath the boulder. My cold body swells along her rigid flanks, moulding to her hard lines, lapping and bubbling and covering her. I run trickling fingers through the mossy growths that clothe her, seep into the tiniest crevices, whisper soft sounds of pleasure to her. I learn her every curve and plane, knowing her form intimately. I feel the smallest possible tremor under my fluid lips, the slightest suggestion that this stone admits of sensation. I lick her skin all over, my mouth lapping on her unceasingly in inexorable, tireless rhythm.

Only water is more patient than the rock, more persistent, more strong. I will caress her till she yields.

It comes sooner than I expect, though perhaps hours have passed when I am woken from my cool reverie and my quiet lullaby shattered by her abrupt exit. She takes flight in the shape of a duck, rocketing into the sky with a struggle that splashes water everywhere. It takes me long precious moments to recollect myself and return to the chase.

I am a hunting-hound, lean and leggy, hide white as snow except for the bloody red of my long ears. My nostrils are aflame with the scents of the night and my ears ring with the clumsy crashing flight of the duck climbing through the canopy. She will not flee far. She is too proud. I race in her wake like another shadow cast by the moon. She leads me down through the trees, over the road and into the barley field beyond. She is heading for the Levels. I run with my nose lifted to the sky, my ears straining. Though the open land under the full moon seems as bright as daylight I cannot see her, she is too distant, but I can still track her. I hear her wing-beats falter.

My feet are in water, mud squelching up between my clawed toes. This must be the marsh. I leap from tussock to tussock and patter through the shallower pools. I can hear the grumbling quack of a great many ducks ahead. Elvers skitter from beneath my paws. The bitter tang of the Sedgemoor floods my nose and mouth. I pause, lap twice at a muddy pool and cock my head to listen. I can see only grass and stars and the glint of black water.

There is a flock of ducks roosting in the mire. I inch my way forwards, working round until I am down-wind and the warm sour feathery smell of them fills

253

my head. Drool runs from my lips. They are quarrelling and muttering among themselves. Something has disturbed them. I creep forwards until I can see the first few birds. The flock has camped in the shelter of a crumbling windmill that perches on a low knoll, but now they stand quacking and staring about them with mad little eyes. The arrival of another duck would not rouse them so.

They are only birds. She is not there.

Throwing open my throat I let forth a long baying howl and the flock explodes into panic, the air filled with the rattling sound of their flight. Across the deserted marsh I pound, right up to the wooden skirts of the building.

She is the mill.

I leap and stretch myself and became one with the sky. I am the wind blowing across the marsh. I bear the scent of rotted vegetation and rich mud, the sharp aroma of bog-myrtle, the whisper of grasses, the booming call of bitterns. I lean into the wooden arms of her sails and feel them creak beneath me.

I am attenuated to the point of annihilation. She is pushing me to my limits. Her strength frightens me – but she has no plan. There is no pattern to her movements. *Find me; chase me; fight me* – she flees in every direction at once.

The sails are starting to turn. The mill groans as the mechanism within is forced into life. I push harder and a tile slides from the roof. The spars rise and fall, picking up speed, their substance protesting but unable to resist my thrusts. The creak of the arms is now a rhythmic grunt underlaid with a swishing sigh. It is the sound of the bed under the pounding of ardent lovers. I feel her heart thumping within her wooden breast, racing faster and faster. I am blind and unthinking, feeling only her movements beneath me, my only will to stir her to the foundations. If I can bring her to a climax then I will have won. More than that; if she is an Immaculate, then with the breaking of her vow half her strength will slip from her like sand through her fingers.

The mill explodes. She is a cascade of autumn leaves scattering under my caresses, dancing before me, slipping from my grasp. I chase her across the marsh back towards the hills. She twists and flickers, she tickles my fingertips, I throw her high and chase her low but cannot seize her. She eludes all but the briefest touch and that tantalises me beyond endurance.

Then I let her go and she sinks to the ground, a drift of auburn and russet and umber in the long blond grass of a summer meadow.

I am wildfire, eating the grass. I will consume her. She incandesces under my flickering tongues. This is going to kill me.

She is the rain, falling from a summer thundercloud, drenching my flames, smothering me in her wetness.

I am the thirsty earth, cracked and dry. I soak up the sweet moisture she pours upon me, drinking her in great gulps. Her being is mingled with mine. I swell and enfold her. I have never held anyone so close, never known such intimacy. She does not struggle but lingers, locked in my heart and I am soaked in her and full of her and it is pure bliss.

She is a mole, velvet-furred, burrowing through my flesh. Her powerful hands tunnel in my earth and she kicks me with clawed feet. She is sculpting me. With a flex of her shoulders she opens me to the air and a molehill erupts on the pale face of the meadow.

I am a grass-snake, every inch muscle. I throw coil after coil around her form and tighten upon her. I feel her warm body quivering under my deadly grip.

She is another grass-snake. What is she doing? We are wrestling together, coils within coils, a knot of writhing flesh. Tongues flicker in a blur of tasting as we wrap around each other, each striving to get on top. She is flexing and moving beneath and above me like living whipcord and it is too much, I want to use hands to hold her down, I want to use legs to pin her, I want . . .

We change together, without thought, without hesitation, wills united in a common purpose. We are still intertwined, still crushed together in terrible struggle. Her mouth is on my throat. Her thighs are locked around my hips. I am thrusting into her. I am in her. Full length. Yes . . . I have her, Galiena, moon-pale, soft as wood-ash beneath my fingers, her long hair tangled about my head, her mouth sweet and starving beneath mine, fingers sliding up and down my spine. We are rolling in the crushed meadow grass. She kicks and pushes me over so she is on top, she ends up straddling my hips, holding herself up with one hand on my chest. Her eyes are full of storm-clouds. I cup her face and she whimpers, licking at my fingers. I push her thighs further apart and thrust further into her. She writhes on my iron-hard member. She pushes herself up from her knees and then sinks again, driving herself on to me, sliding her hot, tight, soaking-wet purse up and down my stiff prick, and she does it again, and again, in quickening beat. She arcs her back and pushes her breasts out; I cannot keep my hands off her, I put them on her thighs and stroke her slowly, from hips to slender waist to ribs to breasts, and I cover these with my palms and they are like the Grail raised in my worshipping hands.

And I am still thrusting.

And I see, too late, the trap I have set myself.

Oh no. No. I am lost.

I quicken, and it is like a wave of fire that rises in me and falls upon my head. Ecstasy hits me like a whip-lash, flaying my prick raw. I scream, and I keep on screaming because it does not stop. My spine arches

256

and I jam into her yielding body like I would stab her through the heart. I shriek her name. My body is burning. The world is on fire. My vision turns crimson, but I can still feel her under my desperately clenched hands. I hold on to her for my life as the surge of all-annihilating pleasure rips through me.

Then the wave recedes, at last, with a terrible hissing undertow that threatens to drag me into utter black-ness. I am left broken in its wake. I can't see. My eyes are full of blood.

I hear her whisper my name.

I keep blinking, and my vision clears slowly. Galiena sits motionless upon me, her hair hanging around her face like a cowl. My hands still grip her waist; I fear that they may have been digging in very hard.

She has won.

Every muscle in my body hurts. There is a sticky wetness at our joined crotches that I dread to investi-gate – though I am still rigid, still throbbing with the aftershocks of pleasure. But I feel so weak. The moon has left me and I am empty.

She reaches forwards to brush the red tear-tracks at my temples. Her whole body is faintly luminescent, her eyes wide and very dark. I have never seen anything more beautiful. Why doesn't she pull away from me? The line of her mouth is soft. I wish – vainly – that she would kiss me, but she sits back again, rocking on my prick. That is not triumph I read in her eyes; for the first time since I met her, she looks afraid. I wonder if I have hurt her.

She swivels her hips, then licks her lips gingerly. I stare in wonder. She begins to describe swirling circles with her groin, her cleft still clasping my prick. Her hair is swept from shoulder to shoulder as she twists her neck. The moon-lines on her skin are writhing. I stroke my fingers softly across the small swell of her belly and into the sweaty tuft of her pubic hair, and she

moans at my touch. I don't quite believe this. Her eyes
plead. Her skin is very hot. Gently I begin to match her
movements with a counterpoint thrust of my hips. She
gasps. My prick is still swollen and willing, filling her
tight hole. I start to trace the pulsing silver lines across
her skin with my nails and she rewards me with a look
so grateful, so terror-stricken, that my heart nearly
stops. She is grinding down hard on me now, her teeth
bared, hardly breathing. My hands reach her breasts,
trace the radiating lines back to the source at her out-
thrust nipples. She throws her head back.

She comes, and the orgasm discharges straight down
through me into the earth, hitting me with a second
climax like a blow. This time I do black out.

I come to, and Galiena is still astride me, crouched low,
her hair lying in drifts on my face and chest. She is
weeping – silently, but her whole body is shaking. The
lines on her skin are just blue scrawl now. She is so
small.

I pull her gently down on to my chest and she does
not resist, allowing me to slip my arms around her. She
feels cold. It is not a very warm night, despite the
season; if it were not for the cramps racking my own
muscles, I would have noticed already that I too was
feeling chilled. There is a sow-thistle or some such
crushed under my left buttock which is quite painful. I
roll us both over on the flattened grass so that we are
lying on our sides, Galiena still in my arms. She slides
one hand up around my shoulder-blade to clasp me to
her. I kiss the tears from her face.

Her lips are soft.

It is the last hours of the night and we are lying
damp and shivering in a Polden haymeadow, two
naked people bruised and sore and besmirched with
blood. Our clothes and shoes are probably miles away.

It will be a long walk home, my love.

BLACK LACE NEW BOOKS

Published in May

PLAYING HARD
Tina Troy
£6.99

Lili wrestles men for money. And they pay well. She's the best in the
business and her powerful body and stunning looks have her gentle
men visitors begging for more rough treatment. Her golden rule is
never to date a client, but when James Travers starts using her services
she relents and accepts a date.

An unusual and powerfully sexy story of male/female wrestling.

ISBN 0 352 33617 X

HIGHLAND FLING
Jane Justine
£6.99

Writer Charlotte Harvey is researching the mysterious legend of the
Highland Ruby pendant for an antiques magazine – a ruby that is said
to sexually enslave any woman to the man who places the pendant
round her neck. Charlotte's quest leads her to a remote Scottish island
where the pendant's owner – the dark and charismatic Andrew
Alexander – is keen to test its powers on his guest.

A cracking tale of wild sex in the Highlands of Scotland.

ISBN 0 352 33616 1

CIRCO EROTICA
Mercedes Kelley
£6.99

Flora is a lion-tamer in a Mexican circus. She inhabits a curious and
colourful world of trapeze artists, snake charmers and hypnotists.
When her father dies owing a lot of money to the circus owner, the
dastardly Lorenzo, Flora's life is set to change. Lorenzo and his
accomplice – the perverse Salome – share a powerful sexual hunger, a
taste for bizarre adult fun and an interest in Flora.

**This is a Black Lace special reprint of one of our most
unusual and perverse titles!**

IBSN 0 352 33257 3

Published in June

SUMMER FEVER
Anna Ricci
£6.99

Lara Mcintyre has lusted after artist Jake Fitzgerald for almost two decades. As a warm, dazzling summer unfolds, she makes the journey back to her student summer-house where they first met, determined to satisfy her physical craving somehow. And then, ensconced in Old Beach House once more, she discovers her true sexual self – but not without complications.

Beautifully written story of extreme passion.

ISBN 0 352 33625 0

STRICTLY CONFIDENTIAL
Alison Tyler
£6.99

Carolyn Winters is a smooth-talking disc jockey at a hip LA radio station. Although known for her sexy banter over the airwaves, she leads a reclusive life, despite the urging of her flirtatious roommate, Dahlia. Carolyn grows dependent on living vicariously through Dahlia, eavesdropping and then covertly watching as her roommate's sexual behaviour becomes more and more bizarre. But then Dahlia is murdered, and Carolyn must overcome her fears in order to bring the killer to justice.

A tense dark thriller for those who like their erotica on the forbidden side.

ISBN 0 352 33624 2

CONTINUUM
Portia Da Costa
£6.99

Joanna Darrell is something in the city. When she takes a break from her high-powered job she is drawn into a continuum of strange experiences and bizarre coincidences. Like Alice in a decadent Wonderland, she enters a parallel world of perversity and unusual pleasure. She's attracted to fetishism and discipline and her new friends make sure she gets more than a taste of erotic punishment.

This is a reprint of one of our best-selling and kinkiest titles ever!

ISBN 0 352 33120 8

If you would like a complete list of plot summaries of Black Lace titles, or would like to receive information or other publications available, please send a stamped addressed envelope to:

Black Lace, Thames Wharf Studios,
Rainville Road, London W6 9HA

BLACK LACE BOOKLIST

Information is correct at time of printing. To check availability go to www.blacklace-books.co.uk

All books are priced £5.99 unless another price is given.

Black Lace books with a contemporary setting

THE TOP OF HER GAME	Emma Holly ISBN 0 352 33337 5	☐
LIKE MOTHER, LIKE DAUGHTER	Georgina Brown ISBN 0 352 33422 3	☐
IN THE FLESH	Emma Holly ISBN 0 352 33498 3	☐
SHAMELESS	Stella Black ISBN 0 352 33485 1	☐
TONGUE IN CHEEK	Tabitha Flyte ISBN 0 352 33484 3	☐
FIRE AND ICE	Laura Hamilton ISBN 0 352 33486 X	☐
SAUCE FOR THE GOOSE	Mary Rose Maxwell ISBN 0 352 33492 4	☐
INTENSE BLUE	Lyn Wood ISBN 0 352 33496 7	☐
THE NAKED TRUTH	Natasha Rostova ISBN 0 352 33497 5	☐
A SPORTING CHANCE	Susie Raymond ISBN 0 352 33501 7	☐
TAKING LIBERTIES	Susie Raymond ISBN 0 352 33357 X	☐
A SCANDALOUS AFFAIR	Holly Graham ISBN 0 352 33523 8	☐
THE NAKED FLAME	Crystalle Valentino ISBN 0 352 33528 9	☐
CRASH COURSE	Juliet Hastings ISBN 0 352 33018 X	☐
ON THE EDGE	Laura Hamilton ISBN 0 352 33534 3	☐

- - - - - ✂ - - - - - - - - - - - - - - - - - - -

Please send me the books I have ticked above.

Name ....

Address ....

....

....

.... Post Code ....

Send to: **Cash Sales, Black Lace Books, Thames Wharf Studios, Rainville Road, London W6 9HA.**

US customers: for prices and details of how to order books for delivery by mail, call 1-800-805-1083.

Please enclose a cheque or postal order, made payable to **Virgin Publishing Ltd**, to the value of the books you have ordered plus postage and packing costs as follows:
  UK and BFPO – £1.00 for the first book, 50p for each subsequent book.
  Overseas (including Republic of Ireland) – £2.00 for the first book, £1.00 for each subsequent book.

If you would prefer to pay by VISA, ACCESS/MASTER-CARD, DINERS CLUB, AMEX or SWITCH, please write your card number and expiry date here:

....

Please allow up to 28 days for delivery.

Signature ....

- - - - - ✂ - - - - - - - - - - - - - - - - - - -